A Certain Magical Index

Index

18

KAZUMA KAMACHI

ILLUSTRATION BY
KIYOTAKA HAIMURA

HOLY SWORD ASCALON

A Soul Arm created by a sorcerer who based it on the legend of a holy sword from the sixteenth century. It was designed with the theoretical value of "something that can slay a fifty-foot-long evil dragon." Fashioned from a lump of steel, its total length is about eleven feet, and it weighs nearly 450 pounds. The base of the blade features an escutcheon.

*"I mean, I don't think
I did anything bad…"*

Member of the British sorcerer's
society New Light **Florice**

c o n t e n t s

"Wh—? *Cough! Cough, cough!!* T-T-Tatemiya, how do you have that ultimate weapon?!"

Amakusa-Style Crossist Church follower **Itsuwa**

"Ta-daa!! I call it the Great Itsuwa Cinderella Operation!! It's the great fairy peeping maid!!"

Amakusa-Style Crossist Church follower **Saiji Tatemiya**

"............"

Academy City Level Zero **Touma Kamijou**

"Hey!! Y-you just ate it! You ate my food!!"

Formerly Roman Orthodox. Sister in the Agnes Unit **Angeline**

"I'll give you mine, so distance yourself at once from the cardinal sins of wrath, gluttony, and envy."

Formerly Roman Orthodox. Sister in the Agnes Unit **Lucia**

"*Om, nom...* I didn't eat it."

Nun managing the Index of Prohibited Books for the Puritans, one of the three British ruling factions **Index**

"Bring me two heads. Your enemy will be an old friend. Don't pull any punches."

Second princess of the Royal Family, one of the three British ruling factions **Carissa**

"I assure you, I have no acquaintances within the enemy ranks."

Head of the Knights, one of the three British ruling factions **the Knight Leader**

A Certain Magical Index

VOLUME 18

KAZUMA KAMACHI

ILLUSTRATION BY: KIYOTAKA HAIMURA

NEW YORK

A CERTAIN MAGICAL INDEX, Volume 18
KAZUMA KAMACHI

Translation by Andrew Prowse
Cover art by Kiyotaka Haimura

TOARU MAJYUTSU NO INDEX Vol.18
©KAZUMA KAMACHI 2009
First published in Japan in 2009 by KADOKAWA CORPORATION, Tokyo.
English translation rights arranged with KADOKAWA CORPORATION, Tokyo,
through Tuttle-Mori Agency, Inc., Tokyo.

English translation © 2019 by Yen Press, LLC

Yen On
1290 Avenue of the Americas
New York, NY 10104

Visit us at yenpress.com
facebook.com/yenpress
twitter.com/yenpress
yenpress.tumblr.com
instagram.com/yenpress

First Yen On Edition: February 2019

Yen On is an imprint of Yen Press, LLC.
The Yen On name and logo are trademarks of Yen Press, LLC.

Library of Congress Cataloging-in-Publication Data

Names: Kamachi, Kazuma, author. | Haimura, Kiyotaka, 1973– illustrator. | Prowse, Andrew (Andrew R.), translator. | Hinton, Yoshito, translator.
Title: A certain magical index / Kazuma Kamachi ; illustration by Kiyotaka Haimura.
Other titles: To aru majyutsu no index. English
Description: First Yen On edition. | New York : Yen On, 2014–
Identifiers: LCCN 2014031047 (print) | ISBN 9780316339124 (v. 1 : pbk.) |
    ISBN 9780316259422 (v. 2 : pbk.) | ISBN 9780316340540 (v. 3 : pbk.) |
    ISBN 9780316340564 (v. 4 : pbk.) | ISBN 9780316340595 (v. 5 : pbk.) |
    ISBN 9780316340601 (v. 6 : pbk.) | ISBN 9780316272230 (v. 7 : pbk.) |
    ISBN 9780316359924 (v. 8 : pbk.) | ISBN 9780316359962 (v. 9 : pbk.) |
    ISBN 9780316359986 (v. 10 : pbk.) | ISBN 9780316360005 (v. 11 : pbk.) |
    ISBN 9780316360029 (v. 12 : pbk.) | ISBN 9780316442671 (v. 13 : pbk.) |
    ISBN 9780316442701 (v. 14 : pbk.) | ISBN 9780316442725 (v. 15 : pbk.) |
    ISBN 9780316442749 (v. 16 : pbk.) | ISBN 9780316474542 (v. 17 : pbk.) |
    ISBN 9780316474566 (v. 18 : pbk.)
Subjects: CYAC: Magic—Fiction. | Ability—Fiction. | Nuns—Fiction. | Japan—Fiction. | Science fiction. | BISAC: FICTION / Fantasy / General. | FICTION / Science Fiction / Adventure.
Classification: LCC PZ7.1.K215 Ce 2014 | DDC [Fic]—dc23
LC record available at https://lccn.loc.gov/2014031047

ISBNs: 978-0-316-47456-6 (paperback)
        978-0-316-47457-3 (ebook)

1 3 5 7 9 10 8 6 4 2

LSC-C

Printed in the United States of America

CHAPTER 5

Mercenary and Knight: Encounter and Clash

Another_Hero.

1

October 18, 12:30 AM

On a mountain trail outside Folkestone, in southern England.

Spread out before him were three knights and their commander, the Knight Leader. As well as the wielder of the Curtana Original, the mastermind behind the coup d'état: Second Princess Carissa.

Here and elsewhere, the blades targeting Third Princess Vilian's life were innumerable. But there was one man who blocked their path.

William Orwell.

A ruffian mercenary who, at one time, was in a position to be knighted.

In his hand was the Ascalon: The product of a certain author, it was a legend embellished to the extreme. Everything about it was calculated to realize the effects of a sword that had never existed, a Soul Arm said to have the ability to theoretically slay a fifty-foot-long evil dragon.

And the action he took with it was an extraordinarily simple one.

He didn't plunge into the enemy lines, cutting down knight after knight like a man possessed.

He also didn't use some sort of trap or trick to make fools out of the entire group at once.

He simply swung the Ascalon from high to low.
To cause the ground at his own feet to explode.

A dull *boom* and a shock wave burst.
An immense wall of dust rippled through the air, a curtain drawing over the knights' vision in an instant. The rumblings that shook the ground were earthquake-like, and even the brawny warhorses whinnied in fear.

"Damn!!" cursed the Knight Leader.
Several of his knights fired off arrows at ground zero, but it was all in vain.
As the evening breeze blew the dust away...
It was empty. All that was left was the ground where the Ascalon had hit and the eerie cracks in it.

"I see. You're thinking of Vilian's safety first and foremost. If the battle here gets chaotic, you could all just die," muttered the second princess to herself, soothing the steed she rode with a light touch. "...It may look like you're dealing with things calmly, but you're also exposing your weakness. In your prime, you would've been able to fight us *and* protect that unsatisfactory sister of mine."

"How shall we proceed, ma'am?" asked the Knight Leader.
Carissa exhaled, seeming to find this dull. "Bring me two heads." She reaffirmed her grip on the sword, which lacked a blade. "I'll make sure the Curtana Original is working and get used to wielding it. I want results by the time I'm finished."

"Understood, ma'am."
"Your enemy will be an old friend. Don't pull any punches."
"I assure you, I have no acquaintances within the enemy ranks."
With only that, the Knight Leader walked into the darkness, without even so much as getting onto his horse.
The enemy was close.
At this distance, his own two legs would get him there faster.

2

Third Princess Vilian was in the arm of a certain mercenary.

Said mercenary carried her in one arm and a sword larger than her in the other, but his movements weren't weighed down. As a matter of fact, William Orwell's voyage was not that of a normal human at all.

You couldn't say he was running. Much like a thrown ball, each step arced over twenty meters at a bound. He used not only the ground but tree trunks and branches as footholds, leaping and leaping.

The blue moonlight was striking.

The biting cold was comforting.

The unique feeling of weightlessness seemed like a release from the clinging sense of entrapment.

The mercenary and the princess moving under the night sky were like two characters in a picture book.

It wasn't a real throne room, where she was toyed with as a pawn in worthless political games. It was a scene out of a children's story, of a king's lands, where anything could happen.

"Hee-hee..."

A smile formed on the princess's lips.

She didn't know why she had laughed. Maybe it was her relief at escaping a direct crisis. Maybe it was her joy at finally outdoing her sister Carissa, who had always seemed like an unscalable wall. Maybe it was the fact that even one person was willing to stand up for her. Or maybe the scenery before her eyes simply struck her as beautiful.

Whatever the reason, she laughed.

She opened her mouth wide and laughed for the first time in a long time. A defenseless laugh, having cast off all her fetters as princess of a kingdom—a laugh like any other girl would have.

"Ah-ha-ha!! Ah-ha-ha-ha-ha-ha-ha-ha-ha-ha-ha!!"

Her arms and legs swung; she laughed so hard she thought she might slip out of William's hand, but the mercenary didn't particularly stop her.

Instead, William Orwell eventually descended onto a dark mountain path.

He let the princess down gently. Vilian asked him with a conspiratory giggle, "Well, what will we do now?"

"Run, Your Highness. Somewhere safe."

As he answered, William proceeded into a thicket a short distance from the trail. There was a small hill there about a meter high, probably made out of dirt, with a rag resting on top. William removed it to reveal a horse made of metal, its four legs folded up.

Vilian looked at the letters engraved on the silver horse's surface, then made a dubious face. "Bayard...?"

"It doesn't have effects like the ones the sixteenth-century author dreamed of, but it has camouflage to escape magical searches. As long as nobody sees you with their naked eye, the Knights will not find you."

"I—I see."

"Bayard has been programmed with the location of a Necessarius hideout. Unlike those old fools in Canterbury, no sorcerer who knows real combat would forsake you."

The third princess let out a very slight sigh.

The mercenary continued to inspect Bayard, completely unaware. "I will follow you anon, so please get onto Bayard, ma'am. I will take care of the Knights. I will be sure to keep any pursuit to a minimum, so you may rest assured—"

William's words stopped midsentence.

The reason had to do with Vilian's fingertips.

The third princess's face was downcast, and she'd reached out to softly grip his clothes.

"Please stop," she said abruptly, smiling a little. "What would you have me do after fleeing from here? My life would be saved, but what then? My sister will have control of all Britain within moments, and as I hide, alone and afraid, they will drag me out to the gallows. Either I will be killed now or killed shortly after. Isn't that the only difference here?"

Her smile had no life in it. William Orwell watched her in silence.

"And there is no guarantee the Necessarius hideout Bayard will bring me to will take me in. Even if I am of the royal family. They have no need to take the risk of protecting me, the third princess, who has no real strength or authority to begin with."

The princess's eyes wavered as though she was looking for him to refute her.

"So please, stay your efforts. I've given up trusting anyone. Yes, that's right—even the Knight Leader, who was always there to offer a helping hand, tried to kill me during a coup d'état. And you're the same, aren't you? Once something compelling occurs, you'll betray me in the end, won't you? So stop this, please. I do not trust you. I choose not to."

Vilian's words continued alone, carefully controlled to avoid faltering.

"I am sure I will go to my death hating this country and the world. You have no need to fight any further, either. You may try your hardest and wield your sword for someone who doesn't trust you, but it would all be empty, wouldn't it?"

This, in other words, was what the third princess, Vilian, was saying:

Abandon me.

No matter how strong the mercenary, he was but one man. If Carissa's forces, having taken control of the nation itself, were to clash with him, it was obvious that William Orwell would not escape unscathed.

That was why she spoke thusly.

Vilian was ordering him to be disgusted with her and leave this place.

"..."

William released the Ascalon to the ground beside him—

—to move both of his now-free hands.

"Hya?!"

The unintentional yelp came from Vilian. The mercenary put his hands underneath the princess's arms, then picked her up as though she were a small child.

"U-um, I..."

Ignoring Vilian, who was terribly surprised, William placed her on Bayard's saddle. After that, he lightly stroked the metal horse's neck area. As though this had sent some kind of signal, Bayard's legs slowly unfolded and it rose.

Now that Vilian was looking down at William, he took her hand and wrapped it firmly around the reins before he spoke.

"Please rest assured."

He did not smile.

He did not know how to set others at ease, so he displayed it through his actions.

"Even if you don't trust me, my reason to fight for you will not change at all."

"Wait—"

Before Vilian could finish, William Orwell lightly rapped the back of his hand on Bayard's body.

In response, the metal horse began to move.

The sudden burst of motion threw the third princess backward, and she unintentionally tightened her grip on the reins. Bayard had fully automatic controls, so she wouldn't be able to figure out how to disengage it quickly. In the meantime, the distance between them simply opened wider and wider.

"You fool…"

Unable to jump down, either, Vilian gripped the reins with her small hands tightly enough to crush them.

She'd said all that to get that mercenary away from the jaws of death, and all it had done was isolate him even more. The fact made her clench her teeth in frustration.

"Those weren't the words I wanted to hear, you blasted fool!!"

3

William Orwell stared into the darkness until Bayard had vanished from view.

Eventually, he relaxed his shoulders, then picked Ascalon up off the ground.

Feeling a person's presence, he slowly turned around.

"The third princess is that way, then?"

The familiar voice belonged to his old friend and chief of the Knights.

"But why do you stand in my way now? Acqua of the Back is a member of the Roman Orthodox Church's God's Right Seat. He should have no reason to risk his life for our nation's third princess."

The mercenary replied not with words but with action.

The lump of steel was over eleven feet long and weighed over four hundred and forty pounds. He swung it sideways.

The sound of air splitting.

A flash of light.

Not many would have been able to notice that he'd flipped the huge sword over, then used the sharp, thick spike near the base of the back to launch a giant nearby boulder.

The mountainside near them exploded into pieces. Earth and sand flowed across the path, completely blocking off the thin trail continuing behind William. It functioned both to prevent anyone from pursuing the third princess and to block William's own escape route.

While the knights around them were surprised and set their guards, only their leader, his old friend, nodded quietly. "I see. No matter what your attachment, it doesn't change what you need to do. That way of thinking is so truly like you."

"..." William, holding the heavy Ascalon in one hand parallel to the ground, glanced about at their surroundings.

A semicircle with an approximately thirty-meter radius, with the mercenary at its center. That was the encirclement the silver-armored knights had created. Swords, spears, axes, bows, maces, and many other weapons glinted in the moonlight.

They numbered a bit under forty.

As he watched the Knight Leader, who stood at the center of them, William's lips moved slightly.

"...More men to die."

His few words caused the atmosphere near the knights surrounding him to become highly charged, but once again, the Knight Leader alone nodded frankly.

"We may be bolstered to a degree by the Curtana's power, but even now, not many would be able to keep up with you," he admitted, sticking his thumb to his chest. "I will duel you."

"This is a battlefield," spat William. "I've no interest in your courtly chivalry. If you want me, then all of you come at me. If you would prefer not to die needlessly, then remove yourselves posthaste."

"Don't worry," said the Knight Leader, shaking an arm.

Suddenly, there was a longsword in his hand with a blade about an inch wide.

The two-and-a-half-foot sword was optimized for knights to use while riding their horses. However, the silver-colored surface of this particular sword was covered in something dark red and coarse.

"I meant it in the old sense—a duel to the death."

Pok! The surface of the Knight Leader's dark-red longsword bubbled.

It wasn't a mere chemical reaction. Each one of the bubbles was the size of a basketball. They were giant, clearly bigger than the sword's thickness, and in the blink of an eye, they multiplied into dozens, even hundreds. Then, all at once, the entire shape crumbled.

A new blade began to form.

A ten-foot-long sword, much like the Ascalon William wielded.

"Hrunting?"

The name appeared in an old legend. Tempered in the blood spatters of enemies it slayed, the mythical magic sword was said to grow sharper with each strong opponent it killed.

"...The decade since you left—it's right here. I am no longer the one who fell to you at Dover."

The Knight Leader, holding a Soul Arm of the same name as the legendary sword, spoke quietly and simply.

"Allow me to use my decade to test the fruit your decade has borne."

*　　*　　*

That was the signal.

Each wielding his weapon in order to kill a superhuman monster, the clash between mercenary and knight began.

Sound vanished.

Light scattered.

William and the Knight Leader had simply jumped directly at each other, hitting the Ascalon and Hrunting together. Despite the simple act, the aftereffects that flew all around them were enormous.

A few moments later, the blast of wind came.

With a thundering *boom*, a dome-shaped shock wave expanded out from the two. The blast winds reached one hundred meters out, mowing down the fully armed knights encircling them. Trees were ripped out, the mountainside was chipped away, and the asphalt trail shattered like glass.

By the time the shock wave passed, neither of the two combatants was where he had been before.

They had jumped into the night sky.

Footsteps banged like gunshots, ringing through the darkness at a moment's delay. Thirty feet in the air, their gargantuan blades clashed two, three times. The sparks were like lightning bolts; the shock waves billowed out, one after another; and the onlooking knights were hit with an expansion of light and heat like being in the path of an exploding firework.

Some cried out.

Some crouched and tried to take the hit.

The shock waves pounded them all down equally.

"I see," said the Knight Leader after landing on the peak of a thick tree, glancing down briefly at his subordinates.

This was probably the reason William Orwell had let the third princess escape earlier. It wasn't that he would struggle to protect her while fighting, nor was it a sense of despair, wanting to safeguard the princess's life even if he died. It was no more than an attempt to avoid getting her killed with his own strength.

The Knight Leader turned a new glare on his old friend, who landed on the top of another huge tree.

At first glance, it would have looked like the two men had been fighting physically by hitting their swords together, but the battle's true essence was in *sorcery*. After all, even if you built your muscular strength with reckless abandon, you'd never get that much destructive force out of it. As soon as you crossed a certain line, your own muscles would compress your organs, ending in self-destruction.

The secret to their battle was meticulousness. Before this had started, each man had inferred all possible side effects that would come about as a result of putting out unreasonable strength or speed, then continuously picked out which ones to use during the clash of their overwhelming power in the meantime. During their battle, hundreds, thousands of ill effects would come about, their type changing from moment to moment depending on the situation. If a caster let even one of those slip through during a high-speed battle, then a moment later, he would die.

It was easy for a person to say they were going to overcome their own limitations, but to succeed only after going *that* far…And even if they did go that far, they could never completely get rid of the limitations of their own physical existence. Depending on the case, developing tricks to use as tactics, such as Kaori Kanzaki challenging others to short contests using her sword-drawing technique, worked for victory. But whether it was through the power of sainthood or that of the Curtana, a person was never stronger in battle just because they had a stronger raw power. When all was said and done, anyone who wielded immense strength also needed technique and the capacity to control their immense strength.

William was strong.

The Knight Leader was strong.

One couldn't stand in their position merely having acquired some sort of power. It was because these two had mighty skill from the start that they could add on special powers and step into the realm of what defied imagination for normal people.

Conversely, if one blocked the magic the other was using to supplement their high-speed combat, they could bring down the caster indirectly…However, this didn't apply to the two fighting here and now.

William possessed the innate disposition of a saint as well as a group of spells he'd developed in God's Right Seat.

The Knight Leader possessed the Curtana and the all-British Continent, along with sorcery he had optimized for knights.

These symbols, which served as their sorcery keys, would not be easily snatched away. Furthermore, both of them being extremely talented casters, the two of them had acquired mind-sets that would not easily shake during the process of overcoming numerous wars. Even if one or two of their limbs were cut off, their magic would likely never run out of control.

The two only watched each other's stances, continuing to glean information that went beyond mere soldiers.

Being old friends meant nothing. The time that had passed and the roads they had traveled down, constructing spells unbeknownst to each other, were moot.

"Hmph." The Knight Leader sniffed. "You are certainly talented for a saint…but you don't seem capable of giving full play to your abilities."

"…"

"I can sense your wounds throbbing with every attack. You won't use your forte, water, or your high-speed sliding movement. Is your Academy City defeat still dragging you down?"

William didn't answer. All he did was slowly swing his ten-foot-long giant sword to reposition it.

"Is there a reason to go that far to protect the third princess?" said the Knight Leader, also moving as if in response. At the giant tree's summit, he shifted his dark-red Hrunting smoothly.

He noticed the knights under his command struggling on the

ground below but still trying to grasp their bows with shaking hands. He didn't spare them another glance.

"Certainly, the benevolence and morality that form her basis are remarkable," he continued. "But not, I should think, enough to operate a nation. The more important problem is this: What is the most efficient political move to direct this country? If you were to ask me which would save the United Kingdom as it is now, military might or virtue, there is only one real answer. Her Highness Carissa appears to be concerned, but it does not seem to me that the third princess could wield the Curtana Original. Not in terms of her personality *or* ability."

" … "

"I won't say the Curtana is all that matters. But the fact remains that it is an effective combat strength. The Knights will make the best choice for the kingdom. With that choice being Her Highness with the Curtana Original in hand, our position is to support her with all our might—"

The Knight Leader abruptly stopped at the sound of a chuckle.

The mercenary's shoulders were moving slightly, up and down. But the smile on his face wasn't the wild one the Knight Leader knew, the one he'd give when faced with a sturdy opponent.

It was a laugh.

"You talk overmuch, my friend," William Orwell said, outright denying all the things he'd just heard. His expression implied that it was absurd to even bother remembering them. "Have you fallen to where you cannot even take up your sword and fight a man, without layering excuse upon excuse for yourself and others both?"

There was no voice in response.

Boom!!

Leaping from the canopies of the ancient trees, the mercenary and the knight clashed overhead.

The incredible force of their departure crushed the limbs they'd been standing on.

William and the Knight Leader had both jumped straight up

from the tops of the trees. Then, making gravity yield through brute force, their bodies seemed to slide right through the air, and their swords—they collided without mercy at the midpoint.

Sparks exploded.

An inexhaustible shock wave obliterated.

Having completely lost their forward energy to the initial attack, the mercenary and the knight began to descend vertically. But for them, gravity was no threat. They ignored it and swung their swords again from point-blank range.

Duga-zzzaa-guga-gigigigi!! Blade and blade snapped in a complex pattern.

With no footholds in their aerial battle, they couldn't place their body weight behind their slashes. Instead, William and his foe used the energy from parrying each other's attacks to rotate their bodies, then repeat their attack from a different angle—repeating, repeating, repeating, and repeating again.

They looked like two gears, their teeth locked together as they descended.

Gears with thick blades, shaving away at the other like a circular saw.

Their 360-degree exchange made the most of their situation, but it wouldn't last forever. The ground was still getting closer. And the moment they landed would be a chance to break the deadlock.

It came a moment later.

Their feet made contact with the undergrowth-laden ground.

"‼"

"‼"

A thunderous *boom* rang out.

William Orwell and the Knight Leader each went away from the other, about fifty meters from ground zero—exactly like pebbles blown away by a huge bomb.

But the regroup hadn't come about of their own intentions.

As they landed, they both took another step forward and unleashed a mighty strike, but each was thrown back by the other's attack power and sent sliding across the ground.

Scrriiittch!! William's soles scraped nastily.

It was the sound of the black soil tearing away along with the underbrush. Almost like a railroad track, only the line William went along had been carved out of the ground.

Because of the aftereffects, the battlefield had shifted away from where the knights had fallen.

William's back was almost touching the slanted surface of the landslide hundreds of yards across that he'd caused in order to cut off his own escape route. Meanwhile, the Knight Leader repositioned his dark-red longsword. William wouldn't be retreating any farther than this. Not because of how thick or high the wall was, though. Surmounting that wall was synonymous with giving away the route leading to the third princess.

And the Knight Leader could tell by looking at William.

His body weight was already starting to lean forward, into his giant Ascalon.

Just like he was at the starting line of a short-distance sprint.

But the Knight Leader was about to charge, too.

"The reason for your anger is the third princess, is it? Both of us have slain many on the battlefield who we decided were enemies. What good is it now to take up the sword for a reason like that?!"

"Insignificant. Your excuses are insignificant!!"

"Hmph. You mean to tell me you'd rather not cut down those who might submit to surrender, even on the battlefield?! I suppose it is very much like you to say that!!"

A burst of noise.

The Knight Leader, dark-red longsword in hand, plunged toward William, and the mercenary responded by charging toward the chief of Britain's knights, putting them on a direct collision course.

"But to think you would make an enemy of the military to protect 'Virtue.' Are you quite certain there is worth in supporting that girl?!"

Sparks and a shock wave scattered around, spreading, and even during that time, they moved at a high speed.

Blade clashed with blade, and they glared at each other from point-blank range.

"I have no need for rambling about my stance just so you can hear it," William spat.

Scrape.

William's Ascalon pushed back against the Knight Leader's sword.

"I will demonstrate my reason for fighting through this body and sword of mine!!"

The mercenary briefly pulled his own sword back. Then, to bury the slight empty space that opened up, he slammed the blade against the Knight Leader's dark-red longsword. The incredible impact caused the Knight Leader's balance to be shaken ever so slightly, and William followed up by unleashing a second strike.

The chief of the Knights wouldn't perish from just that, however. He swung his dark-red blade around to parry, then let the force of the impact send him backward.

A distance of thirty feet opened up between them.

…Mercs fight without considering military or political reasoning. Even whether or not the third princess is princess of this country holds no meaning for him.

The Knight Leader, reading his opponent, gripped his longsword handle with even more fervor.

Flere210—the one who transforms tears.

As his magic name implied, the Knight Leader's reason for taking up arms was to transform cold tears into warm ones.

But that alone is still shallow. It is far from enough to kill me, you wannabe mercenary.

"…"

On the other hand, William, having finally stopped moving, regripped his own sword's handle in his hands.

The Soul Arm Ascalon.

Over ten feet long and over four hundred pounds, created by a sorcerer who had calculated the values from a legendary, mythical blade related in a sixteenth-century tale—it was a sword that possessed the capabilities to theoretically slay a fifty-foot-long dragon.

The double-edged sword's blade didn't have a uniform edge. Each part had a different thickness and angle to it, allowing its user to wield it like an ax as well, or a razor, or a saw. It was even equipped with a can opener–like spike and a wire running across the blade like a jigsaw, giving insight into just how eccentric the sorcerer who had created it truly was. Scales, flesh, bone, muscle, tendon, fang, claw, wing, fat, organ, vein, nerve…The creator seemed to be serious in their intent to make it something that could break down an entire dragon by itself.

In the Knight Leader's hands was a dark-red longsword: the Soul Arm Hrunting.

Almost thirteen feet long, its weight was unknown but probably the same as other longswords of its type. A Soul Arm with the same name as the magic sword used by the mythical Beowulf. Each time it killed an enemy standing in the way, their spattered blood would supposedly strengthen the sword and sharpen its blade…But more than likely, the Knight Leader's sword applied the angelic power of telesma as blood spatters, gaining immense destructive force by compressing and sealing large amounts of it.

Its steel no longer obeyed normal physical laws: a lightness that didn't match its actual mass; a hardness to take an attack from the Ascalon and not be scratched; and above all, a supersharp blade that would probably kill William in one clean hit. It explained a few things.

…In the end, it's the same as the crosses in Crossism—an application of Idol Theory, thought William in calm analysis. *By applying the Curtana and the Hrunting, swords that symbolize the United Kingdom, they further increase their ability to control alien powers within the kingdom's territory…Hmph. I had wondered how he was using more telesma than an average saint's body…As loyal as ever to his theory of knights, to entrust his own life to his sword and his nation.*

As he thought the final words, William Orwell bent his lips slightly.

The Knight Leader, not noticing it, said, "We don't need secrets in a one-on-one fight. I'll explain the details if you like."

"This coming from someone who has deceived the queen."

"The second princess's plan is effective, but to be honest, I've been slightly bored by it. Well, I'm sure she'll allow me to do things my way, if it's only a short break taken against a mercenary."

"I see. But that's not necessary," denied William. "I've figured you out, but an enemy like you will need more than that to be defeated."

"That was fast," the Knight Leader muttered, appreciative and impressed. But then:

"And unfortunate. This battle will only happen once. I would have liked to fight you at your strongest."

Ga-boom!!
The darkness of the night rumbled with a strange force.
The Knight Leader hadn't moved a step from his position.
He had, however, recklessly swung his sword.
But range didn't come into play.
William dodged to the side immediately upon hearing the noise, but he was already too late. His left shoulder, including his collarbone, already had a hole of an inch or two carved out of it.
…That wasn't…Hrunting…?!
His attack was clearly different from the ones that had come before.
Faster than the blood could spurt out, William had already regripped Ascalon in his right hand.

"Did you know this? Beowulf is famous for his magic sword Hrunting, but in the most important battles, strangely, *the sword played almost no part at all.*"
There was no sound.
The Knight Leader stepped up to William faster than sound could travel.
Hrunting came at him in a horizontal swing, and William caught it with Ascalon, using just one hand. But apart from that, the noise of slicing wind reached his ears. He felt a strange chill, and as he channeled all his strength to swing his head out of the way, a shallow wound ran across his cheek.

"In Beowulf's infamous battle against Grendel, he used the strength of his own arms. In his battle against the water monster, an old sword in the enemy's hideout. And then, during the final battle of his life against the wicked dragon, a different blade once again."

The Knight Leader moved anew.

With William's balance slightly askew from his dodge, the Knight Leader released Hrunting from its locked clash with Ascalon.

And then he swung a longsword.

William parried with Ascalon, but his balance was off. His body lifted into the air.

Boom!!

With a huge noise, William Orwell flew.

"The story has one thing to teach us. To divide your fate—to always have more than one trump card ready."

As the Knight Leader's lips moved, the mercenary's body slammed into a giant tree and crumpled down to its base.

Ignoring the cracking as the tree began to fall, he continued, "As I thought, this is as far as a wannabe mercenary can go."

William stood, blood spurting from his left shoulder but Ascalon still in his right hand.

The Knight Leader's words reached his opponent's ears.

"Duels don't need secrets. I'll explain the details if you like."

4

On a freight car on the Eurostar line headed from London to Folkestone, Touma Kamijou pressed himself to the roof to keep himself hidden.

The train was traveling fast. He didn't know what a foreign train's average speed was, but they probably didn't reach close to two hundred miles per hour normally. They'd been going at low speed using diesel, which they did when there were power transmission issues in the city of London, but then the train had suddenly sped up, presumably because electric power had been reestablished.

There were few trains running, since it was the middle of the night and close to the last train time. More importantly, with most of the United Kingdom region embroiled in a coup d'état, regular schedules were not being maintained. It was only because there were no other trains on the line that this one could shoot along at this ridiculous speed. That said…

"*Mgha-gha-gha-gha-gha-gha-gha-gha-gha-gha-gha-gha-gha-gha—*"

…With the relative 186-miles-per-hour wind blast pressing directly into his face, Kamijou's expression was currently twisting into strange shapes.

The knights patrolling inside the train couldn't find him as he was shivering madly from the chill, and there was a simple reason for that.

Nobody in their right mind would ever hide themselves in a place like this.

…And, personally, it wasn't as though he wanted to be on the roof or anything. At first he'd certainly been hiding in the freight cars. But the knights patrolled at uneven intervals, so if he wanted to escape detection, staying in one place was actually more dangerous. Because of that, he'd been sneaking around to match the knights' movements…and before he realized it, this was where he had been driven.

Yeah…I've heard of illegal immigrants clinging to the walls and roofs of freight train cars to smuggle themselves from Mexico into the U.S. I wonder if this is what it was like…, thought Kamijou, remembering a documentary he'd seen in his dorm in Academy City.

In his case, though, his goal wasn't just to arrive at his destination, either.

*Index…*He gritted his teeth slightly.

When the coup had broken out, Index had been with the second princess, who was said to be the one behind it. He had no idea what sort of state Index was in now, but it was clear from the situation that her safety was not guaranteed.

After all, she held the knowledge from 103,000 grimoires in her head.

The idea that anyone who wanted to bolster their national combat strength even a little bit would use her for evil purposes wasn't a strange one.

To be frank, this wouldn't be simple or easy. It wasn't something an amateur would be able to confront alone.

...But it's not like I have to beat the enemy boss and all the forces protecting her. Kamijou spared a glance at his right fist. *For now, I'll slip through and rescue Index. If that's all I'm thinking about, this should go better than if we brought a whole bunch of people into the enemy camp.*

But just then, Kamijou caught something out of the corner of his eye.

When he looked over, he saw the top of a silver helmet near the area where the freight cars linked together. The person wasn't merely trying to move between cars—they seemed to have their hands on the ladder.

A patrol...? Crap, is someone climbing up here?!

The armor-wearer was to his front. Frantically, he headed for the rear of the car. With the train whizzing by and the relative wind blasts urging him on, he started to slide across the flat freight car roof. Feeling a chill that it would be over were he to fall off into the gravel passing by at such a speed, he came to the tiny gap between cars and jumped down into it.

Freight car junctions weren't like regular trains—they didn't have passages between them. Each car was isolated, and the place Kamijou had jumped down to was no different: small and surrounded by a metal railing.

The gap between cars was cramped, so it looked like he could move between them if he jumped over the railings. A shudder ran through his spine as the rails and gravel sped past his feet, but he still moved to the adjacent car.

Damn, he swore to himself. *This thing's going pretty fast. I feel like we should be in Folkestone by now...*

But it didn't matter if they were arriving in ten minutes or one. If they found him, that was it. There was nowhere to run on this speeding train. If a group of knights converged, his right hand alone wouldn't really be able to deal with them, either. He didn't have a precise grasp on their numbers, but the train had originally been on the move to transport additional troops to the second princess. It looked like he could safely assume somewhere from one hundred to two hundred were packed on board.

...*Sheesh. This is a little beyond the level of street fights.*

Using both hands, Kamijou slid the door aside and slipped himself through.

The cars near where he was hidden were actual freight cars, loaded with many articles of equipment instead of personnel. Heaps of swords and spears were messily bundled together by category, reminding him of firewood. They weren't the arms and armor you'd see decorating mansions; each one of them was an honest weapon, maintained to kill.

Still, though... In the unilluminated freight car, Kamijou sighed.

He couldn't speak much English. He could probably understand some if he broke words apart into letters and syllables like in textbook English, but locals would blend words together and leave bits out to make it easier to talk. With such fast pronunciation, he couldn't understand any of it.

But even he could tell that the knights on this train were ruffled by something. It seemed an emergency had happened. The exact reason didn't come across to him, but he thought he made out one name that they repeated.

William...

He was pretty sure it was a relatively popular name for westerners, and he didn't have any idea who it could belong to.

There were probably a lot of people with that name in the United Kingdom. He considered that this William was a sorcerer from Necessarius, but he decided it wouldn't do him any good to think about it anymore.

And then:

<"Hey.">

*   *   *

The sound of someone suddenly talking to him from the back of the freight car nearly stopped Kamijou's heart in his chest.

It was a girl's voice.

Kamijou whipped around to look and saw, in the shadow of a heap of silver suits of armor, something wriggling about. It was a person. A girl, with her hands behind her back and both feet fixed to the car with separate cuffs.

Wait, those clothes...? he wondered. Her outfit looked almost like a lacrosse uniform. *Feel like I've seen them before...Are they a fad in London?*

Without paying attention to Kamijou as he thought, the girl spoke. <"You don't look like a knight. Or some kid apprenticed to them. Did they catch you and put you on this train, too?">

Her voice sounded languid indeed, but he didn't have a clue what the quickly spoken English meant.

She seemed to guess the problem from the look on his face. "Hmm? Oh, I get it. Sorry 'bout that. You look Japanese, so maybe I should speak your language?"

"W-wait, you could tell I'm Japanese...?"

"Whenever you see an Asian for the first time and they've got that creepy, faint smile on their face, that means they're Japanese."

...Is that how other cultures think of the Japanese ingratiating smile? thought Kamijou, suddenly tired.

The girl, however, didn't seem to notice. "Anyway, I'll ask again. You're not with the Knights, right?"

Unable to figure out what she was after, he looked back at her again.

The girl was probably around fifteen, with white skin and blond hair. There were four physical restraints, one on each of her limbs. They weren't modern handcuffs—more like those wooden planks with the holes you see when they put people on a guillotine.

When Kamijou didn't respond, the blond girl frowned unhappily. "...You don't understand Japanese? Or is my pronunciation wrong?"

"N-not at all. I understand you. I understand, but..."

"Oh, okay. I'm Florice. I was, well, pretending to be in a little sorcerer's society, but...I guess that doesn't matter. Help me out, would you?"

5

A gash about two inches wide had been dug out of William Orwell's left shoulder.

A significant amount of fresh blood flowed freely from the dark-red wound. Ignoring his now-powerless left arm, the mercenary readied his giant sword with just his right hand.

The distance to the Knight Leader was about thirty feet.

Both were spaced to clash within an instant, but the Knight Leader didn't move at all.

Then, as though making a light practice swing, his dark-red longsword cut through empty air.

"!!"

A slash came at William from beside him, a completely different angle, aiming to lop off his head.

After he crouched to avoid the strike, several rays of flashing light crackled all around him.

A moment later—

Matching the longsword's movements as the Knight Leader swung it like a baton, invisible slashing attacks came at William from every direction. The underbrush tore apart as clawlike scars scored thick tree trunks, and several leaves floating in the night air split apart one after another.

Whether it was from the sound of the wind, some other sense, or even a supernatural premonition—William swung his head and jumped back to dodge. He caught one swing on the thick side of Ascalon's blade and repelled it, fending off all the Knight Leader's attempts to kill him.

Zzzz-ghh-ghh-ghh-ga-ga-ga-ga!!

—A flurry of sparks came next.

Swinging his greatsword fast enough to exceed the speed of

sound, sometimes protecting his backside without turning around, William spoke.

"I am sure you do not believe that merely modifying the range of your attacks will kill me so easily."

"...Another thing you saw through quickly," the Knight Leader said with a bitter face as he whipped his dark-red sword around. "As always, apart from when you absolutely need to speak, you're detestably silent."

Right now, what the Knight Leader wielded were *patterns*.

Many legendary weapons appeared in myths about warriors and knights Scandinavian, Celtic, Charlemagnian, and Germanic, but they all had a certain fixed pattern.

"I had thought to compensate for my weaknesses one by one by mastering many knightly ways and combining them...but it would seem that if you pile complexities upon complexities, everything starts to simplify toward a single, simple attack. Perhaps it's also not too dissimilar to the death of a star like our sun. Stars that grow too massive explode and create a black hole...A theoretically simple gravity field but overwhelming in its strength at the end of the day."

A single strike, born from layers atop more layers of every spell imaginable.

Due to its nature, magic-based disruption or nullification would be extremely difficult. In order to unravel the knots, it would be necessary to follow every road the Knight Leader had investigated.

"Still, that wasn't a black hole in the sense of a complete and total end. There are several ways a star can die. If a star's mass is below a certain amount, it can apparently turn into other things, such as neutron stars or interstellar clouds. My single attack is no different—it seems that because it is incomplete, it still possesses the attributes of a sword."

The Knight Leader's slender fingers regripped his longsword's hilt.

"Theoretically, the attributes of swords of this level can't be fully compressed into one category and are instead split into several. The easiest way to understand it is this: 'severing power' that can slice through anything; 'armament weight,' to create immense destructive power; 'durability' to prevent it from breaking; 'movement speed' to move faster than anyone can follow…In rare cases, a 'specialty usage' is needed to kill a specific monster, and 'precision' allows it to move automatically to strike at vital spots. And there are also the patterns, which I'm controlling now."

"…In other words, it's attack range, yes?"

The Knight Leader had probably reanalyzed the laws used by the Scandinavian Gungnir and Mjölnir, the Celtic Fragarach and Brionac, and others like them before putting them all together and concentrating their properties. His personal brand of evolution had given shape to an entirely new spell, just like how the life of an over-expanded star ends with the creation of a black hole.

Plus, even outside of European legends, the sort of which the Knight Leader liked to work into his spells, other similar legends—the ingredients for this black hole—existed throughout the world.

"As a result of reanalyzing many cultures, legends, Soul Arms, and weapons in order to compile this skill system, I came to realize something: It is the wish of all men to seize victory from a place their opponents' attacks cannot reach, burying them in a flood of unopposed strikes…I dislike that it reeks of uninteresting gun societies, but I am forced to admit it is effective in its own way."

And the ingredients to make that a reality are…

"Hah!!" William used Ascalon to parry a long-range strike that raced toward his temple from the side. It struck the sword's thin wire that was strung like a jigsaw located along the sword's front, sending sparks flying. When they stabbed into a nearby tree trunk, it was a blade, only a few millimeters long, that looked like dark-red rust.

"Sword shards."

The Knight Leader casually revealed the trick he should have kept hidden.

All the while, he swung the dark-red sword around like before.

"Some excellent armaments and Soul Arms will retain much of their original power even after being reduced to fragments. After all, the sword used by King Charlemagne was forged using shards of the holy spear."

"Someone poised to fight France resorting to use the legend of a French king?"

"How unusual for you to speak when it isn't necessary." The Knight Leader grinned.

Roar!! Guided by the sword's motion, rust blades went after William from dozens of directions.

"I will use anything I can. And if you're going to go that far, even the Curtana's etymology comes from French. Come to think of it, it meant a sword whose tip had broken, turning it into a 'shortsword.'"

At that, the Knight Leader abruptly stopped moving.

This time, William was the suspicious one.

"Don't make that face," his old friend said, repositioning Hrunting. "I already told you I don't like to acknowledge a worthless gun society. A proud and noble knight lives by the creed of defeating an opponent after he has used all the strength in his own hands."

"…You plan to point your sword even at powerless servants in order to brag about your pride?" William clicked his tongue softly.

The sword Ascalon, held in his right hand, emitted a red flash of light.

Except—the light was more than one color. It glimmered and shifted depending on the blade's angle, like the surface of a CD.

But strictly speaking, that wasn't entirely accurate, either.

The eleven-and-a-half-foot Ascalon didn't have just one blade. It had many parts with different thicknesses and angles, one like an ax, another like a razor, yet another like a saw. There were even a can opener–like spike and a jigsaw-like wire running down the sword length equipped to it.

The source of Ascalon's glow lay in those functions.

With many methods of attack to choose from, Ascalon changed color depending on which part was active and how it was used. Red for the ax-like blade, blue for the razor-like blade, green for the can opener–like spike, yellow for the jigsaw-esque wire…Mana would be supplied to a specific part of the Soul Arm, chosen in real time depending on what would provide the most destructive force in any given situation, and the section that was used would determine the light's color.

"I would have liked to not use it, if possible."

"That's not like you. Are you holding back against the one representing the evil dragon?" The Knight Leader smiled and gripped Hrunting's hilt tightly.

There was more than one thing an evil dragon symbolized in Crossist teachings. For example...

An invading force of heretics or an alien people. Even...

A fallen angel stained with evil.

6

Inside the freight train, Touma Kamijou was standing face-to-face with a girl bound by her hands and feet.

She said her name was Florice.

...If he'd known the entirety of the incident tonight, maybe the group name "New Light" would have immediately popped into his head. However, Kamijou was no more than an adventitious amateur participant. Necessarius wasn't exactly sharing all its information with him. Aside from Lesser, who had been gravely wounded before his eyes, he didn't really know the names or faces of any of its other members.

"Hey, stop standing around and help me already."

"Help...with what?"

"Don't you have eyes? These things. Help me get them off."

She grunted and held out the wooden shackles constricting her ankles.

Kamijou saw them and scowled. "...What the heck did you do to end up in those stiff-looking things?"

"*I mean, I don't think I did anything bad. Ha-ha-ha,*" laughed Florice. Then, she added in whispered, quickly spoken English, <"...I was a little impressed when those knights rescued me from the Necessarius church, but then they put me in chains and threw me onto this freight train. I can't believe it. Turns out they were trying to silence me right from the start! Shit. This is where trusting those civil servants will get you, Bayloupe. You idiot…And I'm not about to end my life clean after the mission like Lesser, either.">

"What?"

"Nothing at all. Aren't your circumstances basically the same? Pissed off the knights, and now they're bringing you in or something?"

"I snuck on board to get to Folkestone."

That was in itself a very interesting few words, but Florice turned a deaf ear. For now, if she knew he wasn't one of the knights, there was no problem.

"Anyway, here. Help me get these off, will you? Thanks to this Soul Arm, there's a two-meter box keeping me in. So…well…there. I can't even get to the key hanging right over on that wall."

"Huh? This is what you wanted?" Kamijou reached a hand for the key chain hanging on the wall, but then stopped abruptly.

Florice made a dubious face. "What's wrong?"

"Nothing. It's just that my right hand is called Imagine Breaker. The short version is, if the key is magical, then as soon as I touch it, it'll shatter. And then we won't have any way to get you out of those cuffs." As he explained it, he suddenly looked up. "Wait. I don't even have to bother with taking care with the key, right? If I just break the magical restraints directly with my right hand—"

"Huh? Uh, hey, wait, wait wait wait!! I don't know what you're trying to do, but—?!"

As Florice busily muttered, Kamijou grabbed her ankle restraint with his right hand.

With a *snap*, the shackle fell to pieces.

"See? Should've just done this from the start."

"Uh…Ah…"

Kamijou then went around behind her and destroyed the shackles binding her hands, too. "And there we go. Ha-ha. This means you'll have a life debt to pay, my Florice—"

"Wait, gwaaah?! If you break them without thinking, you'll—"

*　　*　　*

Bfweeee.

Naturally, an alarm went off in the freight train.

He sensed people rustling about in the cars in front of them and behind them, and then he began to hear the physical clanking of armored footsteps.

Florice turned a bloodshot death glare on Kamijou. "N-now what?! The game's only ten minutes in, and it's already over!!"

"N-no, it's too early to give up!!" said Kamijou offhandedly, heading for the iron door.

Since it was a freight train, there was a large sliding door on the side wall of the car, in addition to the doors in the front and back, used for loading and unloading freight. Kamijou unlatched it, then used both hands to nudge it open a little.

A gust of wind blew into the car.

"Where are we?"

"I don't know—probably close to Folkestone by now?"

As he listened, Kamijou glanced outside the door again to where the train was headed.

Spread out before him was a flat green plain. But as far as he could tell from how fast the ground was zooming by behind him, it was painfully obvious what would happen if he jumped out carelessly.

So he said, "We'll just have to jump."

"Are you stupid or something? If you want to kill yourself, then leave me out of it!!"

"No, not that. We're coming up on a river! If we want to escape, that's our only chance!!"

"What? We can't do that. It'd take a miracle to survive diving from a high place using water as a cushion. It happens all the time in Hollywood but never in real li—"

"Let's go. If we hold hands, there's nothing to be scared of!!"

"Huh? Huh? Wait—we're actually going to die, you moron!!"

The freight train passed over an old stone bridge.

Florice was still going on and on, so Kamijou grabbed her arm and leaped out of the open sliding door.

The surface of the water was about ten meters or so down.

Florice, as though terrified of the drop, clung to his torso and, with the blood vessels in her temples bulging, shouted, "It's all over!!"

"No, we're fine! If we use the water's surface as a cushion—!!"

"That river?! That river is only three feet deeeeeeeeeeeeeeeeeeeep!!"

"...!!"

Kamijou's eyes became points.

He swung his neck around to look overhead. Several knights holding longbows were on the freight train as it passed over the stone bridge, but the way their shoulders had relaxed made it look like they were completely astonished. Yes, sort of in the *Well, it's our job, so we could fire, but it would definitely be a complete waste of tax-payer money* kind of way.

"Gah, damn it!!" shouted Florice when suddenly a light came out of both of her shoulders.

There were some kind of metal pieces attached to them. Ignoring the law of conservation of mass, two slim metal rods, akin to umbrella handles, snapped and stretched out to the left and right.

"Grab hold!! I'll try to cancel our speed with my wings!!"

With a *bshhh* noise, a film of light spurted out, connecting the two umbrella handles together. It was like a cockroach spreading its wings. When Kamijou saw it, his face drew back slightly.

This was what he was thinking:

Um. Did you hear me explain what my right hand does?
You're going to slow us down using magic?
...I've got a really, really bad feeling about this.

7

Ascalon, shining in a rainbow of colored lights.

The Knight Leader's longsword, entirely the bloody, dark-red color of rust.

Thirty feet, separating sword and sword.

"Here I come," announced William Orwell quietly.

"Come on, then," answered the Knight Leader softly.

Roar!!

The Knight Leader's long-range slashing attacks flew at William from every direction.

He'd analyzed the spells and Soul Arms appearing in the stories of knights from various cultural spheres and joined them together. As a result of his compression, like a distended star collapsing into a black hole, he'd created a single firing-range attack as an evolution of his references. On top of being a thorough investigation of several attacks that could land a one-sided strike at an enemy from impossible distances, the slender, rust-like sword shards joined together to fire, making the Knight Leader's slashing attacks come from all sides.

Meanwhile, William used only his right hand to swing his big eleven-foot sword upward, then turned his wrist to brandish its back surface.

The sword glowed crimson.

Like this, it represented an ax.

The mercenary unleashed a straight vertical strike, but not to beat back the attacks coming at him from every direction.

He aimed at the ground.

Boom!! The very earth itself shook.

The earth sank deep around William in a radius of about twenty yards. It reached where the Knight Leader stood as well, and in an instant, countless slashing attacks carved through the air over the mercenary's head, which was now ten feet lower.

"Wha—?"

Whether because his certain-kill strike had missed or because his footing had become unstable, the Knight Leader's movements became ever so slightly imbalanced.

In terms of time, it was only a moment.

But by swinging his blade straight down, William Orwell could use his crouched posture to its fullest, explosively straining his muscles to rush right up to his foe.

Ga-boom!! The violent sound of his footstep followed a moment later.

The ground, already sliding away, began to completely fall apart.

Ascalon's glow shifted from red to blue. He turned his wrist and flipped the double-edge sword over once again, then reset his stance, this time aiming the thin, razor-like edge forward, before swinging it in a horizontal arc to cleave through the Knight Leader's torso—

All as if to say how long or short his attack range was didn't matter in the slightest.

As if silently implying it would be impossible to disrupt their fight's outcome with such petty tricks.

However…

"I don't remember saying my attack range was the only pattern I could control, you wannabe mercenary."

Sound disappeared.

Then the Knight Leader simply vanished from before William's eyes. Even with his kinetic vision, he couldn't follow the enemy's motions.

"'Movement speed.'"

A voice from behind him—

Without turning around, William thrust his sword behind him at the approaching wind pressure.

Kreeeee!!

Steel clanged together.

A dull pain came back to William's wrist from the contrived position. Resolutely ignoring it, the mercenary pivoted, body and all.

The blade's color went from blue to green. He turned his wrist over and put Ascalon's blade spine forward. The can opener–like spike attached about midway up shot for the Knight Leader, who had taken his back.

"'Armament weight.'"

But then came an unexpected impact.

An even more powerful recoil than the earlier strike he'd parried from an unstable position assailed him. It was like someone bashing a shovel into a boulder, and William's body almost careened in the other direction.

The mercenary's feet slid, inch by inch, over the black soil.

A preparatory movement of only one inch.

During it, the Knight Leader raised his dark-red longsword aloft.

"'Severing power.'"

"?!"

The eeriness in those words made William give up his parry.

He immediately jumped back to create distance instead. He dodged the Knight Leader's blade by millimeters, and it struck the black soil with a clatter.

Kaboom!!

The earth split.

William hastily jumped farther to the side, lest the crevice swallow him whole.

And as he did—

"'Attack range.'"

—*dj-bah!!* rang an unpleasant sound.

A shallow cut opened in William Orwell's side.

It seemed the man could walk the walk, too, he thought.

Attack range wasn't the only thing he could control. "Severing power" to slice through anything, "armament weight" to create immense destructive force, "movement speed" that nobody could catch up with...and—though he hadn't seen them yet—in all likelihood, "durability" to absolutely prevent destruction, a "specialty usage" needed to kill a specific monster, and "precision" to make it aim for vital spots on its own.

As a result of performing compression upon compression upon the mythical Soul Arms and spells that appeared in warrior cultures from across western Europe and elsewhere, he'd arrived at simplified attack patterns...and he had obtained them, now using them freely as his method of attack.

"You'll die," the man holding the dark-red "weapon" said quietly, looking at the blood flowing from William.

The Knight Leader's weapon was no longer Hrunting.

It wasn't even a sword.

"I've seen your all. As you are now, you cannot overcome my blade."

Just a weapon.

It would annihilate all its foes, human and monster alike...A tool that never should have been made.

A single strike from it was overwhelmingly sharp, overwhelmingly heavy, overwhelmingly fast, overwhelmingly hard, overwhelmingly long, possessing exclusivity to cleave through monsters that blades could not cut, and accurately guiding their destruction through the most efficient weak points.

Earlier, the Knight Leader had compared his attacks with a stellar explosion. In contrast to those stars that never accumulated enough mass and changed into neutron stars or interstellar clouds, one should call his current attack an "ultimate black hole" created at the end of a star's overexpansion.

One could try to dodge, if not for its "attack range" and "movement speed." One could try to block, if not for its "severing power" and "armament weight." One could try to break it, if not for its "durability."

If the Knight Leader used all his power, he'd end this with his next attack.

If he cut William Orwell in two, the battle would be decided.

Why hadn't he done so before now?

Was it sentiment?

"Will you throw down your sword and leave the United Kingdom?"

The Knight Leader slowly moved the "weapon" gripped in his hands.

"Or will you and your sword become part of its soil?"

The longsword's tip pointed at William in the distance.

"I'll let you choose. Which would you like?"

The result was plain to see.

William Orwell was not unharmed. Thanks to the gash in his left shoulder, he'd lost feeling in one hand. Because his side had been cut, he'd been losing even more blood. And more importantly, because he'd lost his battle in Academy City, he couldn't even display his true potential.

If the Knight Leader's strongest-class attack was as he'd advertised, then no matter how much the mercenary struggled, he would never have a chance at winning.

Which made it obvious what he should do here.

"...Before I choose, I will ask this," said William, still holding Ascalon. The Knight Leader frowned, and William continued, "Do you believe, beyond a shadow of a doubt, that if you support the second princess and kill the third princess, this nation will be saved?"

Mercenaries didn't normally speak much.

Which meant there was a reason he had to deliver these words.

"The first princess's intelligence, the second princess's military prowess, and the third princess's virtue...Can you state for certain that the one you choose and the ones you forsake are the correct ones?"

"...I cannot call it ideal," said the Knight Leader after a pause. But the light in his eyes never wavered. "But history is already on the move. We cannot turn back time, so all we can do is join a side. The most beneficial side for this nation's future."

William nodded. "I see."

And then he moved.

He brought up his bloodied left hand to join his right on Ascalon's hilt. Its white cloth, wrapped to prevent sliding, quickly turned red.

"Have you made your decision?" asked the Knight Leader, still not moving. "Will you flee in defeat or die?"

"No." William Orwell rejected the choice itself. "These are my two options: kill you or not kill you."

"...I see. You've made your choice, then." The Knight Leader sighed.

He didn't say it directly, but William's goal was probably to rescue the third princess.

The mercenary's retreat would secure a perfect success for their invasion and subjugation of the entire nation, which would ensure the third princess's execution. As the last bastion against this fate, he was unlikely to run.

"You will not withdraw, no matter the outcome?"

"There is no point in talking," answered William immediately.

The head of the knights sucked his teeth. "Frankly speaking, I haven't the heart to pass judgment on the third princess. And there are distasteful things about how the second princess, Carissa, does things, too."

"…"

"But Carissa is already on the move for revolution. Any knight in this nation would tell you she isn't the type of person to let excuses stop her."

The battle was already over.

The Knight Leader, his finishing blow at the ready, spoke his final words to his old friend.

"Now that history has begun its upheaval, no half measures can be allowed. If this revolution drags on in the form of internal strife, the United Kingdom's national power as a whole will diminish, and foreign enemies will take advantage of it to easily attack and defeat us."

Was it in accordance with a knight's chivalry, which asked for mercy unto enemies?

That was where the reason lay for the head of the Knights taking up his sword and fighting, from beginning to end.

"To save this nation, our only choice is to lay down our arms at once and create a new order. And the question there is who will stand at the top. If Her Majesty returns to the throne, we will not escape our current crisis. Which means it must be someone else. Between the first princess's intelligence, the second princess's military prowess, and the third princess's charisma, which of them will be able to fight back against the approaching crisis should she ascend the throne? One barely needs to think about it."

"Nonsense." William Orwell cut it all down with a single word. "Did you think adding more unnecessary words in the name of justice would fill the hole of your own barbaric acts?"

"And yet you still do not speak of your own intentions even now."

"Is it something that needs to be spoken of?"

That was all the mercenary said, ignoring the pain from his wound-covered body.

The Knight Leader, however, had predicted this response. "You want to warn me of the danger of the nation losing its virtue to engage wholly in military matters. But I would answer that there exists no absolute, correct order of precedence. We can only decide which card to choose."

William, possessing many a means to attack, wielding a sword that had the gall to have his knight's crest on the side, said, "I see. But I have already shown you my reason."

"What?"

"Pah. *That* is something I've no need to speak of."

He didn't need prospects of victory.

Gripping his bloodstained sword hilt even more tightly, the mercenary stared straight into the face of the knight.

He was always that kind of man. The Knight Leader narrowed his eyes slightly and brought the tip of his sword away and directly above, assuming a downswing posture.

"Severing power," "armament weight," "movement speed," "durability," "attack range," "specialty usage," "precision"—an ultimate attack that connoted all of them.

"Then..."

The Knight Leader had no hesitation.

He said one last thing to his enemy he'd known for so long.

"If you will not withdraw, you will die here."

The two moved at the same time.

Bang!! The blast of a shock wave rang out through the night.

William Orwell sprinted only forward, using all the strength at his disposal to close with his enemy as fast as he could.

Meanwhile, the Knight Leader took a step but not to move. It was to shift his center and bring the sword he held in both hands down with all his might.

He had no need to run up to his enemy. All he had to do was swing his sword down to unleash an attack with incredible range. Its overwhelming movement speed would prevent evasion, its overwhelming severing power and armament weight would prevent defense, and its overwhelming durability rating would prevent the Knight Leader's blade from breaking.

This was what it meant to kill for certain.

Sure enough, the Knight Leader swung the longsword down without mercy a moment before the mercenary plunged into close range.

Shh-pow!! went the sound of slicing air.

And a moment later, a slashing attack that was too enormous to be from a sword crashed toward William from directly above. The warrior reacted instantly and repositioned Ascalon above his head, but—

Ga-keeeee!!

Their slashes collided and bounced away.

Even the Knight Leader's attack, which should have been a certain kill, was canceled out.

"?!"

...It's not worth talking about, thought William as he ran. *A certain-kill technique that is sharp, heavy, fast, hard, and long-range...If he could really attack in such a way, I would never have survived with a mere gash in my left shoulder!!*

Yes.

The Knight Leader could certainly use all those categories of spell freely, especially as methods of attack.

However.

William had never seen him wielding more than one at once.

Which meant he could use only one pattern at a time. If he prioritized "severing power," he'd lose "attack range." If he prioritized "attack range," he'd lose "armament weight." Each one of the Knight

Leader's attacks had brought that specific facet to its extreme, which meant he couldn't use them together.

He hadn't held off from using this omnipotent certain-kill attack earlier because he'd been hesitating. On a real battlefield, there was no point in keeping combat power in reserve.

That hesitation existed simply because there was no such convenient certain-kill move to begin with.

And that gave William a chance.

If the Knight Leader prioritized only "attack range," then the mercenary could physically block it!

"Oooooooooohhhhhhhhhhhhhhhhhhhhhhhhhhh!!"

And now William had the Knight Leader in his own range.

He swept his eleven-foot sword sideways.

"!! 'Movement speed'!!"

The Knight Leader's arms moved at a high speed and barely blocked the mercenary's strike.

"Not enough."

But there was no weight or hardness there.

The Knight Leader's body tilted backward at the full-force attack.

It was a loss of less than a second.

But in that time, William turned the blade over with his wrist and focused on the spike at the base on the back. Then, he swung Ascalon again.

Its light color shifted to white.

Large swords like the ones William and the Knight Leader were using lost power at super-close range. The sharp spike had been attached to the base of the sword as a means of dealing with that.

William's magic consolidated to one point, giving it even more penetrating power.

If this couldn't be stopped, it would be the Knight Leader who would fall.

"'Durability rating'!!"

"Too slow."

A moment after William Orwell spoke the words:

The spike that was attached near the sword's base for use in close combat—probably made originally to rip out an evil dragon's thick nerves from the inside using the principles behind levers—slipped past the Knight Leader's defense and stabbed mercilessly into his right breast.

Everything.

Everything was to save the third princess, embroiled in a military coup d'état and soon to be put to death.

Da-paaaaaa!! came the blast.

There were no birds still around to fly up out of surprise.

After all, every bird and beast had run away after over half the trees around them had been cut down.

8

Meanwhile, there were others hiding on a train aside from Touma Kamijou.

Agnes, Lucia, and Angeline.

They were riding an extremely normal passenger train made of ten cars. It was headed from Edinburgh to London. The line was a straight one, going from north UK to south.

Still, probably because the political chaos had stopped all the trains, it was bounding along at a speed that was normally impossible, racing past every station it was usually supposed to stop at.

The cold wind struck Agnes Sanctis on the cheek.

They weren't lingering inside a car or on a roof. Their plight was the wall. Lucia was good at causing her giant wooden wheel to burst apart and using those fragments for attacks, but this time, she'd stabbed the sharp fragments into the aluminum wall to use as footholds and railings.

In a state like a free climbing practice ground, Agnes twisted and peeked through the window. Normally it would be filled with crowds of students and employees alike, but now only the bald-faced fluorescent light lived inside. However, there were tools and devices to adjust swords and armor inside, along with what looked like a communication Soul Arm—the knights had probably brought them on board.

As she scanned them, Agnes muttered to herself. "...It looks like they're still concentrating on keeping watch over the sisters captured in the next car up. The extra knights seem to be gathered in the next one back, too."

Lucia and Angeline nodded to her.

"...That must mean we're halfway between the two groups," the former hissed.

"...I-in that case, if we disconnect the cars, we can set all our friends free without fighting the knights head-on," the latter whispered.

Most of the sisters in the former Agnes unit had been captured in Edinburgh. They hadn't been beheaded on the spot, either because they wanted to go through a proper religious court to make it a lawful enactment of justice, rather than an unreasonable massacre, or they were going to have a grand execution of all former enemies during the second princess's coronation ceremony.

Either way, it was clear what Agnes and the others needed to do.

"...Let's get started," Agnes whispered. "Sister Lucia, Sister Angeline, use your projectile weapons to attack the knights keeping watch through the window from outside the car."

By targeting the knights from outside the window, they could trick them into thinking the attackers were attacking them from somewhere off the train. They might eventually deduce where the snipers were, but that wouldn't present a problem if they settled things quickly enough.

"...I'll destroy the train-car link with the Lotus Wand, then launch a direct attack on the knights while they're confused. You two back me up," she went on.

"...P-please be careful. Surprise attack tactics when we have the initiative are okay, but if we fight head-on, I don't know if all three of us combined could take down even one of them."

Angeline looked worried. Without thinking, Agnes tried to lightly smack her upside the head, but she was holding on to only the wood shards sticking out of the wall. Her posture shook, and she hastily regripped the stakes.

They all nodded to one another, then got rolling.

Lucia and Angeline shifted footholds, going from one wood shard to the next as they headed for the train's roof. Without watching them go, Agnes used the wall to proceed to the rear of the car. She was after the connection linking the two train cars.

"Tutto il paragone. Il quinto dei cinque elementi. Ordina la canna che mostra pace ed ordine."

Her weapon, the Lotus Wand, was hanging from her shoulder by a rope.

When the words formed on her small lips, the wings of the angel statue crouching on the wand's tip began to open up like a flower.

"Prima. Segua la di Dio ed una croce, due cose diverse sono connesse."

When Agnes got close enough to the connection, she used one hand to regrip a wood shard sticking out of the wall and the other to grasp the Lotus Wand.

Her wand ignored distance and struck space itself directly. The power of this spell depended on the force with which she swung the wand—in other words, Agnes's physical strength.

But I know a naked arm won't rip off a steel connection. She glanced at the gravel speeding by her feet. *If I hold the wand to the ground and use the overall force of the train itself, then hit the connection with it, I should be able to destroy it...*

Twisting slightly, she checked the connection's position coordinates, then slowly lowered the bottom of her wand to the gravel.

That was when it happened.

All of a sudden, the door connecting the cars opened and a man clad in silver-colored armor exited.

Agnes, who had been essentially clinging to the automatic door in order to get to the connection, quickly tried to hide herself, but she was too late.

But.

The communication Soul Arm sitting in a seat in the car made a soft noise. If the knight moved his head just a little, he would have noticed Agnes, but he hastily ran over toward the Soul Arm.

As he listened to what was coming through, he said, "That Imagine Breaker snuck onto the freight train headed for Folkestone? Damn him. Was he trying to take a swing at Her Highness Carissa…?"

"…Nice one, kid! I freaking love you!!" Agnes hissed.

She gestured to Lucia and Angeline, who were standing by on the roof, then took a different aim with the Lotus Wand.

Ga-boom!! went a thundering sound.

At the same time that the train's automatic door crashed inward, the ceiling above the knight's head collapsed all at once. The knight frantically tried to pull his sword from his waist, but the three sisters let a concentrated attack rip.

Even presented with a surprise attack from three directions, the knight accurately parried Lucia's and Angeline's attacks.

It didn't seem likely they'd be able to defeat one of the knights borrowing the power of the Curtana Original and the all-British Continent, even if they landed a clean hit.

So Agnes, instead of aiming for the knight himself, attacked the floor of the train at his feet.

"…?!"

The fact that the knight immediately reacted with all his strength may have been the deciding factor. No normal human would have ever fallen through the train's floor, but the silver-colored armored foot broke through it like a sheet of Styrofoam.

Of course, it would take more than that to bring down a battle-hardened veteran knight.

Blast. If I add too much more force, it'll split this car clean in half. If that happens, the Puritan captives gathered in the next car up will slip out of our grasp…!!

Thinking that far in an instant, the knight immediately stopped, which one could probably call a wise decision.

But when he did.

Wham!! A dull noise rang out as a blunt strike from Agnes's space-ignoring Lotus Wand crashed mercilessly into the knight's body. Directly hitting a sensitive spot, ignoring his thick armor.

Where she'd hit was a vital spot on a human body.

Put more precisely, she'd hit him in the crotch.

Like the losing samurai after an *iai* match in a period film, the knight remained still for several seconds.

Eventually, he croaked, "...That...that attack...was unchivalrous..."

He didn't go down in one hit, probably once again because of the Curtana's magic.

Agnes Sanctis sniffed, stuck out her chest, and argued, "Well, good thing we're freaking nuns, then!!"

Wha-bam-bam-ga-bam!! Several more unpleasant sounds repeated, coming from the same place, and the knight's armor shook and trembled. They couldn't read his expression behind his helmet, but it probably would have been a sight to behold.

"Hmm. Just like I thought—looks like my attacks that can ignore distance are the most effective. I can hit their physical bodies behind their thick armor with them," said Agnes, poking the body of the now-disabled knight to check if he would resist.

Angeline's face went red with panic, and possibly to take her mind off it, she headed for the communication Soul Arm and listened in on the other knights' information.

"U-um...It looks like that spiky-haired boy is running away from the freight train with a sorceress from New Light?"

Lucia sighed in spite of herself. "My word. What on earth is going on? Well, perhaps it's business as usual for that young man."

"A-also, they tried to dive into a river, failed, crashed into the river, then got washed downstream and coincidentally picked up by the third princess, Vilian, as she was fleeing. They're saying they're making a mad dash for it while going at it with the Knights' pursuers."

"What is going on?! Japanese Momotaro?!" snapped Lucia unconsciously.

Angeline's shoulders gave a start. "W-well, don't ask me......?! S-Sister Agnes, please help me out here— Eeek!!"

When Angeline looked over at Agnes again, a yelp escaped her.

She watched as Agnes, who seemed to be trying to get information out of the defeated knight, had her hands moving in a somewhat questionable manner as she used her Lotus Wand.

"Oh. I see—you like being stroked better than being hit, do you? Ah-ha-ha. You're trembling. What are you trying to say? Oh—oh, oh my. You're reacting in that spot, too? You're even more sensitive than before. Fu-fu-fu. For a gentleman to feel it more when his hole is played with—you're a pervert. In that case, why don't I shove this wand in directly, all the way?"

"U-ugyaaaaaahhhh!! Wh-when did Sister Agnes change into full-power forbidden mode?!"

"...Sister Angeline. Is this worth being surprised over now? Sister Agnes acted like that during the *Book of the Law* incident in the under-construction Church of Orsola, remember?"

"Well, no, b-but I thought Sister Agnes was actually a pretty, purehearted maiden!! I mean, that boy saw her naked and that was enough to make her faint!!"

"Yes. Sister Agnes is the sort of person who takes great delight in the skirts of others being flipped but deplores her own skirt being flipped."

"I-isn't that the *worst* sort of person?!" cried Angeline in a flurry.

Lucia sighed painfully. Angeline did the same kind of thing. "Let's stop there," she advised Agnes. "This is nothing more than a simple way to rip information out of him, no love or lust involved, but if we don't cut it out now, this knight seems like he'll be corrupted on his own."

"Y-you think you can stop Sister Agnes when she's tripping to the max like this?!"

"Returning her to her senses is a simple matter. I just gave you the answer, too." Lucia set her stare on Agnes's rear end—she was too engrossed in handling her Lotus Wand to notice their conversation. "Sister Angeline, it's your turn. After all, Sister Agnes is the sort of person who hates her own skirt being flipped."

9

Two silhouettes stood out against the dark night.

One was William Orwell.

One was the Knight Leader.

Before, they'd been moving with the drive to exceed the speed of sound, but now they were stopped. The Knight Leader's longsword, having failed in its defense, remained fixed in an awkward pose in the air, while the spike near the base of William's sword had avoided the block and pierced the knight in the right breast.

The spike attached near the base on the back was not nearly so kind as to be the size of a regular nail.

No: It was almost a stake, suitable for a greatsword totaling over eleven feet in length.

While it may not have resulted in instant death, any honest prediction would have involved the ribs on his right side all breaking.

Hidden in the darkness, their expressions contrasted.

One in agony.

One in transcendence.

However—

The one making the agonized expression was William.

And the transcendent, aloof one belonged to the Knight Leader.

It may not have been a strike certain to kill, but William's attack should have had enough destructive force to comfortably disable his opponent.

But in reality, there wasn't a single scratch on him.

Supposedly stabbing into his right chest, the spike didn't draw a single drop of blood—it didn't even tear the fabric of the Knight Leader's shirt.

It felt unnatural, like a sponge, and even William found himself giving a confused look.

…He redirected the impact…No, that isn't it. This is…?!

"Do you know of a Scandinavian warrior named Thororm?"

With the spike pressed to his right breast, the Knight Leader spoke, his expression unchanging.

"Legends say the warrior used sorcery and had the ability to bring a sword's sharpness to zero. Therefore, it is said that no attack would wound him, and his sword would carve into enemies without fear of retaliation."

"That...can't be..."

"I have created a spell that can bring the attack power of any weapon I am able to perceive to zero. Whether the attack is born of science or magic, for that matter. Theoretically, it could disable even nuclear weapons, but as for actual proof...Yes. I'm sure it would manage against the anti-divinity slashing attacks the Far Eastern saint uses."

The Knight Leader slowly shook his head.

"I told you—always have more than one trump card ready," he continued. "Its effects on an individual weapon last ten minutes at most. Arrows and bullets need only fall to the ground, and once bombs fail to explode, they certainly won't suddenly go off after ten minutes without an additional external factor to initiate them. But none of that has to do with you. I can only create a ten-minute reprieve...but when an enemy gains that much time on a real battlefield, it's clear what sort of fate lies in store."

The Knight Leader glared straight at William.

"You caught me with a terrible surprise attack at Dover. It's no wonder I came up with a countermeasure."

"!!" William, feeling the Knight Leader would grab Ascalon's blade with his bare hands, quickly pulled the sword back behind him.

Then, with the slight distance he'd made, he let loose one slashing attack after another, each one using a different method.

The light was red—a thick blade like an ax to rip a dragon's flesh.

"Zero."

The light was blue—a thin blade like a razor to slice a dragon's fat.

"Zero."

The light was green—a spike like a can opener midway up the blade to strip away a dragon's scales.

"Zero."

The light was yellow—a jigsaw wire running along the blade to remove a dragon's organs.

"Zero."

The light was purple—a giant saw on the back to cleave a dragon's bones.

"Zero."

The light was pink—a hooked spike attached to the pommel to tear out a dragon's teeth.

"Zero."

The light was white—a close-range spike near the back of the base to scoop out a dragon's nerves.

"I've already made that zero!! ...Finally out of options?!"

The continuous rumbling, clattering noises suddenly ended.

The Knight Leader grabbed Ascalon, its attacks unleashed from point-blank range, as though handling a sheet of Styrofoam. William gripped his sword hilt even more tightly, and the two stared at each other.

The Knight Leader, who stood in a position of absolute advantage, used his other hand to regrip his dark-red longsword.

"It's over."

The two of them, having stopped moving, glared at each other at point-blank range.

The Knight Leader spoke in an unwavering voice as he admonished the mercenary's greatsword. "Perhaps sorcery that doesn't utilize a weapon—your runes, I'd say—may be able to kill me. Would you like to try?"

It was obvious from his tone that his proposition wasn't serious.

William and the Knight Leader were equals in speed. If William neglected his body-controlling spell to use different magic, that would get him cut down immediately.

"This power was lent to me through the Curtana Original in order to protect the United Kingdom. A lowly mercenary who gives no thought to consequences and disrupts the state for naught but his own emotions cannot kill me."

The Knight Leader's dark-red longsword aimed at William.

Ready to kill the man with a single stroke, the knight offered these last words:

"Go to heaven—along with the third princess."

"...You still don't get it," William spat. "This really isn't enough to go through the trouble of talking about."

"What...?"

The Knight Leader, dubious, looked at Ascalon, whose movements he'd prevented by grabbing it.

More specifically, to its side—attached with a metal fitting, to a single emblem.

"You...What are you thinking? What are you plotting?"

"How persistent. After all this, you'd still ask with your words?"

Upon hearing that, the Knight Leader's face grew even more dubious.

William Orwell was no mere optimist. He could have possibly been more intimately familiar with the tragedies of war than the Knight Leader himself, who had remained in Britain this whole time.

A mercenary like that should understand which politics to back to save the nation at this stage—military prowess or charisma. If he removed Carissa and supported Vilian, with her ideals, they wouldn't even be able to fight off France alone, since it was now a pawn of the Roman Orthodox Church.

This man always had his feet on the ground.

But it didn't seem like this path toward destruction was what comprised William's unwavering spirit.

Wasn't the Knight Leader misunderstanding something?

What on earth was this mercenary named William Orwell fighting for?

The Knight Leader looked once again at the weapon William gripped.

More specifically, at what was attached to its base—the escutcheon.

No...

The escutcheon was originally made to be used by a certain mercenary upon being knighted.

In the end, the opportunity had been lost, and it left an unignorable, eternally blank space in the hallway in Buckingham Palace.

No.

The escutcheon divided the shield into four parts, with each of them painted in a blue-hued pattern.

On top of them, in green, were three animals distributed around them: a dragon, a unicorn, and a silkie.

No!

Four partitions and three animals.

Those could represent only one thing.

No!!

The blue undercoat was England, Scotland, Wales, and Northern Ireland.

The green animals were the Royal Family, the Knights, and the Puritans.

The escutcheon represented perfect harmony among the groups in the United Kingdom.

This mercenary wasn't trying to kill one and back another.

Even the second and third princesses didn't matter—he wanted to combine the strengths of the three sisters and the queen.

"...Are you serious?" The Knight Leader moaned. "Is that what you're thinking?"

Meanwhile, the stiff muscles in William Orwell's face loosened just slightly.

As if to say welcome to his opponent who had finally thought that far.

"I already told you. There is no point in speaking of it."

"It's impossible."

"I don't care," said William with surprising lightness. "My reason is not one I need to explain or defend, nor one I need everyone else to understand. As you said many times over, these are merely the trivial personal emotions of a mercenary. I won't use words to tell you to understand. All *you* need to do is silently carry out the acts you believe in."

"..."

Oddly, after all that, the Knight Leader was at a loss for words.

Nevertheless, the mercenary was right. He couldn't stop his blade here.

However he considered things, making this revolution succeed was for the sake of the United Kingdom.

If the second princess didn't ascend to the throne in this critical situation, there was no telling how many enemies would be upon them.

Therefore...

...In the end, what I must do doesn't change.

They'd both given their reasons.

They didn't need words for them.

One of them would win, and the other would lose.

That was all that existed in their world.

But now that you've lost all your weapons, you've lost your chance at winning.

The Knight Leader had already grabbed Ascalon's blade and stopped it, and his own sword could be upon William at any time.

Thororm's Spell, which could reduce a weapon's attack power to zero, had a duration of about ten minutes. He would need to discharge his duties before this strong enemy named William Orwell regained his weapon.

"I'll end things now."

"I'm sure," came the flat response, which the Knight Leader winced at.

A moment later, William Orwell used all his strength to pull Ascalon's hilt to him—and suddenly, the hilt itself fell out.

The Knight Leader was left holding Ascalon's temporarily powerless blade, and now he was the one about to lose his balance.

Hmm? Did he cause it to break? he thought.
But that wasn't correct.

On the end of William Orwell's hilt was a blade over three feet long.
It was one final superior sword, hidden within his eleven-foot greatsword.

Normally, whether the sword was western or eastern, the forger would prevent the blade slipping out of the hilt the instant you swung it by burying one part of the blade's steel inside the hilt (or creating a hilt by enclosing it between two sheets) and locking it in place with screws or wedges.
Ascalon was the opposite.
Its creator had stored an even smaller sword within the greatsword by placing it so that it lay alongside the steel buried in the hilt.
It was a gimmick workable only because Ascalon was so enormous.
And.
Because the blade had been hidden, the Knight Leader hadn't been able to perceive it.
William turned his back to his opponent, hiding the sword behind his giant frame. Then, going along with the momentum, he quickly twisted and loosed a strike swung around from the side.
Vwohhh!! came the sound of atmosphere splitting apart.
"?!"
For the first time, the Knight Leader's face changed. As he used all his might to retreat, it tore his suit and ripped a straight wound in his chest.
Yes.
Was it not a hidden blade flung from a sleeve that had killed the mythical Scandinavian figure Thororm?
The stinging pain pressed more weight than sharpness against the Knight Leader.
The weight of the trump card. The weight of a renewed fighting spirit. The weight of a strike made without a word.

It almost proved William Orwell was just. In response, the Knight Leader let out a roar.

"Raaaaaaahhhhhhhhhhhhhhhhhhhhhhhhhhhhhhhhhhhhhhh!!"

But he wasn't the only one who shouted.

With one final blade in hand—or perhaps it was the Soul Arm Ascalon's true core—William Orwell pursued the Knight Leader as he jumped back again, attempting to dive into close range.

The wound carved into him, the dripping blood, dulled the Knight Leader's movements.

But it still wasn't a fatal injury.

The Knight Leader had two methods. One was to use his dark-red longsword's attack power to cleave William's body. The other was to use Thororm's Spell to sap William's sword's attack power.

I'll break his sword, decided the Knight Leader instantly. *It won't be victory unless I slay him after crushing that weapon, the symbol of his resistance!!*

He believed in his own justice. Therefore, the Knight Leader denied simply fleeing and tried to thoroughly trample his opponent's view.

Ignoring the pain of the shallow cut in his chest, the Knight Leader set to breaking William's final weapon. If he could only do something about that blade, he'd be left to launch a one-sided attack.

"Zer—!!" he was about to say but stopped.

There was no blade in William Orwell's hands.

They gripped a hilt, but the blade that should have been on top of it was absent.

I...Where is it?!

The spell of Thororm the Knight Leader used selected a target from weapons he himself perceived, then brought their attack power to zero.

In other words, he couldn't influence a weapon he couldn't perceive.

That was when the Knight Leader saw a glint of light.

Directly above the sword hilt William held stretched an extremely thin wire. And the mercenary's thumb was hovering over what looked like a hidden button on the hilt.

Did he shoot it upward first?!

Orwell was probably expecting to throw off the Knight Leader's timing, then he would reel in the wire to reconnect the blade to the hilt and use it for a second attack.

If he succeeded, he'd certainly deal heavy damage.

But now that I know, that's it! Ze—!!

Just as the Knight Leader was about to direct his gaze above William's head, something moved out of the corner of his eye.

It was a branch, about two meters long and thick as a human arm.

It had broken off and fallen to the ground earlier; William had stepped on it, using a seesaw-like motion to kick it upright.

The blade's body above and the fallen tree below.

He could use either as a weapon, but it was obvious which was the more dangerous.

Did you think I'd hesitate and give you time?!

The Knight Leader, without flinching, looked upward.

He would return the blade's attack power, which would probably deal a fatal wound to him, to zero.

I have you n—!!

Convinced of certain victory, the Knight Leader funneled even more strength into the hands gripping his dark-red longsword.

But then something changed.

The sword hilt William held—and the thin wire connecting it to the floating blade—was, strictly speaking, a micro-size tube, and from inside it began to spurt a resinous fluid. When it made contact with the air, it solidified like glue, positioning stakes in every direction, now reborn as a primitive club.

Yes:

William Orwell's most beloved weapon had turned into a giant mace.

"!!"

"!!"

Will I make it?

This was the final attack.

If the Knight Leader endured this, he would win, and if it pushed him back, William would win.

With the mace already right before his eyes, the Knight Leader focused his mind.

Zero!!

The wannabe mercenary, using all his strength, swung the mace down.

The knight chief, without thinking of defense, swung his amber-red longsword in response.

The two giant weapons crossed.

Boom!!

A terrible quake, strong enough to crush human flesh, resounded around them.

In that moment.

At the last possible instant.

The Knight Leader's spell had gone off.

The attack power of the spiked mace William Orwell held had gone to zero, and even if it had made a direct hit at supersonic speed, it wouldn't have been able to wound his opponent whatsoever.

In the darkness, the two men had stopped.

It would have been clear to anyone what the result was.

"...Hmph."

The first one to make a sound was the Knight Leader.

The one who freely manipulated the very patterns behind the armaments that appeared in legends, using them as ways to attack. For his final strike, he'd chosen "severing power" that could cut through anything. Its destructive force would cleave the earth at a mere touch, and even if his opponent was a saint, a direct hit would unavoidably lead to death.

"What a dull ending."

"..."

The mercenary didn't respond to the Knight Leader's words.

The knight's body shook and swayed to the side.

William's mace was buried in the side of his neck.

More specifically, the mace's—and the sword's—hilt.

Even more specifically, the small metal attachment, fixed to the hilt as a part of the device that fired the sword blade, was sticking out just slightly, and that was buried in the Knight Leader's neck.

The man selected a target from all the weapons he could perceive and brought its attack power to zero. Conversely, even if something was right there in front of him the whole time, unless he perceived it as a weapon, he couldn't influence its attack power.

"Ten years since you left...I thought I'd...really made myself stronger, but just like Dover, you did me in with a surprise attack..."

The dark-red longsword the Knight Leader held had veered off course thanks to William's strike, and now it slipped from his hand and fell to the ground.

"Still...though...Knights, too...A disagreeable man, put to shame... To think that on that escutcheon...representing harmony among the three factions and four cultures...would be written even my name..."

The score was settled.

"...Come to think of it...You've always been...that kind of man..."

His body swayed even more to the side, then crumpled to the ground.

He hadn't died.

Just like a *mineuchi*, a strike with the back of the sword from a Japanese katana, he'd passed out from being struck in the neck.

Its attack power hadn't been affected, but the Knight Leader wasn't a weakling—a single metal clasp couldn't kill him. And William Orwell, knowing that, had entrusted his final attack, the difference between dark and light, to that little piece of metal.

His reason was obvious.

"I'm no more than a ruffian, a shallow mercenary wannabe. But it does mean I can fight more freely than a rigid knight," muttered said mercenary to himself. "...Unfortunately, I don't have any blades with which to slay an old friend."

The words were, unusually for him, just idle talk.

10

Touma Kamijou had arrived in Folkestone.

He was trembling madly after getting soaked in the river's water, but he didn't even have the time to complain about it right now. Perhaps it was because he was right in the middle of enemy territory, but he was beginning to feel as though something was wrong.

Dammit, where's the Eurotunnel terminal?! I hope they didn't bring Index away from there...

Kamijou stared into the darkness of the mountain grove with no real light source.

Kamijou had run into the mysterious sorceress Florice and the third princess, Vilian, on the way, but neither of them was currently nearby. They'd encountered a Born Again Amakusa patrol, and he'd entrusted the two ladies to them. They'd apparently received intel from Agnes that Kamijou's group was in Folkestone, so Born Again Amakusa, which had come right nearby using an aquatic rescue machine, sent out scouts to look for them...For some reason, as soon as Florice saw the Amakusa, she shouted, "Y-you tricked us, you bastard!!" but Kamijou wasn't sure what that was all about.

Apparently, a strong enemy called the Knight Leader was protecting Second Princess Carissa in Folkestone, and he'd even taken down Kaori Kanzaki, a saint, putting her out of commission for a time.

The Amakusa didn't want anyone pursuing the wounded Kanzaki, and when an important person like the third princess came into the picture, they necessarily had to choose to fight a defensive battle. At the moment, they seemed to be hiding and watching for an opening in the knights' recon to move out with their aquatic rescue machine.

"You know, if we break down our 'rank' and arrange our people, we can let a few go with you."

When the Amakusa had suggested that, he honestly wanted nothing more than to take them up on it. But Kamijou thought it over a second time more calmly.

"No, you all concentrate on the rescue machine. We can't let Vilian get captured again, and aren't you doing healing magic on Kanzaki or something? In that case, if you got her back onto the front lines as soon as you can, that would be safer than sending people with me."

"But..."

"Once I rescue Index, how am I going to get out of Folkestone? What I want is for you guys to protect the goal line. It would make things easier for me, too."

With that, he got Born Again Amakusa to reluctantly agree after he indirectly integrated into their "large ring." They really didn't seem to want to leave others to their fate.

The knights' highest-priority target to destroy was the third princess.

It made more sense for a force like Born Again Amakusa to put their people toward protecting Kanzaki and her.

...But Itsuwa was getting all red for some reason, and everyone else put her in a stranglehold. Did she want to rescue Index that badly? They must have made friends during the fight with Acqua of the Back before, thought Kamijou calmly, which would have gotten him speared if Itsuwa had heard him.

In any case, right now, he was alone.

"...?"

Suddenly, Kamijou's head lifted. He could hear something.

When he realized it, a moment later, his ears were slammed with the sound of an explosion like a shock wave.

What is...?! Kamijou crouched down instinctively and turned in the direction from which it had come.

He couldn't see past the darkness.

It was clear that getting closer wouldn't do him any favors, but if he didn't dive into the danger, he wouldn't be able to rescue Index.

Slowly, Kamijou crept toward the source of the sound.

The way held a narrow, paved road, covered in fallen leaves. After a certain point, cracks appeared in it, then breaks, until it got to the point where he was actually having trouble walking on it. Finally, he saw exhumed black soil and thick, mowed-down trees.

As always, there were no streetlights.

But there was a light source.

"Is that…?"

A horse and wagon?

Something was there, about ten meters ahead of him. On the front of the awfully old-fashioned vehicle hung glass lamps enclosed in open box-shaped reflectors. Maybe they were lanterns, like the things on the end of flashlights. They were likely not imitations, instead actually using fire. At times, the light illuminating the dark swayed unsteadily.

But that wasn't the only light.

Blade hitting against blade, and steel armor, too, breaking into sparks.

It was a true battlefield where man fought against man.

If he looked very closely, the carriage wasn't in good shape.

With one of its four wheels broken, it was unnaturally tilted.

And the battle was unfolding around that broken carriage. No—he wasn't sure he could call it a battle. At least, it certainly didn't look like an equal fight.

Several knights, clad in silver-colored armor, jumped in from various angles.

At their center stood a man holding a sword over ten feet long.

A flash.

Kamijou's eyes couldn't make out the details—it was just a skirmish unfolding with overwhelming speed—and as a result, spectacular sparks flew one after another from the silver armor, each of them blown far, far away.

One of them crashed right next to Kamijou.

It was no coincidence.

The man standing at the middle had moved only his eyes, not his head, to level a glare on Kamijou.

A brawny body.

Clothes mostly blue.

A giant weapon.

They all combined to give Touma Kamijou a terrible chill. This sensation wasn't so vague as a mere premonition—it was the *experience* of having been literally driven to the precipice of death that triggered the warning signals in him.

Their root cause looked Kamijou in the face and said, "Hmph. I would have preferred not to see that hateful face again."

"Acqua...of the Back?!" shouted Kamijou in spite of himself.

A big man who wielded particular might even in God's Right Seat. Once, they had been able to defeat him in Academy City, but the opponent was one against whom they needed the full Amakusa roster plus the saint Kaori Kanzaki's powers to just barely eventually win.

He's...alive?! I thought there was that huge explosion in the underground city lake...Are you telling me he survived even that and then escaped Academy City?!

Kamijou's thoughts, while disturbed, presented several possibilities to him.

His tensed body shivered. *But why would Acqua show up here? Don't tell me God's Right Seat is trying to stir up this awful coup d'état even more?!*

He didn't know what reason the man was in town for, but he wasn't a person Kamijou by himself could do anything about.

Unconsciously clenching his teeth, he inadvertently mumbled to himself, "...Damn, all this stupid coup business is already a mess. This is a pretty unlucky coincidence!!"

"I doubt it is coincidence."

Despite standing at a distance from Kamijou, Acqua actually responded to his mutterings.

As the sharpness of Acqua's five senses caused Kamijou to renew his caution, the man offhandedly gestured to the broken carriage. "If your long-term goal is to resolve the coup d'état, and your short-term goal is to recover Index again, then the basis for our actions aligns in several points."

"What?" Kamijou followed Acqua's fingertip with his eyes.

When he did, he saw the broken carriage's door was half-open, and a cloth, which looked like a nun's hood, was sticking out. It wasn't a normal one. It was white fabric embroidered in gold, like a teacup.

"Index!!" he cried without thinking, but there was no answer.

He wanted to run right to her, but it was too dangerous to shift his attention away from Acqua of all people.

But while Kamijou kept his guard up, the soldier himself didn't seem that interested in him. With casual movements, he went away from the carriage, turning his back to Kamijou.

"If recovering her is your goal, then be swift about it. In a certain way, this place is more dangerous than the conquered city of London."

"...?" Kamijou gave him a dubious stare—the God's Right Seat member was displaying a strange lack of hostility.

But the situation didn't end there.

"Hmph. By the looks of things, the Knight Leader's been taken down."

A sudden voice.

Kamijou and Acqua turned around just as a single woman came out of an interval between trees.

A member of the British royal family, she wore a predominantly red dress garnished here and there with equally red leather. In her right hand, she gripped a sword with no blade or point.

"I thought I'd ordered him to bring me two heads so I can get used to this sort of thing...And all he could do was wound you? It seems I need to do everything around here."

The second princess, Carissa.

The mastermind behind the coup d'état.

"!!" Without thinking, Kamijou steeled himself, but the second princess wasn't looking in his direction.

Her eyes set on Acqua, she lightly swung the Curtana Original upward. "He sure did cause me trouble, so. If we don't have the opening performer, that means I need to deal with the cannon fodder myself."

"Your troubles will vanish soon. Your military ambitions will end now, after all."

"You'd better not underestimate me too much. Did you forget the Curtana Original is in my hands?"

As she watched Acqua reposition his giant sword, the second princess smiled thinly.

Acqua's face changed, and his sword moved.

He wasn't aiming at Carissa. Instead, he slammed his sword's side into a nearby giant tree, using the shock wave to blow away Kamijou and send him tumbling.

Meanwhile.

Carissa held her strange sword aloft and said, "This is originally a ritual sword, meant to sever British territory from the planet Earth and to manage and control the interior—but by applying that idea, I can do things like *this*, too."

She swung it down.

Boom!!

A moment later, *Kamijou witnessed the sight of dimensions being cut.*

The range was about sixty feet.

With a strange noise, something passed over in a ray, connecting Acqua and the spot Kamijou had just been in. He could tell that something like a zone, or a wall, was expanding, its width equal to the Curtana Original's. It was colored white, like a plastic model before painting. The object, which hadn't fully become an *object* yet, had appeared before Kamijou's eyes.

"I felt this before, too, when I was *practicing*...The Soul Arm itself is an antique, but when the user—that's me—wields it based on military knowledge, its nature changes a bit, so...Well, my mother has the same trait, so she could probably do something similar."

Joy mixed into Carissa's voice.

"Did you know this? When you slice a three-dimensional object, the cross section becomes two-dimensional. When you slice a two-dimensional object, the cross section appears as something one-dimensional."

They heard a *ka-thud.*

The strange belt-shaped object illogically floating in midair fell down right next to Kamijou.

It had a texture not unlike ceramic, but despite its apparent mass, it seemed to be incredibly heavy. Even after it fell, it continued to sink slowly into the black earth.

"In the same way, when an object with more than three dimensions, or space, is sliced, the cross section is output into the world as a three-dimensional object. The result is that thing—the exposure of the cross section—remains of the object."

Whoosh. The second princess hefted the Curtana Original onto her shoulder.

It wasn't an attack.

Nevertheless, dimensions sliced along with the movement of her sword, and like pencil shavings, colorless belt-shaped objects began to fall at her feet.

"Of course, this thing doesn't care whether it's a higher or lower dimension. It slices all dimensions currently in this position at once. It seems like out of all the exposed cross-sectional objects, the only ones we can perceive are those that appear in the three-dimensional world."

What...the hell? Kamijou was dumbstruck.

If what she said was true, that sword was like a monster weapon that could cut through all dimensions—and he knew what dimensions were, but mostly only in concept. No matter how much steel an enemy used to protect himself, the Curtana Original would probably ignore it and slice through dimensions and his body.

But despite all that...

At this point, Kamijou didn't even feel fear. The scale was just too enormous. The universe was apparently expanding forever because of the Big Bang, but nobody could physically feel space expanding with their own five senses. But that was the kind of power the second princess, Carissa, was manipulating.

"*Omnidimensional slicing magic.*"

Carissa snapped her wrist to whirl the Curtana Original around, and as she littered the ground with cross-sectional objects, the world's wreckage, her smile slowly broadened.

"This is the first time I've used it, too...Seems easier to use than I expected, so. If there's any issue with it, it's that it'll end things so incredibly easily that I'll lose face for it."

At this point, Kamijou was finally recovering from his state of shock and rediscovering his ability to think, little by little.

The second princess, Carissa—mastermind behind the coup.

They'd been able to have a normal conversation in Buckingham Palace, and they had even laughed together. He didn't want this to come down to a brawl if it didn't need to, but it didn't seem very likely to settle things by talking it out. And if he made a wrong move, Index, still unconscious in the carriage, would be in danger too.

...Shit. We'll have to talk it out after fighting!!

Carissa faced them with her sword that could probably slice through far more than a man-made nuclear shelter—like the planet, or space, all at once.

Kamijou threw a sidelong glance at Acqua.

Could he trust him?

No matter what anyone said, Acqua was still one of the God's Right Seat members of the Roman Orthodox Church.

But on the other hand, he'd just been fighting the knights, led by the Knight Leader, on his own.

He could assume they seemed to share a common enemy for the moment.

Kamijou hesitated for a moment, but he was sure there wasn't time to waver. "Hey, can you buy some time?"

"..." When Kamijou spoke to him, the man's eyes set upon Carissa, and Acqua scowled—as expected.

Kamijou ignored this and continued, "Looks like that crazy sharpness is only on the sword's edge. The side of it should be regular steel.

Hit it with your blade and make her falter, just for a second. Then I'll use my right hand to bust up that Soul Arm—"

"Oh, how scary," interrupted Carissa in an obviously sport-ive tone. "Yes, your own patented skill is called Imagine Breaker, isn't it?"

She stopped whirling the Curtana Original around.

The flat, pointless tip came down.

With her sword stopped dead, she said, "Then allow me to intro-duce you to an application of this technique suited for it."

Carissa shoved the Curtana Original's tip into the ground.

Boom!! A shock wave rattled Kamijou's ears.

A dome-shaped, five-hundred-meter tempest of destruction whipped up around the second princess.

She'd probably changed the flow of mana—which she'd focused in order to use her omnidimensional slice—diverting it to a dif-ferent route. The destructive force born as a result didn't reach a high enough output to slice through other dimensions, but instead, it sent a shock wave flying equally in all directions in this three-dimensional world.

It was unquestionably an explosion.

The giant wall turned up the ground, mowed down the trees, and reached where Kamijou was standing in an instant.

"Ah-ohhhhhhhhhhhhhhhhhhhhhhhhhhhhhhhhhhhhhhhhhhhhhhh?!"

With a shout, Kamijou got his right hand ready.

But perhaps it had failed.

This power was so incredibly vast and continuous that Kamijou's right hand alone couldn't nullify it completely. The knowledge left over in his mind after his memory loss forced him to think of Inno-centius and Dragon's Breath.

A fiendishly brutal pressure slammed into his right hand, and with an awful bone-creaking noise, pain splintered through him.

Pushed back by the power, he was launched up from the ground in mere seconds.

And once his body had been thrown into the air, the rest was simple—

Grwshhh!!

—He instantly flew away.

A dome-shaped explosion with a five-hundred-meter radius.

Kamijou, his body fired diagonally up by the pressure, reached an altitude of two hundred meters in the night sky.

When the force pushing him up from below and the force of gravity reached equilibrium, for a moment, Kamijou floated in the air, staring at the scattered Folkestone nightscape.

What do I do...?

It would be a matter of seconds before he began to fall.

And his right hand didn't have any kind of convenient ability to let him land safely from a height of two hundred meters.

What do I do?!

The ever-present force of gravity bared its fangs at Touma Kamijou.

INTERLUDE THREE

Elizard, Queen of England, was riding a horse.

They weren't on refined dirt prepared for equestrians but a small paved road leading from Windsor to London. They'd been running through a dark forest until a few moments ago, but now spread out around her was a gently sloping pasture that reached beyond the horizon.

...Truly—the United Kingdom's flag was made from a combination of flags from England and Scotland as a symbol of our union. Now it's all in shambles. We certainly will need to recover "it" from London to put it back together...

The approximate movement distance was a bit under fifty kilometers.

Compared to the forests and hills from before, the path wasn't very complex. In a car, one might be able to arrive in London in about thirty minutes (ignoring the speed limit).

However—

He may be a warhorse, but even he has his limits.

Elizard exhaled slightly, gripping the reins.

Some thoroughbreds of the racing variety could run faster than a car, but that speed was possible only on soft soil or grass. If you made a horse run full speed over hard asphalt, his hooves would break in short order.

Plus, horse races were like short- or middle-range sprints for the horses; the same laws didn't apply to a long-range run of fifty kilometers.

As a result, the queen needed to keep a speed of about twenty to thirty kilometers per hour and occasionally pause to take a short break so she wouldn't wear out the horse.

He does still have special horseshoes for public roads, and I'm using a spell to bolster his muscular power and stamina...but I still can't make him do anything excessive. Things would be simpler if I could use the large-scale circles embedded all along these old roads to strengthen warhorse power, but...obviously, I can't use them.

Administration of the magic circles built into the old roads belonged to the British government...which meant if she used them, that information would get to the people under the second princess's thumb. If that happened, she'd get caught up in trouble for sure.

It was an aggravating situation, but there was no irritation on the queen's face.

In fact, her look was one of pity for the warhorse she'd been overtaxing.

"Sorry about making you come with me for this tightrope act."

The warhorse couldn't understand human language, but the words escaped the queen anyway. The horse didn't show any reaction, of course, but there was no sense of dissatisfaction, fear, or confusion in his burly galloping. Elizard watched the bundle of muscle as he proceeded on and on with her on his back, reflecting on how she truly was blessed with good subordinates.

Then she was lit up from behind by car headlights.

Thinking it was pursuers from the Knights or the Royal Family, the queen focused her mind on the Curtana Second hanging at her waist, but the reality was vastly different.

A gaudy young person driving a gaudy car drove up beside the horse Elizard rode on. And if the man in the driver's seat was gaudy, then the woman in the passenger's seat was, too.

Actually, upon closer inspection...

"Heeey! My hitchhiking attempt bore fruit!"

"Y-you can't be serious! Were you really waiting that entire time for a car to pass you in the forest?!" cried out Elizard in shock from atop her horse.

Laura Stuart smiled and nodded from the passenger's seat.

Meanwhile, the gaudy youngster in the driver's seat smirked. "Actually, I was super scared at first, since I thought she was a hitchhiking ghost. But now that I'm thinking calmly, she's just some pesky weirdo. I was gonna leave her on the side of the road, but if you know her, could you hurry up and grab her for me?"

"I'm sorry about that. She's an idiot who doesn't know how the world works. I'll take her from here."

After sincerely apologizing, Elizard grabbed one of the arms of the woman in the passenger seat and switched her from the convertible to the back of her horse.

When she did, the man gripping the convertible's steering wheel seemed to finally notice something. "Wait, what? Hey, that's a horse. A horse?"

"...It should be obvious."

"Gya-ha-ha! It just went *brrr* at me, seriously! That's crazy! I don't think I've ever seen a horse this close before. Could I snap a photo before I go?"

"Wait, idiot, no, don't take out a phone or a camera or anything! If the flash goes off, it'll scare the horse! Also, you really shouldn't be using a cell phone while driving—!!"

"Okay, say cheese!"

Ka-click, ka-click, ka-click, went the absurd electronic noise as he released the shutter.

Without thinking, purely on reflex, Elizard had put on a perfect anti-picture-taking queen's smile, but...

"Aw, shit. The horse is real blurry. Nobody'd even be able to tell what this is. Kinda looks like the hag riding it's about to go to heaven or something. Wait, hang on. I've seen her somewhere before. You're one of my aunts, right?"

"…"

Elizard, queen of England, maintained her smile and reached for the Curtana Second.

It had only about 20 percent of its power left, but the ceremonial sword could still cut a little bit of dimension.

With a slashing noise, she cleanly cut off the convertible's radiator, and the spurting coolant prompted the engine to seize up.

With the engine stalled, the convertible stopped on the road, and the queen sniffed loudly at him, but…

"Hmm. That seemed to me a waste of an excellent car."

"Ugh—damn it!" Laura whined. "I could have pilfered the car and used it to head to London to save time!!"

Elizard was now slightly regretful after hearing that, but eventually she turned her thoughts back to the positive.

She regripped the warhorse reins. "Well, we can hardly abandon this boy to a place like this," said Elizard offhandedly as she and Laura Stuart continued on their way to London.

CHAPTER 6

Knight and Queen: Defensive Line Breakthrough
Safety_in_Subway.

1

The second princess, Carissa, stood in the dark forest of Folkestone.
Or rather, the former forest.

Her earlier attack had broken dozens, even hundreds of the trees
that had been around her, mowing them down and driving them far
afield. Now, in every direction were churned-up black soil and jagged half stumps that had barely been left with their roots.

"Hmph. Did I go too far? …Well, this does mean I have a guarantee that my revolution will succeed as long as I have this sword, so."

The second princess rested the Curtana Original on her shoulder
and lightly exhaled.

The omnidirectional dome-shaped explosion wasn't the Curtana's
original usage. As though that was affecting it, the resting sword
shook and vibrated slightly. It would subside momentarily, but it
was eerie—if she did the same thing again, the shaking might break
the sword.

*As always, you need to read the instruction manual for tools in
order to use them properly, so. Temporary measures at the front
aren't enough. I'll need to visit Buckingham Palace and do some real
adjustments.*

The carriage the mercenary William Orwell had ambushed was

also gone without a trace. It was supposed to be transporting the Index of Prohibited Books and all 103,000 of its grimoires, but now she couldn't know for sure if it was alive or dead.

...Well, it doesn't matter. Its only value was as a rational pretext. It is I who holds the reins of this nation now, so. Nobody can complain if I start a war based on an irrational pretext.

With the blade-less, tip-less sword on her shoulder, Carissa used her other hand to take out her cell phone, using her thumb to manipulate it. She chose one abbreviated number from its memory and put the phone to her ear.

On the other end was one of her subordinates in the Knights, who was standing by at Buckingham Palace in London.

"How did it go in London?"

"We've successfully brought almost all the United Kingdom's major cities, including the capital, under our control. London has been restored to order, and there are no signs of any thoughtless uprisings on the civilians' part."

"Oh. Well, it looks like the Knight Leader has lost."

"...!! B-but that's..."

"I know you've already realized it." Carissa laughed sardonically. "Were you hoping I'd deny it?"

Because of how she was using the Curtana Original to send vast quantities of telesma to the knights and the Knight Leader, their leader being defeated would have brought about a fluctuation in the total amount of power.

Still, it looks like they can't help being rattled, so, reflected Carissa, continuing without paying it much attention. "I'm coming back there now. Can you get a Eurostar train moving?"

"I—I received a report earlier that a freight train has arrived on-site to reinforce our troops, but..." Her subordinate's voice sounded somehow shaken. *"Directly after that, it would appear somebody detached the rail lines in several spots along the London-Folkestone line...Repairs are proceeding apace at three of those locations, but considering the possibility they tampered with other lines, we may need to recheck every line going one hundred kilometers out..."*

"I see." *The Asian earlier must have snuck onto that freight train. After they were sure, they no longer had a use for the trains coming after, so they messed with the rail line and started sabotaging our infrastructure.*

A smile escaped Carissa's lips at the guerrilla-like resistance.

She looked up at the starry sky overhead and said, "In that case, call in the Air Force helicopter currently on patrol near Folkestone."

"*Ma'am...Would that be wise? You'll run the risk of being a target for an anti-air spell.*"

"Considering the total quantity of telesma in the Curtana Original, it would take more than a little midair explosion to kill me. It's vital that I head for Buckingham Palace as soon as possible, so."

"*Understood, ma'am,*" came the knight's response. He continued, "*In other news, while you've been away...we've received a telegram from France.*"

"If it's just some assemblyman, ignore it."

"*Well, ma'am, the president technically counts as a member of Parliament...What shall we do?*"

"Hmm, it would be pretty funny to ignore him, too, but put him through to me now. You may listen in. I'll show you your new head of state's diplomatic skills."

This time, the "*understood, ma'am*" response smelled of a slight smile.

A few seconds passed, and the type of noise coming over the transmission changed. She'd been connected to a different person.

"*I-I'm willing to cooperate!*"

The very first thing out of the person's mouth was that.

It was the president of France, who frequently appeared in the news.

"*The Eurotunnel explosion terror incident calls for cooperation.*"

"Hold up, I'm getting some awful noise in the background." Carissa made an easily understood face of displeasure, even though it wouldn't get to him. "Are you calling me from a strip club? There're so many lewd noises that I can't hear what you're saying. Stop sticking bills in the dancers' stockings and be a little more serious about this, if you please."

"Y-you're the one who needs to take this seriously!! I'm telling you I'm willing to negotiate so that we can make the smartest decision for both of us!!"

"Wait a minute. Negotiate? We're supposed to be killing each other. What, do you want me to lick your ass for you? Well, I'm not about to shame someone for their particular interests, but you should make sure nobody powerful catches on to it. Otherwise you'll have a rough election coming up, won't you?"

"E-enough dicking around!! I'm well aware of that!!"

As though he'd breathed heavily into the receiver, actual noise made it to Carissa's ears this time.

As the second princess stuck out her tongue a bit in jest, the desperate French president continued, *"You dispatched destroyers to the Strait of Dover, didn't you?! Loaded with very large missiles, too! I don't know if you're trying to threaten us, but why the hell can't you understand this will deal major damage to our relationship?!"*

"Oh, really?" said Carissa, as though the thought was absurd. "And here I didn't think the one who had a nuclear submarine under the Strait of Dover ready and waiting would have the right to tell me off. As far as we can make out from its frequent coded calls, it seems to have extremely France-like characteristics, and I have a feeling its nuclear payload is aimed right at London."

"…?!"

She could almost hear the man opening and closing his mouth repeatedly.

Ignoring him, she went on. "France is a nuclear power just like the U.S. and Russia, so. I'm aware you have the option, but…Come on, now. Could you be any more obvious about it? Weren't you the ones who got help from the Roman Orthodox Church to use the ban as a shield to convince the EU to take away our nuclear weapons and ability to develop them? In any case, I hope you don't think a single preemptive surprise attack will be enough to finish us."

Boom!!

The source was a distant explosion. It was far enough away that, like distant lightning, the light and sound arrived at different times. Carissa turned her eyes toward the sea, a long ways away.

"Hmm. Don't worry about that one. According to my destroyer's report, it was apparently just a seagull."

As she spoke, Carissa used her opposite hand from the one holding her phone to shake the Curtana Original. *Bam!!* The sword sliced through a hundred meters' worth of dimension and created a fan-shaped white debris object along its path.

Using a foot filled with a part of Michael's LIKENESS OF GOD power, Carissa kicked the giant fan, flinging it into the night sky. The fan swung fast like a helicopter, then disappeared over the horizon.

"…Our nation's radar and anti-air defense weapons can locate and intercept foreign midair objects with that much precision. A big old missile would just be a target, so. They're basically lumps of metal without any concealment magic equipped. You could fire a hundred of them and we could shoot down every last one."

Carissa then created a second giant fan, then a third, and kicked them off into the distance as well.

"*N-no. No!! That submarine doesn't belong to us. Coded calls? They must be faking them to make them seem like France is involved!!*"

"Well, I don't have any proof, so," admitted Carissa easily. After admitting it, though, she counterattacked: "In that case, you would have no issue with us claiming self-defense and sinking this brazen sub of unknown affiliation targeting my nation's capital, would you? France isn't involved in any way, after all, so you'd never try to rescue the crew members, right? …But if you interfere the slightest bit in this operation, you're accepting that we'll label France as cooperating with this 'unknown sub.'"

Booooom!! came another earth-shattering rumble.

This time, it wasn't a destroyer gun. It was the sound of the giant fan Carissa had launched striking the water's surface, then using its massive weight to sink the "unknown" submarine hidden underwater.

"Was that a hole in one? Shouldn't have had it waiting in shallow waters to fire the missile. You won't make it if you try to dive now. That 'unknown sub' fleet won't last another minute."

"*You...You bitch...!!*"

"Let's see. For every time the unknown sub requests help from the French navy, every time it tries to move even a millimeter toward French borders, my nation's destroyers will fire a cruise missile loaded with a bunker cluster. The first target will be Versailles, the second Paris, and the third...Well, I'm sure it won't come to that. If you haven't learned at that point, I can decide then, so...A ruler is judged on how many of his people's lives he can protect. Considering your reaction, you'll get failing marks, won't you?"

Now, all he could do was sit by and watch as the trump card he'd gone to the trouble of deploying sank. He had no other option but to bear it while listening to his countrymen scream.

The French president was struck dumb, and Carissa continued scornfully, "Why don't you pass the baton to your leader-princess? Or is she still sulking in her cradle? You might be proud of having won control over Parliament, but get as many fools as you want together—they'll never come up with a plan that can oppose us. Just go bow down to your precious Saint of Versailles like your life depends on it and ask for the detestable strategist to help...If you don't, your name might go down stained as the most incompetent ruler in history—one who caused a war due to personal pride and led his own country to ruin."

Carissa heard a wail that sounded like a child throwing a temper tantrum, but she ignored it and hung up.

Fwup, fwup, fwup, went the helicopter rotors overhead.

It was the Air Force unit that had been conducting patrol operations in Folkestone. Observational helicopters were essentially attack helicopters with their armaments removed, so this one was extremely small, not even a meter wide. It was originally a two-seater, but it had probably taken time to let one of the pilots disembark in order to allow Carissa on board. She wouldn't have been able to tolerate their late arrival otherwise.

Noticing the princess's presence, the helicopter's pilot stopped abruptly at a height of twenty meters, then began to slowly descend. But the second princess moved before he could.

Bam!! Carissa leaped straight up the twenty meters, grabbed the side of the helicopter with an arm, and dug her sharp heel armor into it. As the pilot gasped in surprise, Carissa opened the door in front of her and entered with the levity of someone climbing into the rear seat of a family car.

"…Helicopters are useful, but the problem is they mess up my hair, so."

After jumping high in the sky using only leg power, Carissa put a hand to her head and made a displeased face.

Then, with her arms folded, she continued, her tone suggesting she was telling her personal driver where to go.

"Could I get you to bring me to Buckingham Palace? I need to go there to rearrange this thing's specs." Tapping the back of her hand on the Curtana Original's side, Carissa went on offhandedly, "And don't be a laggard. If you start to seem useless, I'll drop this helicopter and run there myself just fine, so."

2

"Oww…"

Touma Kamijou awoke to a dull pain in his backbone area.

He was inside a car abandoned in the mountains, up next to the ruined foundation of a building. The car seemed quite foreign—the big sort of gas-guzzling passenger vehicle—but was he even "inside" it? It didn't have a roof. All the doors had been removed, too. It wasn't so much an abandoned car as just a chassis, and Kamijou lay faceup in it.

Past the removed doors was a dark forest. It was still the middle of the night, but his eyes seemed to have gotten used to it by now. The dark wasn't completely blacked out—it had its own values and shading, and he could make out the silhouettes of objects. Truly experiencing the concept of starlight was a relatively rare thing for someone raised in Tokyo.

What...happened...?

Kamijou rose abruptly from the indistinct sofa-like back seat still there, trying to set everything straight in his head.

...I couldn't fully erase the second princess's attack, then got blown away...Didn't it launch me really high in the air...?

Common sense would suggest there was no way he could have fallen from hundreds of meters up and be fine. Having a cushion underneath him to maybe break his fall—it was beyond that level. But he still had all his limbs intact, and not only did none of his bones seem broken, but all he had were a few scrapes.

Then, as he was thinking about everything—

"Must be nice. Have you finally awoken?"

—he heard a low voice. And when he looked over:

"Ee?! Acqua?!!"

—Kamijou nearly assumed a defensive posture without thinking, but his feet got tangled up in the abandoned car, sending his raised hips sinking back down into the back seat with a *plop*.

Acqua of the Back didn't try to enter the vehicle. With a stupidly large weapon in his hand again (though this one different from the time they fought in Academy City), he stood still outside the car.

Carefully observing Acqua, Kamijou asked slowly, "You're... alive...?"

"Those are words that should only be said by those who have attacked someone with the intent to kill and were confident they had indeed killed." Acqua sighed as though it were preposterous. "Still, of course, even I had not thought the power I had accumulated using the Adoration of Mary spell would be made to blow up from within. I immediately built a bypass and then expelled the power from my body, thereby ending things with no trouble. However, it caused my power to temporarily descend to that of an average saint in the end."

Acqua, who relatively enjoyed keeping silent, was rattling on and on about things Kamijou didn't understand. The grudge directed at

, him made Kamijou think, *Wow, he could literally just come over here and crush me,* and he started to tremble.

"Hey, wait, so what the heck happened to me after that explosion?"

"Hmph. Nothing worthy of note. I simply picked you up in midair and landed on the ground."

He said it with such a straight face! thought Kamijou in shock. "Huh? Hey, wait a minute. What happened to Index?! Carissa's attack was like an explosion that went in every direction! What happened to the carriage she was in?!"

"If you are going to ask questions, take a careful look around and think for yourself first."

With an utterly disdainful look, Acqua pointed. Kamijou looked in that direction and saw that the sister in the white habit was sitting in the passenger seat of the abandoned car, passed out.

"...Wait. You picked her up, too?"

"Well, in that situation, two people were likely my limit."

He spoke casually, but Carissa's attack had been nothing less than an explosion. Was Acqua saying that in the span of an instant, he'd grabbed Index from the carriage, grabbed the air-launched Kamijou, and still kept minimal defenses up for himself, all at the same time?

...I keep feeling less and less like I can beat him. Actually, how did I even survive against such a monster when he was in Academy City...?

"Why...did you save me?"

"As you might think, it would have been easier to let you die," Acqua agreed without hesitation. "Are you aware that you are the root cause of this disturbance?"

"..."

"Even so, the situation is different from when I spoke of it in Academy City. The problem is not merely that you have defeated someone of the Roman Orthodox Church. Genuinely, the boss's target was your right hand."

"What? Who's this boss person...?"

"Currently, a man named Fiamma of the Right leads the Roman Orthodox–Russian Catholic federation. And Fiamma is after your right hand and the Index of Prohibited Books, which is required to bring out its true characteristics." Acqua continued his monologue, ignoring Kamijou's confusion. "In which case, one could assume the two ways to quash Fiamma's ambitions are to break your right arm beyond repair or destroy the Index's brain."

"?!" Kamijou didn't grasp the situation, but his body tensed at the crisis before his eyes.

But Acqua himself rejected those choices, apparently: "Obviously, had I intended to do that, I would have left you two, and you would have died."

"...Then why didn't you? What are you thinking?"

"To crush the source of this disturbance," said Acqua smoothly. "However, I am aware that Imagine Breaker and the Index are no more than accessories to the true source. Fiamma would panic if he lost the centerpieces to his plan, but he could always change the plan and restart or even spread far more meaningless destruction in self-abandonment...Therefore, there is no choice but to destroy the source of the sources."

Not expounding on that, Acqua turned his back to Kamijou.

The tall man with the giant sword said, "However, the necessity arose for me to first put a stop to this trivial quarrel, derived from the true source. If the British faction was to increase its power, the possibility would arise for a chance to stop the conversion of the map of the European faction to Roman Orthodoxy...Which, as a result, might also be a factor in reducing Fiamma's aims."

"You have a way to stop all this?"

"I have no need for parlor tricks. I believe you have some idea of how I do things by now."

"But Carissa and the Knights have taken over the whole UK!"

"The obstacle's size is no issue...Well, this new system of Carissa and the Knights based on the Curtana Original does hold its own unique frailties because of what it is, but..."

"Wha—?"

"...Taking advantage of that would not be my way. In the end, I must still face this obstacle squarely."

After nearly spitting the last words, Acqua suddenly disappeared.

He must have left at a very high speed, because Kamijou's eyes couldn't detect it happening.

Acqua of the Back..., wondered Kamijou, putting a hand on Index's shoulder as she sat unconscious in the passenger seat. Would this man, who as an enemy would be devastating, be the thing they needed to turn the tides?

3

Kamijou didn't know what he should do to care for the unconscious Index, but after he waited for a little bit, the girl eventually opened her eyes.

"Mm-mmm..."

"Index! Are you all right? Are you hurt anywhere?!" cried Kamijou, his expression brightening.

Index shifted a little. "...Touma, did you save me from the Knights?"

"That would make sense, wouldn't it?" Kamijou averted his eyes from the girl. "Unfortunately, it's not that convenient."

For a few moments, Index looked at him blankly. Then she cried out, "Wait?! You didn't come all the way here with another woman I don't know, did you?!"

"That would also make sense, wouldn't it? But reality wasn't that kind to me!!" shouted Kamijou. "But I'm glad you're the same as usual."

"Touma, I think I'm ready for dinner."

"Okay, that's too much the same."

"Ah?"

With that, after the now-relaxed Kamijou and the blank-faced Index wandered a little in the dark forest, they were able to join up with members of Amakusa. It wasn't a mere coincidence but rather the apparent result of detecting the large explosion the second princess had caused, and thus the others secretly moving into the region to search for the culprits and victims.

Their temporary base of operations was a large rescue plane that could take off from and land on the water. The rescue machine Kamijou and Index rode on used the slender river to shoot off into the night sky at a speed that would make any professional pilot white in the face.

The plane had seemed large from the outside, but with over fifty people on board, it obviously felt cramped. The one to come to him out of the crowd and talk was Saiji Tatemiya.

"It looks like the second princess used an Air Force helicopter to get into Buckingham Palace a step before us."

He thought he could hear voices from the back of the plane saying things like, "Itsuwa, this is your chance; go for it!!" "I—I can't; I still reek of alcohol!!" "You're imagining it! How many hours ago was that anyway?!" but Tatemiya was standing right between him and them.

"If we want to put down this coup, we're still gonna have to do something about her. Thankfully, unlike the Priestess, the body Carissa was born with isn't special like a saint's. This coup's core is the Curtana Original. If we can just destroy that, we'll be able to take away all the power she has, but…"

Without thinking about it, Kamijou looked over at Kaori Kanzaki when he said the word *Priestess*.

She was sitting on the floor, her back to the plane wall. She had bandages wrapped around a few parts of her, and her exposed skin showed bruises in a couple of spots. When she realized he was looking at her, she bowed her ponytailed head slightly in apology.

"…I am sorry. The former Agnes unit and Sherry Cromwell are fighting the Knights with their lives on the line, and I should have been leading them in the battle…but as you can see, I've suffered a defeat. I'm trying to recover my stamina, but it might be some time before I can move again."

"I mean, I don't care about that, but…Are you even okay?"

"I would love to brag that I'm perfectly fine." Kanzaki's slightly cut lips loosened a little, seeming to construct a smile. She glanced over at Tatemiya, who nodded a bit and carried on for her.

What he said was about what Kamijou had heard from Acqua.

"But if your info that Acqua defeated the one big obstacle—the Knight Leader—is true, then it looks like whatever happened, things have taken a turn for the better."

"...Just so we're sure, he's a member of God's Right Seat, remember? And all I did was listen to what he said. I didn't actually see the Knight Leader defeated or anything. Shouldn't we consider the possibility that it's all part of some plan?"

"Actually, scouts have confirmed a piece of it. We know they were fighting near Folkestone. Considering how Acqua was acting freely after that, we can assume the head of the Knights has been defeated.

"Of course," he added, not really believing it himself, "we can't discard the possibility that even that's part of the trap."

Kamijou thought for a moment. "...If what Acqua said is true, then..."

"All that's left is the second princess, Carissa, with the Curtana Original...Of course, there's also the fact that she's gonna be the biggest pain in the ass."

Still, they had to do something about her to solve this problem.

Then, Kanzaki cut in from the side. "What of Queen Elizard and the Puritans' leader, Laura Stuart?"

"No reports," replied Tatemiya bitterly. "According to the Knights' communication network, they were trying to flee from Windsor Castle into London, but they don't know what became of them."

Kamijou looked between them. "The queen seems like a battle-hardened veteran. Could she think up a winning plan to turn things around even when it's this bad?"

"With her abilities, we can expect that kind of up-front combat power from her. But even if we couldn't, her presence alone creates great value for both internal and foreign affairs...On the other hand, that could give Carissa's plan for a new order a way in..."

Kamijou tilted his head.

Tatemiya summed it up: "Anyway, in order to end this coup as soon as possible, we're going to take down the nuclear core, Carissa. And to do that, first we have to stop the Curtana Original she has from functioning."

As for how to destroy the Soul Arm called the Curtana Original, they could maybe manage with Kamijou's right hand. "But the princess is in Buckingham Palace, isn't she? The Knights have control of the whole country, including London. Are we gonna be able to get inside the palace when it's so tightly guarded?"

"Right now, a frontal assault on Buckingham Palace would be the same as clashing with an entire national military...But the city of London is one place we may be able to sneak into."

"?"

"London has a lot of subway lines underground. One of them is called the Victoria line, and it runs almost directly underneath Buckingham Palace. We don't have to enter the palace grounds—we can mess with them from the subway station nearby."

Tatemiya stopped for a moment, then changed the subject a little. "Besides, why do you think the second princess went back to the Palace?"

"Huh? I mean, she's the leader of this coup, so they can't make it easy to take her down. So she went to a fortress with a ton of security—"

"The Curtana Original's power is immense, and besides, Buckingham Palace doesn't currently have any magical defensive spells supplementing it. She could walk around in person and she still wouldn't be easy to take down. And if she wanted to hide out, she'd have gone somewhere with tighter magical defenses...Somewhere like Windsor Palace—the royal family's other home—or really any number of more appropriate buildings."

"Then why? She didn't go in there for no reason, right? Does making orders from the capital give them added value as a legitimate government or something?"

"Well, sure, it sends a good message. But there's a more direct reason. And it has to do with the Curtana Original, which I mentioned before."

"What's the sword got to do with it?"

"The Curtana Original is too strong. It only works in the UK, but it lets you wield a power rivaling the leader of angels...In which case there's something to be concerned about. The Curtana Original has the power to annihilate foreign enemies, but if the user makes a mistake controlling it and it runs amok, the user is basically the first one who will get caught up in the destruction."

"Really?" muttered Kamijou without thinking.

Tatemiya looked at his expression and nodded once. "Whether it's the Original or the Second, of course, it's held by the highest power in the United Kingdom—the king or queen...But if worse comes to worst and they die, there would be an issue with the sword. That absolutely necessitates a large facility meant for preventing it from going out of control. If a group of facilities, for example, that could accurately escape the power of a berserk Curtana and withstand a huge explosion, happened to be built into Buckingham Palace, where the sword remains for the longest part of the year...

"You know, the Curtana Original disappeared once from history, so they started using the Curtana Second instead. They say the Puritan Revolution was why, but...If the Curtana's power had been complete, this sort of revolution wouldn't have succeeded—the Curtana would have slaughtered the entire resistance faction. But it didn't go so easily, which means..."

"The Curtana Original went out of control once in the past...?"

It was like they were stacking theory on top of theory, but according to Tatemiya, the third princess, Vilian, whom Amakusa had placed under their protection, also seemed to view these "theories" in an affirmative manner.

"Which means," continued Tatemiya, "we can trust the idea that they have measures in place to prevent that from happening. After all, it going out of control in the past gave a revolution the opening it needed to succeed."

Kanzaki picked up on Tatemiya's words from her position sitting on the floor. "If there is a large facility conducting an energy exchange for the Curtana Original, we might be able to interfere with the sword by reversing the mana flow...or so goes the theory. Now that Carissa has entered Buckingham Palace to try to stabilize the Curtana Original, we have a chance to make it go out of control or disable it."

If they could just make the Curtana Original unusable, the second princess's power should fall to normal human levels. The knights wielding the massive UK-only strength would lose the boost effect as well.

Furthermore:

"Carissa and the Knights aren't bound very tightly, either. In the first place, she's not the one leading the Knights—that would be the Knight Leader."

"What? But they were doing the coup d'état together, weren't they?" Kamijou wondered.

"That's only because the Knights decided Carissa's new order would be the most beneficial for the nation. On the other hand, if they decide the UK would suffer for continuing to obey Carissa, the Knights would mercilessly abandon the second princess and withdraw. In other words…"

"Whether or not she can use the Curtana Original is directly linked to whether the coup d'état succeeds or fails…?" Kamijou's face nearly brightened at the vision, but then he paused in thought. "Wait. I thought there wasn't any magical stuff set up in Buckingham Palace. Something about it causing diplomatic issues, since it's basically like throwing your guests into a big trap."

"That's what the subways are for," countered Kanzaki immediately. "There aren't any magical facilities in Buckingham Palace during regular hours, but there are subway lines running underneath it. There's a place where the normal line splits, and a special car equipped with a magic circle waits there. If the Curtana Original goes out of control, it'll move swiftly and carry it underneath Buckingham Palace."

If they did that, then they could still technically say there were no magical facilities whatsoever on Buckingham Palace property. Born Again Amakusa's idea was that a long time ago, they had it on a big horse that stayed put right outside the palace property, and when they opened the subways, they changed it over to that.

For hundreds of years, the Curtana Original had been missing, and the safety using the Buckingham Palace subway had been put together for the Curtana Second. But it was still a Curtana, a Soul Arm, so it wasn't strange that the second princess would use the subway's safety feature, too.

"We're currently keeping in contact with the Coven Compass, an English Puritan aerial fortress," Kanzaki explained. "Once we're ready, we'll have the Coven Compass use its large-scale flash spell, then use the massive quantities of mana from it to interfere with the Curtana Original in the subway and start trying to make it run out of control…That's the idea anyway."

Carefully choosing her words, the young woman continued, "There are five hundred kilometers from the Coven Compass to Buckingham Palace, but English Puritans hidden along the way should have set up Soul Arms to serve as relay points in about ten locations in order to guide the colossal amount of mana. If they succeed, it could possibly disable that bother of a sword or stimulate it to weaken."

"So then, we're going to London now to seal the Curtana Original and then break into Buckingham Palace?"

"That too, but…" Unusual for her, Kanzaki fumbled for words.

Tatemiya took over, his tone one of resignation. "Remember how that special Curtana-blocking car is waiting on a piece of track split from the main subway line?"

"Well, yeah. Why?"

"At the entrance to that branched line, there's a magical barrier that normally looks just like a regular wall. We'll need to break the barrier to secure the route."

I get it, thought Kamijou, looking at his right hand. He understood essentially what he had to do now. "Basically, we'll get to the subway station close to Buckingham Palace on our own, then I'll use my right hand to bust the barrier in the tunnel nearby, right?"

"Yes, but there is one problem."

"What is it?" Kamijou asked.

"Now that London has welcomed in the second princess, it already has a new security system in place. And it'll react particularly strongly to anything related to sorcery. Broadly speaking, if someone with mana is hanging around, security will find them out in no time. Their location gets displayed on a map, and within minutes, fully armed knights will rush to the scene…That means any magicians who can refine mana on their own can't go along on this mission."

"Wait, that means…" Kamijou looked between Tatemiya and Kanzaki as though he'd misheard something; not only Tatemiya but even Kanzaki unthinkingly averted their eyes from him.

"…U-um, anyone who can't completely refine mana or weaker people on a civilian level…That means the only people who can fight in this mission are you and Index," said Kanzaki, shrewdly saying what needed to be said even with averted eyes. As she gazed at the profile of the third princess, Vilian, she continued, "Without Her Royal Highness Vilian of the royal family, you won't be able to interfere with the magical barrier set up in the subway tunnel or the special car with the magic circle. There's no other choice—we need the three of you to do the best you can."

4

It was to be a breakthrough right up the middle of enemy territory.

Kamijou, Index, and Vilian proceeded eastward from near the high-class residential streets in Kensington in the west of London.

Not on foot, though.

London spanned dozens of kilometers from east to west, so it wouldn't be a simple walk-and-you'll-get-there matter. Right now, the third princess was driving them in a small car that rattled down the road. Kamijou felt an incredible strangeness at seeing a storybook princess gripping a steering wheel, but the twenty-four-year-old Vilian offered, "…Come now, I am not *that* sheltered…"

Kamijou felt incredibly bad for having a bona fide princess drive the car, but it wasn't like he or Index could drive instead.

The destination they were heading for was the subway station near Buckingham Palace in central London. They didn't need to get onto the palace property itself, but they had to get a hairbreadth away from it, making their situation relatively desperate.

They'd told him London had tens of thousands of surveillance cameras watching it. But according to Tatemiya and the others, who were now standing by in their rescue machine that had landed in the city, the cameras didn't seem to be functioning at the moment.

"Normally, anyone doing magic-related operations weaves through the cameras' blind spots or plants spells on them to prevent being recorded...but the second princess, Carissa, already has nearly all the state's functions under her control, so she probably couldn't be bothered with them. I bet she ordered the three main London security companies. All the surveillance cameras seem to be off."

"The cameras are off...? Then how did you steal the security company's videos? Is Amakusa really good with the science side's security, too?"

"No, we were just observing from a long way away with a telescope. Surveillance cameras have autofocusing, too, but it doesn't look like they're working at all. The things aren't functioning. Like when someone's eyelids are open but they're not awake."

...They'd analyzed it with an awfully analogue technique, but what Tatemiya and the others were saying was probably true. A sorcerer's society called New Light had snuck into London by taking advantage of the cameras' blind spots. Kamijou, though, was an amateur and couldn't do anything like that. Index didn't know much about science, either. They were driving on back roads for the moment, but if the surveillance cameras' security networks were functioning properly, they'd have been spotted right away.

Staring at the unmoving road cameras from the passenger seat, Kamijou said, "But if we drive down the street like this, with all the noise from the engine with nobody around, won't the knights find us anyway?"

"We'll be okay." The answer came from Index, who was seated in the back. "The knights are using magic for their security right now. Instead of relying on their normal five senses, they're using magically enhanced ones for their security net. There might be a lot of them, but they need to get people to cover dozens of kilometers of all of London...But if we use their magic against them, we can pass right under their noses without their noticing."

"Really," said Kamijou, impressed at what the library of 103,000 grimoires had to say, but then he changed his mind. "Wait a minute, Index. How do you know what magic the knights are using right now?"

"Huh? Well, they're right over on the roof of that building."

"What?!" cried Kamijou in a panic, turning around to where Index pointed. There was indeed a black figure on the building rooftop. But the silvery-armored silhouette didn't notice them and instead hopped over to another building.

...I don't think you'd need this many people to hear a car engine... Was this the cost of relying too much on magic?

Nevertheless, they'd probably get spotted in a heartbeat without Index's (seemingly) random periodic instructions to Vilian like, "Turn here; go slow there."

"But don't the Royal Family and the Knights, like, use the military or the police or something?"

"Maybe they're too busy dealing with the civilians? Amakusa told us they were putting everyone together in hotels and theaters and other big buildings, but if they want to get people who don't know anything to do what they say, using strange magic wouldn't be very direct."

Now that she mentioned it, you could shove a weird wand or crystal ball in someone's face, but pointing a gun at them would be quicker. It was a different story if you fired a warning shot with magic, of course, but wasting shots was probably always a bad thing. *Still, though...*

As Kamijou gazed at the unoccupied London scenery from the passenger seat, he unconsciously looked at Vilian, who was at the wheel in the driver's seat next to him.

She was a fair-skinned, blond-haired woman wearing a green dress—the kind of person you'd see in a picture book. She was like

Index in that neither of them knew much of the ways of the world, but comparing them made their differences in mood pretty obvious. Index would crash headfirst into any science or foreign cultures on sight, but the impression he got from Vilian was of a quietly blooming alpine plant, like she'd vanish without a delicately arranged environment.

Vilian noticed his eyes on her. "Is something the matter?"

"N-no…" Kamijou quickly shook his head.

For some reason, before they'd set off on this mission, people from Born Again Amakusa like Kanzaki and Tatemiya had given him warnings along the lines of, "She might not be perfect, but she does have royal blood in her!" and "If you accidentally flip her skirt, you'll be tried for lèse-majesté!!" But what had all that been about?

"So they were saying that it had to be people who can't refine mana, or else Carissa or the knights would catch us, right?"

"Y-yes," replied Vilian in an awkward tone, squirming in her green dress as though trying to escape Kamijou's gaze. "I'm terribly sorry. I understand it's an essential part of my education as a member of the royal family, but I just feel a sense of rejection toward acquiring knowledge or techniques that could be used for displays of force…Right now, all I can do is touch already active Soul Arms to control them. My sister Carissa seems to have wanted to execute me because she thought I might be able to use the Curtana Original, but even if someone gave me an item like that, I probably wouldn't be able to put it to practical use…"

"Really? Wait, weren't they saying something about needing to have someone with royal blood to get past the subway station barrier problem?"

"Yes…If only my mother or my sister Limeia were here, it would have been perfect…But someone as inexperienced as I, even with the Index of Prohibited Books advising her, might not be able to carry out her duty…"

"I—I really don't think you need to get that down on yourself! Besides, I don't even get why kings and stuff need to learn magic in the first place!!"

"...Is that so...? For this mission, there are apparently several regular servants, cooks, and gardeners heading from Buckingham Palace to the subway tunnel for my sake...If only I had a plan to better protect everyone; even without relying on simple brute force, I might not have needed to make the two of you go somewhere so dangerous."

Vilian was in full-on down-in-the-dumps mode now. She seemed to feel guilty that she couldn't contribute any combat strength during the coup.

Kamijou forced himself to examine the London streets, looking for a way to change the subject. "Anyway...You call these back roads, but even these are different from the ones in Academy City."

"Touma, I don't think a man can really brag about knowing the differences between alleys."

"I wasn't trying to brag," he shot back. "Anyway, I get that we've gotta do something about Carissa the mastermind, and I get that we have to bust up the Curtana Original's functions to do that...But is this huge coup d'état really going to end after beating the big boss, just like that? I'm worried this battle will get bogged down and keep on going."

The city of London wasn't the only place facing difficulties. England, Scotland, Wales, and Northern Ireland...Almost everywhere in the four areas of the United Kingdom was occupied by the knights, led by the second princess. With the problem already having progressed this far, Kamijou honestly wasn't confident that losing one person's support would end the whole thing then and there.

But the third princess, Vilian, said hesitantly, "I believe that if we can just stop my sister Carissa, the coup will end."

"Is that so?" Kamijou tilted his head at her.

Vilian's brow knotted as though she was troubled. "I think there are a lot of different kinds of coup d'états. But with the one currently happening in the United Kingdom, I believe the possibility is low that if they lose the mastermind, the fighting will continue to drag on."

As Vilian spoke, Index nodded along with her. "Amakusa was

intercepting the knights' messages before, remember? They said a mercenary beat the Knight Leader, and now confusion is spreading through the other knights…The leader of the Knights and the second princess are the pillars emotionally holding up the people on the aggressor side. And now one of them is broken. So if the other support breaks, I think the Knights might collapse."

"…If the person demanding that they join her plan is defeated right away, don't you think all the people left would be at a loss?" Vilian explained.

That may be right, Kamijou thought.

"Also, the United Kingdom is split up into three factions—the Royal Family, the Knights, and the Puritans," Index continued, "but that will be important for stopping the coup d'état, too."

"Why's that?"

"Because foreign relations with other countries are something the royal family has complete control over. Meaning, even though the knights are good at fighting directly, they don't have any way to bargain with other countries. The only ones on the state level who could make sure we get equal deals would be Carissa or the Knight Leader, since he's been the closest aide to the royal family this whole time."

"But will they put down their weapons then? If the knights don't know what'll happen next, couldn't they just go out of control?"

"I don't have any proof, but I think it'll be fine. The knights' goal is to protect the United Kingdom, right? That's why they agreed to a Carissa-led coup d'état—they thought it was the most effective way to do that…But if they lose Carissa and realize that continuing the coup would deal massive damage to the country…they'd probably put their swords away at that point. As long as they decide that doing so would keep damage to the United Kingdom to a minimum and be the best thing for the country."

"…" Kamijou fell silent for a bit, then looked at Index in the rear seat. "Kanzaki and Itsuwa aside," he articulated slowly, "when you say stuff like this, Index, I'm not sure how much I can trust the source."

"…Touma, do you think I'm the kind of girl who's totally stupid when it comes to anything besides magic?"

Kamijou nearly told her she was a girl who was totally into eating, sleeping, watching TV, and nothing else, but saying that would obviously earn him a chomp to the back of the head, so he made the wise choice and stayed quiet.

In the meantime, they'd gotten close to their destination, the subway station.

"Stop the car. At this point, I don't think we should have the car noises going off. Buckingham Palace, their base, is close by."

As urged by Index, Vilian parked the small car on the shoulder. After getting out, the three of them took another look around.

It was close to two in the morning, but considering it was the capital of the United Kingdom, there were extremely few people here. Nobody was on the street, and there weren't any cars on the roads, either. Before they'd headed to Folkestone, police had been dispersing curiously onlooking residents, but there was no such commotion now.

The street battles between the Knights and the Puritans were over for the moment, too. Now that they'd gotten the residents under control, maybe they'd gone the route of positioning people all over London, then having them call for reinforcements if something happened.

Kamijou took a look around, but he didn't see anyone like that anyway.

In fact, he couldn't see a single soul near Buckingham Palace, visible past the subway station, either.

Suddenly, Kamijou's right hand was covered in something soft. "Hm...?"

He looked at it again and saw that Vilian was covering the palm of his hand with both of her small gloved ones. They weren't rough gloves for the cold but elegant ones, the kind royalty and nobility wore as accessories.

"...Please take care not to enter the property," she said softly, looking up at his face. "I cannot say for sure, as I am not well versed in magic. However, I have heard my sister Carissa boast in the past that she could accurately detect everything down to the number of insects in the trees."

"Uh-uhhh, yes, ma'am."

He could feel her hands through the thin silk gloves—they were clearly different from a man's rough hands, instead feeling like the soft surface of a marshmallow. Vilian, for her part, didn't seem to take any notice of Kamijou's reaction.

Index looked at them with chilled eyes but added to what Vilian had said: "There are probably knights with sniping spells doing layers of scans from windows and rooftops. Maybe a wide-area application of a spell used for assisting the Robin Hood."

Kamijou heard her and stopped before stepping toward the subway station. "Wait, so then we shouldn't just head to the station?"

"I'll try getting around their search pattern. Follow me."

Index jumped out from their cover. There was nothing there in particular, but she took unnatural detours through empty space on her way to the subway, as though avoiding invisible searchlights. Kamijou and Vilian followed. They had no idea what she was basing her maneuvers on, which made them incredibly uneasy.

Eventually, the three of them made it to the subway station.

After running down the stairs, Index finally let out a breath of relief. "We should be fine now."

"...I have no idea what just happened, but this is where I'm supposed to thank you?"

"I'd like it if you did, but what do we do now?"

"Huh?" Kamijou looked at her dubiously.

Index politely pointed in front of them. "There's this wall thingy with a blip-blop attached here."

All right, everyone, let's translate that from Indexian!☆

"An electrically locked shutter is lowered right in front of us, blocking our entry. What do we do?"

5

No afternoon classes, no holds barred!!

Which meant that Mikoto Misaka, the ace of Tokiwadai Middle School, an elite school for supernatural ability development, was in a family restaurant. The current time was eleven AM. There was still a little time left until lunch, so there were no more than a few customers. Mikoto planned to eat an early lunch here, then go back to Tokiwadai.

As for why she'd go back—it was because it was currently setup time for Academy City's largest cultural festival, the Ichihanaran Festival. Because the event combined school tours with open campuses, it wasn't freely accessible to the outside world the way their largest athletic festival, the Daihasei Festival, was but…On the other hand, the more sensitive a school was to the word *advancement*, the more passion it tended to have when trying to draw in lots of prospective students.

Tokiwadai Middle School hadn't been open for the Daihasei, but parts of it would, of course, be open to the public during the Ichihanaran. Mikoto couldn't be taking it easy now.

Still…, she thought, cutting the huge Hamburg steak on the hot plate into smaller, bite-size pieces. *What is going on with this restaurant? This happens to be the first time I've been in here, but did I walk into the land of huge boobs…?*

She was past the frustrated stage at this point. She looked around in simple astonishment.

Geographically speaking, the place seemed to be used by more high school kids than middle school ones. There was a girl with long black hair, a prominent forehead, a sailor outfit, and huge boobs (and another girl sitting across from her with decidedly smaller ones, whom a shrine maiden outfit might look good on). Plus, probably a teacher from their school, a gym teacher in a green track suit with boobs so massive it was really idiotic at that point. And, sitting in the seat by the window, a glasses-wearing, huge-chested…hologram? It might have been the newcomer Sakura, using an ability, but even still, there was no need to make her chest that large, was there?

Hm? Wait. If basically everyone in here has such an easily identifiable physical feature, then…Does the food here have nutrients that make your rack embiggen?! Wh-what the heck—? That's, like, worthy of a Nobel prize! Well then, in that case!!

Then Mikoto, having come back around into a relatively positive mood, had just begun to chow down on the steak more swiftly than usual when it happened.

Her cell phone, which was on the edge of the table, buzzed.

Just before it vibrated itself off the table, Mikoto snatched it up. *With timing like this, it had better not be Kuroko*, she thought, unfolding the phone. When she looked at the number displayed on the small screen, she nearly tipped over.

It was that spiky-haired idiot.

"Mgh?! *Cough-hack-wheeze-cough!!*" Unprepared for the shock, Mikoto almost choked.

What—? Why?! What does he want?! He almost never calls me... Gah! If he'd just send a text message beforehand, I wouldn't have to be this flustered—Wait, no, in that case, I'd be too nervous to even open the text...!!

Mikoto was all atremble of her own accord now, but she couldn't just hang up on him, either. Calling him back using her phone's call history was a high hurdle itself, too. She reached for the Answer button with a quivering thumb.

I—I guess no Academy City schools have afternoon classes today, so we should have a lot of free time! I can't slack off on setting up for the Ichihanaran Festival, but if I tinker with my schedule, then I should be able to spare a little time...

Grabbing her phone with both hands for some reason, she put it to her ear in proper ladylike style, the kind she never used. The first words that came into Mikoto's confused ears were these:

"*Sorry, Misaka! I need to sneak into a subway station; you got any idea how to open up the electric locks on their shutters or anything?!*"

"..."

Mikoto Misaka brought the cell phone away from her ear, heaved a big sigh, and then, in an extremely composed manner, moved her thumb and hung up.

She set the phone down on the table, then turned to face her giant steak again—

—only to hear the small buzzing of vibrate mode reach her ears.

To calm her mood, she took just one sip of her no-sugar latte, politely wiped her lips with a paper napkin, and finally reached for her cell phone again.

"*Sorry, Misaka! I need to sneak into a subway station—*"

"I heard you just fine the first time and hung up anyway!! Get a clue, idiot!!" she shouted, drawing energy from the pit of her stomach. Eventually, after regaining her usual composure, she gave the phone a scathingly annoyed look. "And why the heck do you need to sneak into a station? Are you trying to go through an employee entrance or something?"

"*No, no. There's some kind of shutter down over the entrance and I can't get in. I mean, it's an emergency so I can't blame them, and we're past the last train at this hour anyway, so normally you'd have the shutters down.*"

"What? Last train?" Mikoto's expression went past dubiousness and into suspicion.

She was sure it was about eleven AM right now. She'd never heard of train lines shutting down before noon.

Then, he seemed to realize Mikoto's doubts. "*Oh, I get it. The time difference. Sorry, Misaka. Did I call you in class or something?*"

"No, that's not the issue...Wait a second. Time difference? Where the heck are you right now?"

"*London.*"

Mikoto nearly hung up the phone again.

That couldn't possibly be right. She glanced at the giant flat-screen monitor installed on the restaurant's inside wall. The screen showed the same sort of news over and over from foreign journalist teams in the pitch-black middle-of-the-night hour. The people in central London had been herded into large facilities like hotels, theaters, cinemas, and churches, and apparently they weren't even allowed to go home. It wasn't a joke—the news was reporting that people had been told that if they left those buildings and facilities, the authorities wouldn't hesitate to use firearms. The United Kingdom hadn't made an official statement yet, but the theory that a coup d'état had taken place seemed to be a very strong possibility.

...But didn't he go to France before...? Mikoto was overtaken for a moment by an ominous premonition but quickly shook her head and rejected it.

It couldn't have happened *again*.

"Do you have any idea how annoying the paperwork to get out of Academy City is? Even for city-approved wide-area field trips, it's a pain in the butt."

"*Yeah, but I really am in London...*" He must have been troubled by this, too, since she could hear a light scratching noise over the phone. "*And I really can't do anything about this shutter here not opening...*"

"I have no idea what you've gotten yourself caught up in, but this isn't the thing to ask a girl for help with," said Mikoto, appalled.

The cell phone groaned for a bit. "*Hmmmmmmm.*"

And then, Touma Kamijou said this one word, mostly offhandedly: "*...I can't?*"

The words *you can* almost made it out of Mikoto's mouth without thinking.

6

"*Hmm, yes. That's a type-225 passive from Marvelous Locks Inc. In that case, if you undo the two latches underneath the panel, there should be a maintenance jack there.*"

After using his cell phone camera to take a picture of the electronic lock panel and sending it to Mikoto, he got an answer back in five seconds. When he heard her remark, he felt like she'd said one thing and he already couldn't keep up with her. Kamijou grunted, choking on his words a bit. "Hey, there's, like, a twenty- or thirty-year difference between tech outside Academy City and inside, isn't there? Do you know a lot about outside tech, too?"

"*Marvelous Locks is a company that cooperates with Academy City.*"

So the tech they're using there is a cheaper version with lower specs," Mikoto replied smoothly. *"Even I wouldn't know anything about stuff made on the outside only, but I don't think I wouldn't be able to get them open. I mean, they're twenty or thirty years behind the tech curve. Even military lab security on the outside isn't as good as the log-in management for throwaway desktop computers sold in Academy City."*

"...Well, I can't even open padlocks."

"That's because your tech level is stuck in the Edo-era," came the stinging retort.

Kamijou got to work fiddling with the electronic lock panel the way she described. "Anyway, it's weird for me to say, since I'm the one who asked, but...you really do know a lot about these things, huh?"

"D-don't get the wrong idea. I only learned it so I could make sure my powers don't mess with electronic locks if they malfunction. I'm not some kind of sneak thief or super hacker or anything."

"Hey, couldn't you have said that a little more simply?"

His fingertips moved here and there, using a handkerchief to at least make sure no fingerprints ended up on it, but he was honestly just doing as he was told. His understanding wasn't keeping up one bit.

Eventually, he heard a *ker-clunk.*

The shutter towering in front of him gave a clatter and began to rise. The knights had already suppressed the main road, so there was nobody around, which made the noise ring much louder than they'd thought, putting Kamijou's and Index's hearts in a flurry, but the knights never caught wind of it.

"It's open! Thanks a bunch, Misaka!"

"Sure thing. Just to be clear, you owe me one."

"Yeah, got it. I'm in a hurry, so bye!"

"Hey, wait! You know how we're setting up for the Ichihanaran Festival now, and there's gonna be a lot of morning-class-only days? I mean, if I plan things out the right way, we could, I don't know, hang out for a—?!"

She was trying to say something awfully quickly, but suddenly the phone call ended. With a "?" Kamijou looked at his cell phone screen and saw that he was getting zero service now.

…Well, if it was important, I can just call her back later, he thought, putting his phone in his pocket. For now, they needed to go inside the subway station structure and into the tunnel, then destroy the magical barrier with Vilian's royal help.

The Vilian in question, though, had a hand to her cheek as she gazed in pure admiration at the opened shutter. "Academy City truly is the frontier of scientific technology…You can even do things like this just by getting help from a friend."

"Uh, right…Well, she is number three, the Biri Biri, so I can depend on her at times like these…Hey, Index, what are you doing over there with the pouty face?"

"…Nothing at all," Index remarked simply, eventually moving her feet and walking over next to Kamijou. But her small feet had the option of giving him a kick to the shin area.

??? Why is there an angry aura around her?

Kamijou had so many questions, but he got the sense from Index that if he carelessly asked any, she'd explode and start biting him. He decided not to mention it again.

He turned his gaze forward.

The shutter had been down to begin with, so there was no light inside the subway station proper. However, the lamps marking the emergency exits and evacuation routes meant that it wasn't completely dark, either. Other lamps were embedded directly into the floor, so for the moment, the passage felt walkable without a flashlight.

After advancing a little, Kamijou looked behind him, thinking things like…

…Oh, right. Wonder if we should have closed the shutter at the entrance. But he didn't know how to open or close it. He'd have to call Mikoto again to close it, and then he'd end up having to call her another time when they were getting out.

"Is something the matter?"

"No, it's nothing…Right, 'cause if we run into trouble in this tunnel and need to make a quick escape, there wouldn't be time to get Misaka's help."

Vilian tilted her head in confusion, but Kamijou stopped talking and made a conclusion himself.

All the way from the subway station to the stairs down to the platform, there were no human figures to speak of, nor were there any signs of a presence. Kamijou wasn't exactly a professional at scouting or searching, but it was kind of like...The place was so silent he figured he'd be able to hear it if anyone was hiding here just from their breathing.

With the lamps indicating the emergency exits and evacuation route as a guide, Kamijou, Index, and Vilian moved in the opposite direction from them and proceeded ever deeper into the subway station.

After descending the stairs and getting to the platform, they could finally see the fluorescent lights.

Still, they weren't the ones that were often installed in ceilings. As though this tunnel was on a separate electrical system from the station, only the lights attached to the tunnel wall opposite the platform were shining.

This, of course, was not enough light to illuminate the entire platform. It was like a hospital after lights out.

Kamijou leaned over the edge of the platform, glancing down the tunnel lined with evenly spaced fluorescent lights. "...It might be past last train, but I don't know about jumping down there..."

Still, they wouldn't get anywhere unless they moved on.

Kamijou and Index got off the platform and onto the tracks. Vilian didn't seem able to do it in one go, though; her long skirt, spread out like a princess's, was getting in the way. He offered Vilian his hands but then withered under the unexpected full weight of her body. With a yelp, they fell onto the tracks.

"E-excuse me. I don't know what sort of manners apply in this situation..."

"Y-y-y-you're absolutely fine! And I don't think they'd teach you how to get someone to let you down from a station platform in a Q and A or an etiquette class!! But if you could please maybe remove yourself from me, that would be wonderful, Princess Vilian!!"

"Touma, that is lèse-majesté."

Index's cold words shot Kamijou through the heart. Meanwhile, Vilian was saying something like, "Y-yes, I'm truly sorry," and hurriedly moving off him.

After standing up on the tracks, Kamijou cast his eyes down the tunnel.

The point Amakusa had designated in advance was apparently only a few dozen meters away. However, it was in the opposite direction of Buckingham Palace.

"That way?"

"Yes. I, too, have only heard of it. This is my first time actually seeing it," said Vilian, her face looking a little nervous.

And then it happened.

They heard the clapping of a metallic footstep from right behind them.

"?!" Kamijou whipped around. *Is it the knights...?*

For a moment, he remembered the sorcerer Lesser from New Light, whose shoulder had almost been severed by a long-range sniping attack. If they aimed for him from the darkness with the same Soul Arm, could he block it with only his right hand?

Kamijou was thinking about things like that, but his prediction was off the mark. Vilian, who along with Index was in a position of being covered, spoke up from behind him.

"P-please wait a moment! They don't seem to be enemies. They're the servants who planned to join us from Buckingham Palace."

"...Does that voice belong to Princess Vilian...?"

The words that came to them sounded like a verification process.

Perhaps because Vilian had just spoken to Kamijou in Japanese a moment ago, the voice from the darkness adapted to them and spoke Japanese as well.

After that, several figures shuffled toward them. What emerged from the tunnel to approach the station platform was a total of nearly twenty men and women. The group burst with variety, containing everything from an elderly man in a faded work uniform to a girl wearing a maid outfit ordered from who knew where.

Vilian passed by Kamijou. While standing in front, she looked around at their faces. "Is this everyone?" she asked.

The maid, about twenty years old, nodded. "Only so many are working on night duty, Your Highness. And today, well...We had to split up to accompany you to Folkestone. Out of everyone who was waiting in Buckingham Palace, this is everyone who comes from a commoner background."

"I...see..." At the word *Folkestone*, Vilian's face clouded subtly.

At the sight of her choking on her words, Kamijou opened his mouth. "I'm gonna assume...that once this mission is over, you're going to escape from London with us?"

"Yes, sir. Originally, we would have come to the subway tunnel and done the work ourselves instead of bothering Her Highness with it, but...Being of common birth, we alone will not likely understand the inner workings of these strange phenomena you call sorcery. Nor are we deeply familiar with royal family secret information. We are here to request your assistance in full knowledge of the dangers."

"Okay." Kamijou nodded. *In that case, we'll have to get this stupid job over with quickly and bring them somewhere safe,* he thought, beginning to walk to their destination—down the tunnel in the opposite direction of Buckingham Palace. The end point was apparently only a few dozen meters down.

They headed for it, more than twenty of them, each with quiet breath.

As always, both sides were concrete walls, with fluorescent lights shining at regular intervals. There were two tracks on the left and right, with pillars in the middle to support the tunnel, also spaced evenly.

"According to Tatemiya and Kanzaki and the rest, there should be a branching track for the special car to get onto the main one..."

Kamijou looked around. As far as he could see, there was no such entrance.

Looking anxious, Vilian glanced at their surroundings, too. "I am quite sure it is around here, though."

"You can tell?"

"Yes, well…It should be, anyway, but…" Vilian's tone was getting weaker and weaker, and then Index interrupted:

"There are markings around here that used mana ahead of time. I think they're so the sorcerers who maintain the Soul Arm don't lose track of where they are."

"Ah, yes. That's right. Now that you mention it, there should be marks to guide the way. Um, drawings, where are the drawings…?"

After Vilian spoke, the maid next to her offered her some annoying-looking stationery: a set of high-quality letter paper and a feather pen. The maid herself held on to the ink bottle.

The third princess frowned. Hesitantly, she moved the pen.

"Yes, I think it was…like this. The guide marks should look something like this. I know little of magic, so I'm not aware of what these mean, though," she prefaced, offering the letter paper. On it was written some sort of symbol, which, as she said, meant nothing at first glance. It wasn't the sort of thing you'd see going about your daily business, but it also didn't have the foreignness of a strange magic circle that made it easy to understand. If someone had told Kamijou it was an uncommon map symbol, he'd probably have believed it.

Only Index, however, that personification of magical knowledge, frowned slightly at the paper Vilian displayed.

"What's the matter, Index?"

"Nothing…It's just kind of weird. They're using the 'heart' as a symbol of an alarm? What for?" she muttered to herself, but it didn't reach Kamijou's ears clearly.

Kamijou and the others came to the conclusion that they just had to look around for the marking Vilian drew. They split up, deciding to check the tunnel walls and floors in different places. The servants, almost twenty strong, aided them as well, thinking that they'd be able to find some hidden markings just fine.

These evenly spaced lights give us enough light to walk but not enough to make it easy to look for a tiny little mark. We knew we'd be coming through a tunnel, so we should have brought a flashlight or something..., Kamijou thought, walking slowly along the wall, his eyes peering through the semidarkness.

Whatever the case was, once they found the mark, it would be up to Kamijou after that. However secure the spell protecting it was, the Imagine Breaker would be the quickest way to destroy it.

Then, the fingers on Kamijou's right hand ran across something rough.

"Ah?" He took his fingers away from the wall, then looked closely into the dark again. It looked like some kind of poster. It was about two meters tall and one meter wide.

He couldn't tell what was depicted on it, since it was dark and the light was unreliable...but its upper-right corner was flapped over, as though the tape had peeled. It kind of looked like it was bowing in his direction.

Huh...?

Then Kamijou frowned.

He brought his face closer to the peeling poster to see what was on it.

Was this thing here before?

And then he saw it.

It wasn't a poster.

It was a wall.

Something with the exact same color and texture as the wall had been loosely taped *to* the wall. A big wallpaper, like the kind ninjas used to hide themselves in low-budget period films.

"This is—" began Kamijou in spite of himself when something moved.

Bshhh!! From the center of the peeling wallpaper, there appeared a faint ray of light that crisscrossed over the whole tunnel wall. The rectangular lattice, the exact same size as the poster, widened in the blink of an eye.

"What the—?!"

"Touma!!" shouted Index, who noticed something had happened, but then she was cut off.

It was a sound like paper scraping.

The tunnel wall appeared to ripple like a wave. Kamijou went on his guard, and a moment later, the rectangular wall divisions peeled away like posters, came off, and assembled into a giant piece of paper.

Several sheets fell to the ground like dead leaves. Those were probably the ones Kamijou's right hand had touched, then caused a chain effect that brought down others.

But all the others danced madly through the air.

A magical…barrier…, thought Kamijou, immediately wanting to grin.

Gsh-gsh-gsh!! roared a sound like a giant's hand crumpling up the paper.

"I mean, I know magic doesn't work on any principles of common sense, but…"

A tempest of papers swirled like a scene out of an office, eventually focusing down onto one point.

And when they did, there was a certain regularity to their shape.

"A wall turning into a person and attacking you? Who the hell even thinks of that?!"

7

With the magical paper sheets having been removed, a new semicircular tunnel appeared. It even came with a special set of rails that could retract and extend like a fire-truck ladder, possibly to force it to link to the main line.

However.

Standing in their way now was, instead, a paper Goliath.

It stood about three meters tall and gave the impression of weightlessness, like paper, but…

"?!"

When the giant swung its fist around horizontally, it smashed through the tunnel pillar on its course and continued hurtling for Kamijou's cheek without losing any momentum at all. The fist was now covered in big hunks of concrete, each one larger than a student bag. Kamijou gave up on using his right hand to intercept it. He managed to barely escape the strike by nearly falling over backward.

There was a short and shrill cry. Did it belong to the commoner maid, or was it the third princess, Vilian? Kamijou didn't even have the mental leeway to devote to that. The giant was trying to obliterate him at this very moment.

He glanced at the monster. It had destroyed concrete in one hit.

Crumple, crumple.

Its internal paper bundles moving, the giant's surface rippled like firm muscles.

Ah, shit! It's just paper, but I guess when you have so much of it, it starts to get real heavy!!

In a sense, it was like swinging around a bookshelf loaded with dictionaries. The giant's arms could quite literally pulverize a person or two.

"Touma, get away!" shouted Index from a short distance afield. "That's a Soul Arm based on how Mokkurkalvi was created!"

Before Kamijou could ask what the heck that was, she laid the giant's identity bare. "It's a model giant from Norse mythology! They designed it to fight the thunder god, Thor, known for being the strongest of all the gods, but the story goes that they used the wrong thing for its heart and they got poor results from it. Whoever made that reimagined the whole thing based on British-style theories. It's a custom model perfectly suited for this place! I think the symbol Vilian drew before was the symbol for its newly designed heart!!"

Another piece of work with a long history, then! Kamijou thought, clicking his tongue. As he did, the paper giant wound up for a swing.

Kamijou unconsciously put distance between them, but the giant kicked the wreckage of the pillar it had destroyed. Pieces the size of soccer balls stabbed up from underneath, their trajectories like uppercuts, striking Kamijou's jaw with force.

"Guh...!!"

Kamijou reeled. The taste of blood spread through his mouth.

But the paper giant's movements didn't end there.

Using its giant foot, it took one step and closed a considerable distance. With Kamijou defenseless, his body weight all tipping backward, the giant once again swung its paper-made fist that had more weight than a stack of textbooks.

Confronted by this desperate situation—

...*This is my chance.*

—Kamijou immediately filled his right fist with power.

The moment the giant approached was the greatest opportunity Kamijou's Imagine Breaker had to attack. If he missed, he'd be instant mincemeat. But if he could stop the incoming fist, it would leave the giant open for a fatal counterattack.

Don't fear—just go!!

Roar!! The two fists flew.

The giant fist could possibly reduce a car to scrap with one hit, but Kamijou's knuckles crashed into the middle of it. Instantly, the giant stopped moving. Its bonding came undone, and it changed into a flood of so many paper scraps. Dozens, even hundreds of huge posters flowed out, almost halfway burying Kamijou's body. As an eerie susurration echoed, his body was moved to the tunnel wall as though caught up in a watery stream.

"Guh...!! Crap. Did I get him?!"

Pain shot up his back and the rear of his head. Kamijou struggled, flailing his limbs, but he couldn't move the way he wanted. It was like he'd been rolled up in a futon. But now that this Mokkur-whatever, this difficultly named giant, had gone back to being a mere collection of papers, it shouldn't function further. He could take his time and maybe have Index help him. Once he crawled out of this paper mountain, he'd be problem-free.

However.

Ksh-ksh-ksh went a sound like paper crumpling, sending something cold up Kamijou's spine.

"You've…gotta be kidding me."

When he looked again, he saw an odd figure. Needly limbs and a spine, made out of only strings of a tiny bit of rolled-up paper. In contrast, its face alone was still the same giant size as before.

Moving its wrinkles, which looked somehow like a human face, the creature brought its right hand behind it as though drawing back a bowstring. It had no stout fist there. In exchange, though, waited a sharpened pile-like tip.

Oh shit, move—I can't get away!!

Kamijou was being held in place by all that paper and couldn't make a move.

The giant was aiming its lance at the center of Kamijou's face.

Without hesitation, the projectile fired with force enough to break through walls.

…Damn it!!

But that was when it happened:

All of a sudden, a figure cut in from the side.

It was one of the almost twenty servants who had joined them from out of Buckingham Palace. The middle-aged gardener, wearing a faded work uniform, clung to the paper giant's arm and managed to throw off the nail's aim.

Thanks to that, Kamijou's head was spared from being crushed like a melon.

Instead, the pile arm jammed into the concrete wall next to him with a ferocious *ka-shook!*

But his savior the gardener was not unscathed.

He'd tried to suppress the paper giant's arm, but its power had been way too high and had flung him away. On top of that, the automaton's body was *hard*, like it had been made by layer upon layer of paste. Its surface was now roughly the same as a fiberglass boulder. Because of that, the gardener's work uniform had been forcibly ripped up, and no small amount of blood flowed from his skin.

Instead of feeling thankful, Kamijou felt the hair all over his body stand on end. "You idiot!! That was insane...!!" he shouted as he struggled to get out from the heavy heap that held him.

The fallen gardener gave this display a thin smile. It was like he was happy that someone else was actually worried about him.

"...I'm sorry...," said the man. "Talk about sorcery all you want and I won't understand a lick of it. But we can fight this thing as long as we have your power, right...?"

Gk-gk went the paper giant as it tried to pull its pile arm out of the wall.

Small fragments of concrete scattered to the ground from the cracks in it.

"If I'm right, then I beg of you: Please do something about this thing. Quickly, before it aims that javelin at Her Highness!!"

8

At the same time as the giant appeared, the servant who had gone in front to be Vilian's shield heard the gardener's words, and her shoulders suddenly relaxed.

Vilian had a bad feeling about this.

And she'd already had several bad feelings tonight alone.

As if to prove that the third princess's instincts were correct, as Vilian stiffened, the young female servant slowly turned around and spoke.

"Please leave this to us, ma'am."

"...?!"

"It seems that if we can buy time for that boy to recover, we should be able to overcome. We've barely learned martial arts, but if all twenty of us press in as one, we should be able to restrict its movements right well."

Yes, civilians would seek solutions such as these. But even Vilian, who didn't know much about sorcery, could tell. Normal rules like that wouldn't work on the strange, mysterious phenomenon occurring before their eyes. If twenty civilians with no power at all rushed in, the paper giant would apply its normally unthinkable strength and rout them.

The servants weren't stupid, though. Maybe they couldn't come up with any hard numbers, but the experiences they'd personally had since the start of the coup d'état probably allowed them to guess that much.

And yet—and yet none of them said a word about that.

It was almost like they were telling Vilian not to worry about them.

One servant, seeming resigned to the decision, removed his shirt. One cook wrapped his necktie around his fist, probably hoping to protect his hand with whatever he could. One tailor spared a momentary glance for the exit but then rallied her courage and returned her gaze to the beast. Even as they did all this, their faces were pale, and it wasn't only their legs trembling—it was their whole bodies.

There was no way they weren't scared.

And yet, when Vilian looked at her servants trying to face down the jaws of death, she couldn't help but ask, "Why...?"

"There's no logic to it, ma'am," answered the young woman, her expression almost a pained grin. "People don't need any unique reason to stand up and fight. We're here because we want to fight for you. That's all the reason we have, Princess."

And then it happened.

The paper giant, whose pile arm had been stuck in the wall right next to Touma Kamijou's face, made a move. As though it decided pulling out the buried pile arm would be impossible, the paper near the end of its arm scattered apart of its own accord. It had sacrificed its volume to regain its freedom of movement, and now it was starting to sharpen its arm into a hard tip again.

Once more, and this time, it would surely impale Touma Kamijou.

This time, it would eliminate the boy with the means to fight it.

When the servants realized that, they began to move.

But then, the third princess gently laid a hand upon her young servant's shoulder.

"I understand how you all feel."
It held a firmness that she hadn't had before.

"However, that is not a good reason for you to die. If that Soul Arm exists to prioritize the elimination of dangerous factors that could defeat its role as a wall, then I am the most well suited to be the decoy."

As she finished speaking, Vilian jumped out. The young woman who had spent this whole time hiding behind others now stepped farther forward than any of them.

"Ma'am, wait—!!"

She heard her servants trying to stop her from behind, but nobody was willing to actually pull her back. It wasn't because they were too stunned to react; no, their fear was already preventing their legs from moving.

It was natural to be scared.

It was natural to want to run away.

Grkk!! Clenching her teeth, Vilian ran down the dark tunnel. She picked up a giant spanner the size of a mop, probably placed near the wall to switch the rails manually in case of emergency, and plunged ever forward. She ran, ran, and ran, diving in a straight line at the paper giant, putting all her strength into the heavy spanner.

People didn't need any unique reason to stand up and fight—that was what the servant had told her. Vilian wanted to believe that as much as the woman did, so she swung the giant spanner in a horizontal arc aimed at the giant's head.

"Oooooooooooooooooohhhhhhhhhhhhhhhhhhhhhhhhhhhhhhhhhh!!"

As she swung out the spanner, she let loose a roar she had never once done in public.

The Goliath responded. After changing the aim of its arm-turned-spear, the paper Soul Arm blasted its sharp edge at the incoming spanner.

Brang!! went the sound of the shock rolling through Vilian's head.

The nail hadn't landed a direct hit, though. The tip of the spanner, now bent about midway up, had struck her in the head.

...If my sister Carissa was here, considering her total power, a contrivance like this would be a light warm-up, not even enough for her to bend her little finger. If she saw how much effort we're having to make, she would only laugh at our incompetence.

As Vilian bent over backward and fell, her gaze never wandered. She tossed aside the wrecked spanner.

Amakusa had told them right at the start that they needed someone from the royal family to release the magical barrier. She'd been lectured on the spell she'd need for it, too.

I may not have much, but even I have a little. If she insists on hurting those who stand up to support me...And if she would try and cause others to suffer using such overwhelming power that this much terror seems like "a little"...

Now she just had to activate it.

In order to successfully use sorcery on her own, Vilian began to move.

That paper giant was the barrier itself that protected the subway tunnel and the special train car meant for the Curtana. And Vilian knew the barrier was controlled by magic only the royal family had.

So Vilian decided she'd put it to the test.

It was her, a member of the British royal family, against this colossus of paper.

To save her servants who had come here for her. To force the Curtana Original to run rampant. *To save all the United Kingdom from Carissa's control!*

Normally, she might have been trembling with fear, tears forming at the corners of her eyes. But now, the third princess glared distinctly at the paper giant.

I will resist!! No matter what, I will resist to the very last moment!!

However, before she regained her footing, the paper giant aimed its pile arm toward her. But the third princess ignored it. With time for evasion or defense a luxury, she began to desperately and rapidly incant the spell to herself.

Her voice made no sound.

As a Soul Arm, automatically, the paper giant tried to eliminate the foreign enemy.

Boom!!

The pile arm flew out.

Its course led straight to Vilian's face.

And then...

"CP! (Change path!) RATTR!! (Right arm to the right!!)"

...Index's words suddenly rang out, causing the paper giant's lance to immediately twist in an unnatural fashion. It should have pierced Vilian through the head, but instead it stabbed deep into the concrete ground.

Then the third princess's incantation caught up.

Strictly speaking, Vilian had been doing the incantation the "right" way, going through each step in turn. But using Index's abbreviation as a reference, she successfully switched over to high-speed incantation.

"IAWTOOSWITRB, SOTG!! (In accordance with the order of she who inherits the royal blood, swiftly open the gate!!)"

As the last letter came out, the greater part of the paper giant's body shattered.

Like death throes, however, the right arm portion alone retained its shape, and even as it crumbled, the sharp, pile-like tip drove toward Vilian's face.

But the princess didn't close her eyes.

Because...

"Sorry about that. You saved us, Vilian."

...right then, the Goliath's arm ceased to move.

All because the boy had reached out from behind and grabbed the creature's arm, as though stopping a street fight.

After that, the giant continued to collapse.

Its original form unraveling, it still turned around to the boy, as though its danger priority had shifted to Kamijou's right hand.

"Leave the rest to me. I'll take it down this time."

Touma Kamijou and the paper giant.

Neither of them waited even an instant.

The Imagine Breaker and the pile arm.

The strikes, each having enough destructive force to kill the enemy, crossed without hesitation.

Ga-bam!! came the roar.

And this time, Touma Kamijou's fist smashed the paper giant beyond all recognition.

The magical creature had been barely managing to keep its human form until now, but currently it exploded everywhere from the spot where Kamijou's fist had hit. The masses of rectangular parchment whipped all the way up to the ceiling, then slowly began to be pulled down by gravity.

"…"

The third princess stared at the sight in a daze for a few moments.

For the first time in her life, she had acted with the clear intent to defeat an enemy. And this scene of all the dancing parchment paper was the result.

Kamijou didn't know what she was feeling, so he decided to leave her be for the time being.

Which was just as well, because that was when his cell phone began to vibrate.

He didn't recognize the number, but when he put it to his ear, a familiar voice came through.

"Oh, thank goodness! I got through!"

"Is that you, Itsuwa…?"

"Y-yes! It is Itsuwa, yes, now with no alcohol left in her whatsoever; good evening!!"

"?" Kamijou tilted his head at the strangely energetic young woman, but of course, she couldn't tell that he did so.

"The operation is a success. Now that Her Highness and the others have undone the magical barrier's lock, we were able to remotely access the special car's power source."

"Oh. That means you can indirectly attack the Curtana Original now, right?"

"Well, about that…Since the special Curtana car is currently stationed right underneath Buckingham Palace, it's now dashing toward you at a breakneck speed! Please get away from there quickly!!"

Kamijou listened with a blank stare.

"A-anyway, we're about to link the core of our aerial fortress Coven Compass to the Curtana Original through that special car," Itsuwa continued quickly. *"When the power's flow reverses, there will probably be a large-scale emission of mana. The knights who detect it will likely go where you are to investigate, and* if you stay there, you'll be at a high risk of being caught in the explosion! *Please get back here as quickly as possible!!"*

9

October 18, 2:30 AM.

The Curtana Original went out of control.

The explosion had a fifty-kilometer radius, centered on Buckingham Palace, home of the British royal family. Still, it was an explosion that had only magical meaning, one that extremely average people living normal lives weren't able to detect.

However, the glass windows of the palace rattled noisily in their frames, reacting to the low frequencies humans couldn't detect.

Then came the sound of someone coughing up blood.

Chunks of blood fell, dirtying the magnificent palace carpets.

It was the second princess, Carissa.

"…A flow reversal from the Coven Compass…"

She'd taken a blow from the total power of the aerial fortress's core, but it was no more than one tenth of what she needed to control the Curtana Original. However, the Curtana itself had been negatively stimulated by the irregular energy forced through it, disturbing it. Shards of power leaked from the destabilized Curtana Original, and they damaged the body of the second princess, Carissa, like knives packed in an exploding bag.

This is why I told them not to be satisfied with taking control of most *positions and not to let their guards down until they'd quashed all of them...Or maybe I'm supposed to respect the cunning of those urchins?*

The power distributed to the knights using the Curtana Original was nearly all lost.

The second princess had lost some of her own strength as well.

In fact, probably about 50 percent of it had been scooped out.

But...

I suppressed it.

Carissa had conviction.

They had probably developed this nasty plan by considering the historical fact of the Curtana Original's loss during the Puritan Revolution, then deciding that the Curtana going out of control would be the foothold they needed to overthrow the head of state. But she would not fall. They hadn't dealt fatal damage to Carissa's forces.

"P-Princess Carissa!" came a knight's voice from the other side of the room's large door. "We've completed recovering and resealing the special train car positioned directly under the palace. Now the Puritans will be unable to interfere with the Curtana Original by reversing the flow."

"Hmph." Carissa wiped the blood left on her lips with the back of her hand. "Then go survey the London area to see what kind of effect all the scattered power from the Curtana Original has had. And then all the Soul Arms stocked in the palace, too. If things went badly, almost half of them could be useless now, so."

Carissa reaffirmed her grip on the blade-less, tip-less sword. "Bring me a Soul Arm interference tool. I'll start rechecking the Curtana Original, so. And temporarily suspend all spec changes and readjustments for the sword. I will place importance on wiping out the remnant forces inside the country for now, above any cheap tricks with the Curtana."

"Yes, ma'am," came the clipped response before the knight left.

On the surface, he seemed obedient, but Carissa knew that the scales in his heart were swaying.

Their organization, the Knights, had originally been led by the

Knight Leader. Carissa, too, had been using the Knight Leader as a window to the Knights. With that lost now, disturbance was spreading through their forces underneath the surface, creating small but new gaps between them and Carissa.

And to top it all off, the Curtana Original had just gone out of control.

It had actually been the result of Puritan sabotage, but on a psychological level, the knights would have to think, even if only for a moment, that the second princess couldn't control it.

They'd already lost their direct leader, and now they were getting glimpses of inferiority from the person above him.

If the old queen Elizard and the Puritans joined forces and began a large-scale counteroffensive, could the knights' spirits endure? It didn't matter that the actual numbers were overwhelmingly in Carissa's favor. It was a problem of the human psyche. Could they keep on thinking they could win? Could they go on believing in the head of state Carissa?

Well, truthfully speaking...If they started a counteroffensive, it would shatter the spirits of half of them, she calculated honestly, even while giving a thin smile.

As she smiled, she put the Curtana Original in her hand on her shoulder.

Now, then. I've no use for cowards, but defections might cause some trouble, so...I suppose I'll just take the initiative, then.

10

Saiji Tatemiya of the Born Again Amakusa-Style Crossist Church was holding a telescope.

He was in a field on the outskirts of London, out of range of the Curtana's rampage. The only thing around him was green underbrush. He couldn't tell how much of it was an artificial pasture and how much of it was nature that had been left alone. In that one spot, members of the Puritan faction scattered across the United Kingdom were steadily gathering.

"Aw, shit," he said. "Looks like we shaved off some of the Curtana Original's power, but it doesn't look like we avoided that big reaction happening."

Tatemiya was sitting on a stepladder, the kind a gardener might frequently use. He was peering through the telescope, his posture almost that of a tennis official.

Meanwhile, the big Ushibuka at the bottom of the stepladder gave a low groan. "Yes. A massive quantity of telesma was emitted in all directions, centering on the second princess. It looks like it's affecting the Soul Arms and other facilities in the city, too. Apparently, three smaller churches have collapsed."

"If the values from the monitoring equipment we left in St. George's Cathedral are correct, the telesma hanging in the city of London is, like, *really* dense," put in the smaller Kouyagi, writing small numbers in a notebook. "At the moment, if someone accidentally uses magic in the city, the entire region of London could ignite, too."

Tatemiya, still looking through the telescope, nodded slightly. "The knights have lost their leader and lack control. And with the Curtana Original having gone out of control added to that, their trust in the second princess is wavering. If we press her hard and fast now, we might be able to mentally wreck the knights without directly clashing with them, but…"

The elderly Isahaya picked up where he left off. "…We'll have to wait for the telesma to naturally disperse, then charge into enemy territory after London is stable. What are the chances of the Curtana Original recovering its power or the Knights' forces converging on Buckingham Palace before then?"

"I can't say anything for sure about the Knights' forces, but the Curtana shouldn't be much of a problem. It has too much power to control, so once it goes crazy, she won't be able to recover its functions very easily. If we calculate using the theoretical values of the power controlling the Curtana Original, it would take at least a month."

"Which means...?"

"A short rest for both of us. And this will be the last time we have to prepare for battle."

Tension ran through everyone, and someone audibly gulped. Then...

"Look, you people...If you know that, then do your jobs already." A woman with fluffy blond hair, Tsushima, sighed from a short distance away.

The group of men, centered around Tatemiya, all made frowny faces and argued.

"Wish you'd stop trying to pick a fight with us," said Tatemiya.

"That's right! This is an extremely serious strategy meeting we're having."

"This is the moment of truth, so we have to make sure everyone's on the same page."

"Mm. I concur with all honesty—we must decide the issue."

The men unanimously gave their objections to Tsushima, but her attitude didn't change. Putting a slender index finger to her temple, she closed one eye and said this:

"Then why is that telescope aimed at Itsuwa in an apron?"

With one thing or another, this was their last supper.

Starting with the Necessarius members who had withdrawn from the capital, people from a rainbow of religions and cultures were assembling in one place—like Born Again Amakusa in their water rescue machine, the former Agnes unit who had been liberated from the freight train, and many more.

The sisters coming and going around Kamijou exchanged various reports.

"Theodosia Electra's team has arrived as well. Now almost all the Puritans' remaining forces in the English region have been assembled."

"Stiyl Magnus's team has yet to arrive. He had borrowed a

transport plane during the Skybus 365 incident, but it seems that when the coup d'état broke out, he ended up in a skirmish at the military airport. He boasted that he would overpower them on his own, so I don't expect any issues, but he may take a little bit longer."

Several other voices added reports. It seemed that the greater part of the remnant forces had assembled in London.

Even as the Puritan sorcerers continued to prepare and fine-tune their respective weapons and Soul Arms, they assigned great importance to managing their own physical conditions—first and foremost eating meals. After all, thanks to the chaos that had ensued ever since the coup d'état began, plenty of people were nearly out of stamina from drawn-out battles and escapes, and plenty of others who knew they'd be working through the night hadn't eaten yet and skipped dinner to take a midnight meal later.

And of course, whenever lots of different people assembled, lots of types of cooking assembled as well.

"Th-this is crazy! It's filling me up...This warm soup isn't just filling my stomach; it's filling my entire body...!!"

"U-um, you're about to exercise, so please, everything in moderat—"

"No, there's no way I'm eating a light salad or something at this point!! I'm going balls-deep! Straight for the heavier meats that drop into your stomach like a bowling ball!!"

"W-well, I mean that about eighty percent full is a good point, because if you get completely full, you'll—"

"Seconds!! I demand seconds, and I'll hear nothing from you!!"

"J-just make sure to chew, and eat more slowly so that you don't upset your stomach—"

"Myaaa!!"

...Countless sisters, large and small, had gone straight into a mode of overeating and overdrinking that was not at all nunlike, and the apron girl Itsuwa of Born Again Amakusa was fluttering frantically among them, not sure what to do, and to top it off, Kamijou felt like apologizing because he was pretty sure even a calico that looked kind of like his cat was chowing down on the food.

With only a small serving plate with nothing on it in hand, and unable to keep up with the throng of sisters and sorcerers and who knew who else, Kamijou stood there doing nothing, somewhat dazed.

Meanwhile, a short distance away from those commotions, the double-headed glutton sisters Index and Angeline were at the same table. At a glance, they seemed to be getting along, sitting next to each other and eating their food, but...

"Ah!!"

"Hey!! Y-you just ate it! You ate my food!!"

"I didn't eat it."

"S-Sister Lucia, you saw it, too, right?! You saw the glutton reach her fork over to my plate!!"

After speaking, the tall, cat-eyed sister (she had her eyes closed in pre-meal prayer, so she wasn't watching, and she didn't care, either) sitting across from Angeline breathed a sigh. "Sister Angeline. We must not doubt our neighbor, whom we must love."

"Mgh?! I-is that right? I'm pretty sure she *definitely* just ate my food—"

"*Om, nom.*"

"See? She just ate it for sure!! She's not even trying to be sneaky about it! She just reached over and ate a meatball right out from in front of me!!"

"I did not— *Burp.*"

"You just said 'burp' on purpose!! S-Sister Lucia, you say something to her!!" wailed Angeline, half crying.

Appearing to give in, Lucia angled her own plate up. "In that case, I'll give you mine, so distance yourself at once from the cardinal sins of wrath, gluttony, and envy."

"Gyahhh!! It's full of vegetables—and only the bitter kind! What is this? Sister Lucia, are you the type of person who brings trials and training into even the food she eats?!"

She took a hesitant bite, then began to thrash about. Lucia hastily offered some vegetable juice, and Angeline drank it all at once and then writhed even more in her seat. Ignoring the hunchbacked, braid-wearing sister practically convulsing, Index set off in search of ever-greater amounts of food.

Still, even Index ran across hard times. They came in the form of Puritan nuns who had been near the table with all the meat-containing dishes on it.

"Oh wow, this brings me back!! Do you remember me? I'm Rachel—Rachel! We always played together, remember? Oh right. Do you want some steak?"

"*Munch, munch.* Who are you and why do you keep grabbing my cheeks?"

"*Ku-ku-ku.* Rachel, I knew you would completely forget about the Index's memory loss issues. Well, she probably doesn't remember me, either. But hey, whatever. I wonder if she's as much of a glutton as she used to be. You want some of mine? Okay, say *aah.*"

"Mgah?! But I just ate a steak before *mghgmgm*!!"

"Eeeee!! She's still just too cute! All she's doing is filling her mouth with food and it's adorable!! Mine too—you can eat my steak, too!!"

"...Uh, uhhh...I—I think I'm done...," said Index, a very rare choice of words for the silver-haired, green-eyed sister.

But the Puritan nuns only increased, saying things like, "Mine too, mine too!" and "Me too!!" and "I'll let you eat mine, too!!"

In the meantime, the regular girl Itsuwa, who was providing all kinds of food, had fallen into her own psychological crisis.

The boy was right near her.

The potato *shochu* had completely broken down in her body, and she'd regained her usual composure.

...But thanks to the sisters spread out all around her creating a tempest of demands for *more food, more food, graaahhhhh!!* she was no longer able to make a move. For a maiden in love (and not on a foppish or whimsical level but on a serious, I-would-die-for-him level), it was a state of considerable suffering.

But then rescue arrived.

It was in the form of the fluffy-blond-haired Tsushima, another of the women in Born Again Amakusa:

"Argh. You're quite obviously getting nowhere as usual, so I'll step in for you. Look, the boy is being swarmed by hungry sisters and hasn't had any food yet. If you brought some to him, it might win you points."

"Wh—That—N-no!! I'm fine, perfectly fine! I don't need to do anything like…?!"

"You don't like making calculated moves? If you keep saying things like that, you'll never close the distance, you know."

"Yes, but I'm pretty beaten up from all the fighting, and I stink of sweat, so I'm not sure I want to face him like this…"

Itsuwa's intent was partially visible, even through her muttering, possibly because they were both women.

But then the unnecessary male group stuck its head in.

"Ta-daa!! For you, Itsuwa, we thought of a grand Cinderella operation!! A presales road show!!"

"Th-that was sudden, and what do you mean by road sho—? *Hic!*"

Itsuwa's sentence ended in something like a hiccup because she was so surprised that she'd caught her breath. Her mouth moved further without much coming out of it as she used a trembling index finger to point at what Tatemiya was holding.

He was spreading something out in both hands.

"Yes sirree!! It is the one, the only great fairy peeping maid!!"

"Wh—? *Cough! Cough, cough!!* T-T-T-Tatemiya, how do you have that ultimate weapon?!"

"Heh. We all know you want someone to give you a push. The designer happens to be based in London, so I got my hands on one right after the coup d'état broke out. It's a huge prerelease false start."

"How did you even have time for that?! And what's going on with how we handle my personal information anyway?!" Itsuwa shook madly. "Ack, you even got my sizes exactly right! That just makes it more creepy!!"

Still, she might have thought this was the key to launching an attack on *that boy,* because she couldn't take it and throw it onto the

ground with all her might, which, you know, would have given him a different kind of show...

Meanwhile, no more than a few meters away from the commotion, Kaori Kanzaki, who had finally recovered her stamina, breathed a sigh, quietly so that nobody would notice.

"...W-well, we couldn't bring most of our things from the English Puritan women's dorm out with us, so the erotic fallen-angel maid must have been buried from darkness to darkness. I brought my pet tropical fish and my friend the washing machine on the water plane, so as long as they're all right, it doesn't really matter."

Kanzaki didn't realize that she was muttering under her breath.

And then Tatemiya whipped around, invoking a foul premonition, and made a declaration:

"No need to worry!! We made sure to protect the Priestess's precious bridal outfit even if it cost us our lives!! The fallen-angel maid and the erotic fallen-angel maid—we've preserved them both, so please, choose whichever you like!!"

"N-nobody asked for thaaaaaaaaaaaaat!!"

Proffered before Kanzaki's eyes as she unconsciously screamed for real was the nightmare she'd just been imagining, the clothes so neatly folded that it seemed like they had just returned from the cleaners. Actually, judging from how Tatemiya, Ushibuka, Kouyagi, and the others were acting, she sort of started to feel stupid for being serious and facing the Knight Leader on her own, then getting thoroughly beaten to a pulp.

"Th-those things are unnecessary!! And if you had enough time to go into the women's dormitory to begin with, you should have obediently brought *yukatas* and things...!!"

"The erotic fallen-angel maid...Unnecessary...? C-could there be a hyper-super-ero fallen-angel maid waiting in the wings?! ...Y-you truly spare no effort..."

"I don't have anything like that!! Wh-what are you even talking about? Hyper-super-ero?! The basic maid premise is barely even there anymore!! You'd be fine with anything as long as it looked sexy!!" blathered on Kanzaki, her face turning red.

But the men of Born Again Amakusa hadn't risked their lives for a one-shot joke.

No, something else lay deeper down.

"(...We've never actually seen the Priestess in the erotic fallen-angel maid outfit with our own eyes! We can't allow ourselves to die without having done that, can we?!)" whispered Tatemiya.

"(...We were all writhing in pain in our beds after Acqua of the Back wrecked us five ways from yesterday. It was a swift technique that took advantage of a moment's neglect,)" Ushibuka agreed.

"(...When we got Itsuwa's report, I thought I was gonna cry tears of blood. We can't go out without seeing something so hot and funny,)" Kouyagi added.

"(...Ungh. And if we've been blessed with this once-in-a-century chance to see a showdown between an erotic fallen-angel maid and a great fairy peeping maid, there will be worth in risking our lives,)" Isahaya moaned.

Not only the young men Ushibuka and Kouyagi, but even the married Nomozaki and the elderly Isahaya were all really getting into it. Looking at them, maybe her irresponsible absconding had made Amakusa's direction distort...Or, at least, so thought the air-headed leadership-worthy Kaori Kanzaki, beginning to seriously worry. Her thinking was beyond big-sister and closer to motherly territory, but make no mistake—she was still eighteen years of age.

The effects continued to propagate.

Angeline, on the receiving end of a bitter vegetable party courtesy of Lucia's goodwill, had stopped her teary-eyed, herbivore-feeling eating and turned her attention to the internal strife (?) occurring in the Born Again Amakusa-Style Crossist Church.

She poked Agnes Sanctis, their leader, who had joined them after-ward (she'd been keeping a huge pizza to herself this whole time; it was covered in all kinds of meat like salami and hot dogs and she was extremely jealous).

"S-Sister Agnes! The Far Eastern religion seems to be having an interesting discussion about wasting their excessive breasts! Should we leave them alone?!"

"Mm. They're basically competing to see who is the most adult-like sexy maid, right? As an organization of two hundred and fifty sisters, we can't quietly withdraw, but we also don't have over-ample bosoms like they do. Now then, who from our camp would be the most effective as a pillar to plan a counterattack...?"

If Kanzaki or Itsuwa had heard her, they would have stormed over with fire streaming from their mouths, but for Lucia, who was listening to their ridiculous conversation, that wasn't the important part. The worst thing was that Agnes and Angeline both, for whatever reason, seemed to be looking in her direction.

Lucia, who lacked feminine sex appeal (but actually had giant knockers), took the initiative. "I'm not doing it."

"I've heard that there exists something called a 'clichéd little devil maid.'"

"I am sure you heard me, yet you seem to be continuing despite that. I repeat—I will not do it."

"There seems to be some special meaning in it being a *little devil* and not just a *devil*."

The girls' discussion began to grow faster and faster.

A short distance away, Sherry Cromwell sat by herself, watching the commotion. She was a woman with disheveled, lionlike blond hair and skin the color of wheat. Her goth-loli dress, mostly black, was damaged in places, which almost served to blend it into the midnight darkness.

She hadn't taken any food in particular.

She had no appetite.

Her stomach was heavy with intense regret born of self-discipline and self-deprecation.

It wasn't that she felt inferior to the knights. In truth, the fact that she'd let herself get so rattled emotionally over some shithead knights was getting to her. No matter how much she tried to deny it, they'd eaten deeply into part of what made her *her*. And she felt like that had just been proven. As though all the experience and results she'd worked hard to accumulate had been snatched away.

"This is the worst...," swore Sherry, lightly rubbing a bruise remaining on her brown skin.

In London, she had sent out her golem, Ellis, to trample the knights, but somewhere along the way, her awareness had ceased. She couldn't even remember what had knocked her out—a desperate counterattack from the knights or the exhibitionist sorceress who had stepped in partway through. The only thing her dimming mind barely remembered was the sorceress picking her up and dragging her away from the chaotic battlefront.

A languid feeling of powerlessness enveloped her whole body.

As it did, a figure unhurriedly approached her.

"I come bearing a snack for you."

"Gah, you again..."

The nun, whose mannerisms were unnecessarily polite, was Orsola Aquinas. Formerly of the Roman Orthodox Church, she supposedly specialized in deciphering grimoires, but before Sherry knew it, they'd ended up as partners working on information analysis and criminal-identification-related jobs.

Whether or not Orsola knew of Sherry's circumstances, she had in any case brought her a mainly vegetable sandwich that seemed easy on the stomach.

"We will probably be busy soon. It is important to remember to eat while you are able to. I hear that one's stamina sometimes decides the outcome of a battle."

"...Oh, buzz off. It'd be just like me to die for some stupid condition like that—*Bgh?!* Did you just smile while shoving that sandwich in my mouth—*Mgghbgh!!*"

Nearly choking, Sherry had to start chewing to avoid the threat to her life.

Orsola was busy pushing the entire sandwich-laden serving plate at her, giggling quietly.

Sherry violently snatched up the sandwich and said, "…Come to think of it, I heard you were late getting out of the women's dorm."

"Everyone was all in a fluster and left without me. They spoke of bringing only what they absolutely needed, but I ended up with more luggage than I expected."

"Hah, that's just like you." Sherry snorted just for show.

But there was no insult or derision in it. For a few seconds, she stayed silent, and then she looked back at Orsola's face again.

"Let me guess—*this* was part of all that stuff you risked your life to bring out?" Still sitting, Sherry kicked something lying on the short grass.

It was a statue of a child, carved in marble.

On its base was the word *Ellis*.

"Ah-ha-ha. Have I been found out?"

"Nobody asked you to do that…" Sherry sighed, appearing truly displeased. "This thing's a failure. It's not something you had to risk your life to take…In fact, I would have rather it disappeared already. Would've been a load off my mind."

"Now, now. You need not force yourself to take a load off your mind, do you?"

"…"

"Clearing your regrets and rejecting the dead are different things. Do you not think the phrase *to break ties with the past* is misleading? Who in this world could say for sure that those who treasure their memories of the departed have no right to live new lives and build new families?"

"…Don't act like you know," muttered Sherry offhandedly. But she didn't complain any more than that. She pushed the statue of Ellis's base away with her foot, then watched the failure from above without a word.

For a few moments, there was no sound.

But unlike before, this silence was a gentle one.

"Oh yes, that's right."

"What is it now…?"

"Miss Sherry, your dress appears to be in shambles from repeated battles, so I prepared a replacement outfit for you. I must say, I was right to bring every single thing I thought might be necessary when leaving the women's dormitory."

"No, this is just my style, so I don't mind if my clothes are—*Bgfftt?!*"

"Ta-daa! Evidently, this is called a goth goddess maid!!"

"It makes a mockery of everything gothic!! Actually, aside from looking vaguely western and old, there're no similarities whatsoever!!"

"Oh?" said Orsola, inclining her head slightly.

It was an unusual reaction for the sorceress Sherry...or so she thought, but the brown-skinned golem user actually had a personality that got quite frequently excited (especially in battle).

Still, even Orsola seemed to understand that the goth goddess maid had been unfavorably received. Holding the unique maid clothing spread out in front of her, she frowned, troubled.

"How strange indeed...Amakusa is well-known for penetrating cultural spheres all over the world and swiftly adopting new trends. They were discussing such things as erotic fallen-angel maids and great fairy peeping maids earlier, so I had no doubt this would be at the cutting edge of current trends..."

"Ugh. You're an old-lady character, mentally! I can't trust anything you say about trends and fads!!"

"Still, it would be a waste to discard it without using it...Oh, then why don't we do this? If there is nobody to wear it, then I will just have to—"

"Hey, wait, wait a second!! Stop that! If someone like you with no conscious knowledge of her own enormous breasts wore a ridiculous maid outfit like that, something catastrophic would happen!! No, stop, you idiot—"

11

About one kilometer away from the Puritans' camp was a mercenary.

William Orwell was standing next to a line of dairy-farm facilities that included an animal shed for milking the cows and a silo.

Of course, the farmer's home seemed to be built elsewhere, so there wasn't a human soul around at the moment.

His giant sword Ascalon, over eleven feet long and about four hundred and fifty pounds, was an intricate, complicated construction of several different blades. William went through each of their functions, checking them, sometimes disassembling pieces and continuing to make adjustments.

…The problem is with my left shoulder rather than my sword, it seems. I have applied some healing magic since then, but…

Suddenly, William brought his face up.

The movement was like a wolf reacting to a distant howl heard from beyond the darkness.

In fact, that impression wouldn't have been wrong.

He had caught a magical transmission traveling to him from afar.

"Can you hear me, William?"

"…Hmph. It seems even our devil's luck is in competition," he gruffed, despite the fact that his lips loosened slightly—slightly enough that even he didn't realize it.

The familiar voice belonged to the Knight Leader.

"The Curtana Original seems to have gone out of control in London. It also seems to have been intentional, by someone adopting the safety directly under Buckingham Palace… Were you involved in that? Well, anyway, thanks to that, the knights' unified will is on the verge of breaking down…Nevertheless, it must have been caused by my own defeat, so I can't say anything too haughty."

"It is likely to be the work of magical experts this nation possesses."

William put a few disassembled parts back together, continuing to build them into the form of a single large sword.

"Also, would not the knights' will solidify were you to return to the lines of battle?"

" … "

"You waver," noted the mercenary bluntly. "Then you would benefit from watching how the others act. I know not how long time would wait, but it would be better than going to your fate without thought."

"*If I was to stand before you once more as a result, what would you do?*"

"It would not change what I would do. I would only bring you to your knees a second time."

A tsk. "*I can't stand you.*"

William couldn't see his expression along with the words, but the Knight Leader seemed to be grinning painfully.

William abruptly stopped checking Ascalon for issues. "If I recall, your spell of Thororm can target a perceived weapon and render it useless for ten minutes. Could you not foil the Curtana Original using it?"

"*Idiot. There's an exception to every rule. In the first place, it should be incredibly obvious how disrespectful to royalty it would be for a knight to permanently carry a weapon that ensures the head of state's death. When I constructed the spell's theory, I intended to show my loyalty by including something that would prevent it from killing anyone related to the royal family.*"

"...Unfitting, from a man who tried to behead the third princess with an executor's ax."

"*Yes, and that's why I wasn't using my own weapon on Her Highness. I was forced to use a normal weapon.*"

At some point, the Knight Leader had unthinkingly lapsed into his old banter.

"*Since you're going off to certain death now, I have one piece of advice to give you.*"

"And what is that?"

"*At one point in our previous battle, you were concerned about this. That my strongest class of attack would have been equipped with everything—severing power, armament weight, durability, movement speed, attack range, special usages, and accuracy—and that it wouldn't have allowed any evasion, defense, or counterattack. It would be certain to kill...But in reality, I could only use one pattern at a time. I couldn't use multiple at once.*"

The Knight Leader paused for a moment. Then, as though resolving himself, he spoke.

"The second princess, Carissa, and the Curtana Original probably make that attack a reality."

"…"

"If you truly plan to defeat her, then make all due preparations. If you make light of her, thinking there is a trick to her strength or that you could turn things around as long as you find a weakness…you won't be able to overcome her."

"No matter who the enemy, it does not change what I must do."

There wasn't even a moment's hesitation before William's answer.

The man who didn't speak more than was necessary wouldn't even energize himself through his own words.

"I will sever the roots of this disturbance. But if removing her from the Curtana means I will not have to take her life, then that is another choice available to me."

There wasn't even the slightest discrepancy between William Orwell and Acqua of the Back in the way they acted.

It had been the same as when he'd attacked the Imagine Breaker boy. He had simply thought that by crushing the right hand of the one (he thought was) at the center of the disturbance, he could return the boy to a normal life and stop the global war between science and sorcery at the same time.

"I don't know against whom or where you will take up the sword next, but if we are to meet again, then we shall."

"Yes. In any circumstance, we must both do everything in our pow—*Ngh?!*"

Then, the man who normally refrained from any pointless talking made an unusually meaningless grunt.

In fact, it set the Knight Leader's nerves on end. *"What is it? An enemy attack?!"*

"…Blast," William hissed. "The third princess has realized I'm here and is on the approach! A magical smuggler seems to be aiding her. They're headed straight for me." He quickly cleaned up his tools, then, pressing to his body the transport shoulder pad at Ascalon's base, hefted the weapon.

"…I said something somewhat embarrassing not long ago. I had hoped it would stabilize her mind, but I see I should have refrained from doing things I am not familiar with after all!!"

"*Well, I don't get it, but you're saying something fairly embarrassing right now*," said the Knight Leader.

The mercenary ignored him and immediately left the place behind.

And so, their last suppers ended.

What waited for them now was a conflict to decide the fate of the United Kingdom.

A true battle, with no possible guarantee that both sides wouldn't end up dead together.

And yet, naturally, they gathered.

INTERLUDE FOUR

Queen Elizard had finally arrived at the outskirts of London, but her horse was the one who had exhausted his stamina. After all, he had run the nearly fifty-kilometer distance entirely over an asphalt road he was unaccustomed to. For a horse, it had served excellently.

"I do apologize. I've been doing nothing but pushing you hard. If I'm able to regain my political authority, I'd want to make you the first decorated horse in the world," said Elizard considerately.

Her hands held a bucket with water in it. They were on a plain, but a little farther ahead was a man-made pasture. She had gone there to pilfer the water from the stable's supply.

In passing, the warhorse tried to point his head in the direction of London, as if to respond, *What are you saying?! I can get there—I still have a lot left in me!!* But even he wouldn't last if she didn't make him rest now. The queen decided to be a little more forceful with the reins. She pulled the horse's head down and made him drink.

The horse was in a state of some excitement, but when the water passed down his throat, he came to realize how tired he was. He gave a low whinny, then folded up his four legs and sat down on the ground. In that position, he began to chew on the short undergrowth next to the asphalt.

...I truly am putting everyone through a lot of trouble.

It wasn't just this horse. The queen thought of all those fighting in the United Kingdom and narrowed her eyes in slight amusement.

She glanced at the Curtana Second and thought, *...I do feel like this would be faster if I put it on full power and rushed in, but* I'd rather avoid doing that for too long.

Then...

"Ph-pheeew. As I thought, these things called warhorses are tiring if one is not accustomed to them."

Coming in with the line that ruined the confidential mood was a blond woman whose hair reached down to her waist—Laura Stuart.

Elizard gave her a scornful look, the complete opposite of before, and said, "You're too soft. You're probably tiring him out more by not moving your body in time with the horse's rhythm anyway."

As if in response to her cutting tone, her horse stopped eating the grass and turned his head in Elizard's direction. His gentle eyes seemed to be saying, *Now, now. My job is to carry people and items, after all.*

I swear. The horse looks far more competent than she does.

Then it happened.

Elizard heard a rough rustling noise.

When she pointed her sharp gaze toward it, she found a figure.

"Oh my. What a big appetite you have for a horse. Would you like one of these carrots?"

A mild voice belonging to a young woman struck Elizard's ears. The queen, who had turned around with the nearly powerless Curtana Second in her hand, relaxed. "Limeia?"

"Yes, Mother. It is I, Limeia, the first princess." The monocle-wearing royal, still holding orange carrots in one hand, grinned.

Elizard turned dubious upon seeing her daughter's face. "What are you doing in a place like this?"

"Oh? Well, I was actually waiting for you, Mother. Based on what I've gleaned from the knights' communications, and assuming you would head for London from the spot they lost track of you, I decided this route was the most probable one for you to pass through."

"...What are you here for? Knowing you, we're not about to shake hands and join forces. In fact, with the way you think, you'd want to beat me up, take the Curtana Second, then create a foothold for a strategy to attack Carissa."

"Well, I had thought a bit about doing just that, but…Even though it's lost most of its power, fighting the Curtana Second in a fair match seems painful to me. For the 'brains,' I'd like to play out my role a little more wisely, Mother."

"…Very meaningful words and smiles coming from my daughter after dropping all sorts of incorrigible Soul Arms at her feet. Also, the wire coming from the bushes over there is a claymore mine, isn't it? Civilian cars could be passing through here, so remove it."

After Elizard offhandedly pointed it out, Limeia stuck out her tongue in jest, then pulled the wire strung across the road.

"And there we go. By the way, is it true that a horse's favorite food is carrots?"

"…They're vegetarians, so they'll eat them. But they don't particularly like them above everything else. His main diet consists of grass."

"Oh. That ended up being quite similar to how goats don't actually eat paper. I'm sorry."

Limeia was about to pull the carrot away, but the warhorse stretched out his neck, seeming to say, *But why? I'll eat anything I can get, you know*, and chomped down onto the orange vegetable.

"That's a good boy." Limeia smiled, petting the horse's head.

Elizard gave a fed-up sort of expression. "You really do act honestly, even to those without influence or interests."

"Of course I do, Mother. I am not about to place my trust in those who know who I am. I want to trust those who treat me kindly even when they don't know I'm the first princess."

"…I'll admit that's an important part of being a ruler, but…Confound it. Why must all my daughters be so extreme in one way or another? My eldest plots so much she has trust issues, my middle is so focused on fighting she gets everyone around her involved, and my youngest is too considerate of others to have any opinions of her own…" Elizard clawed at her bangs.

Limeia, on the receiving end, wore an unenergetic, thin smile on her lips. "Oh, how surprising. Are you in a position to lecture me? Is there no issue with the way you brought us up—with your hands-off, incredibly Spartan policy? Especially Vilian—if you had wanted to, you'd have been able to provide her a life where she wanted for nothing."

"Rubbish. Not personally cultivating your own personality invites dependence. Especially for Vilian's virtue. Twist it a little and she could become wholly reliant on others. Easy salvation is strictly forbidden. Looking at the long-term, the way I did things wasn't wrong. Unlike the three of you, after all, I have my head screwed on correctly."

"Oh. And who, pray tell, ten years ago when that crowd wanted to offer Vilian as bait to acquire South America, went in with her Curtana Second swinging, bowling over every single one of the self-serving politicians in the Royal Family faction?"

"D-don't even go there. I only did what I had to as a parent."

Elizard spoke out to deny it, but Laura, who was idling about nearby, said to herself, "...Well, that was a naïve thing to do."

"That's right, and in an extreme sense, Carissa has also set forth some quite extreme methods."

"...Then you think Carissa's aim is to expand the Curtana's functionality, too?"

"Most likely." Limeia nodded. "The Curtana Original, which applies the angelic leader Michael's LIKENESS OF GOD to the head of state, only works within the United Kingdom. But if the Curtana's effects could manifest even outside the country, the queen of England would turn into a man-made calamity trampling the whole of Europe—as an executor of a heavenly judgment decided by man, bringing forth on her own far more casualties than even a hydrogen bomb or the bubonic plague."

"That sword is like a baton that controls the giant spell built into the geographical requirements of the four cultures that make up the United Kingdom. The knights will bring their full force to bear in the defense of the mainland, and in the meantime, Carissa with the

Curtana will destroy Europe by herself…And she might just manage by doing that, too. After all, if she can fully unlock the Curtana Original's powers, I'd bet none of humanity's magic would even scratch her."

If that really happened, then unless an actual angel or a magic god appeared, it would be very difficult to oppose Carissa.

"…But is that really the whole of it?" mused Limeia.

"What?"

"Edinburgh, in Scotland…New Light was acting as Carissa's disposable limbs. I let some spies into their base of operations. Hu-hu. I can't say anything until I know for sure—a clichéd line but one intellectuals are especially qualified to use, don't you think?"

She used the word *spy*, but she wasn't talking about the sorcerers under the British royal family's employ or military operatives. Limeia especially disliked professionals and elites within such structures of authority. In all likelihood, the people working in Edinburgh whom she was referring to were her own comrades. Ones she'd built bonds with during her frequent escapades from the palace—but without wearing the face of the princess or using any of her authority.

That self-reliance, that independence to put in so much of her own effort is highest among the three sisters…If only a general distrust of people wasn't at the root of it…Doesn't exactly make me happy for my hands-off approach. Elizard sighed.

Then, she spotted Limeia giving her warhorse another carrot and eyed her dubiously. "Hey. Where in the world did you get that from?"

"Oh, you don't know? The Puritans' remaining forces were just gathered nearby and were having their last supper, too. It seems they left behind the devices and food they wouldn't need for the battle with the intent of coming back for them if they won."

"Wha—?"

"It's fine. I made sure to have my pet taste test the leftover food and ingredients. There's nothing here that would trouble anyone to eat, at least."

Ch-ch-ch. The first princess made a soft noise with her tongue. It was the sign she used when calling over the small indoor dog she was always fawning over.

But even after giving the signal, there was no sign at all of her pet coming to her.

Confused, the first princess scanned her surroundings, and then saw a small cage, which was broken for some reason—and a calico and an indoor dog who had jumped out of it, now glaring at each other from very close range, rumbling and growling, as if to say, *Who the hell are you?!* and *This is my nation's territory!!*

"Oh, oh, what a cute calico. I've always been interested in Asian varieties, but in person, they're even more adorable than I thought."

Smiling like a completely unguarded child, Limeia picked up the calico. The little dog began to whine, as if to say, *Hey, wait! I'm the one who put my life on the line to taste test those carrots, remember?!*

But Queen Elizard was concerned over a different matter.

"Oh, bugger!! They were having such a delicious time until just a moment ago?! I bet they were pulling photos of their loved ones out of their pockets, saying things like, *We're getting married after this battle is over*, and such!! Damn…Am I fated to always miss the juiciest parts of everything?!"

"Everyone seemed to be quite adamant about heading into the heart of London for some reason, if it helps."

"And they left me behind?! D-damn it all. Can you make it, horse?! We must get to London posthaste!!"

The warhorse unfolded his four legs and rose, as if to say, *Sure thing! That's how a queen should act.*

Elizard hopped onto her mount, then used one arm to grab Laura Stuart, who, like before, was idling about, and soon situated her on the back of the horse.

"Hey. Is the flag prepared?"

"Fifty-fifty is about what I would say. The thing itself was blended into the general exhibits in the British Museum. Not many came to the realization that it is in fact a Soul Arm. Also, if the museum-employed Charles Conder did the work I had hoped from him, it might actually be somehow usable."

"A normal member of society? His life would be on the line if the knights detected his actions...I need to give more respect to the gentlemen in this country," said Elizard before falling silent for a moment.

She thought to herself.

She thought of the people who had prepared at this campground then headed to London. She thought of those assisting them, risking their lives even though they couldn't use magic.

...Hmph. Being able to use the Curtana's authority on the outside is a problem. And so is Carissa turning nearly invincible using the position of angelic leader to trample over Europe.

The queen's face changed.

As she looked in the direction of London, her expression grew more dangerous.

But have they forgotten that Carissa, armed with the Curtana Original, can already bring out that power within the borders? The thing you're about to fight is someone who might destroy all of Europe single-handedly, someone more terrifying than a hydrogen bomb—a man-made calamity in the flesh!!

"Damn them! They can say it's for the fate of Britain, but they are idiots for going off to the final battle with nerve and guts alone, without any trump cards! They can get themselves killed for all I care!!"

"Ufu-fu. Despite your tone, Mother, you seem quite happy about it."

CHAPTER 7

Princess and Queen: Fabulous Villains
Curtana_Original.

1

3 AM.

Kamijou, with the members of the Puritans, stormed into London.

Still, for once, they didn't just walk in like naïve fools. To swiftly head for Buckingham Palace, they split up into over twenty large trucks.

Even now that they'd entered London, they faced no real inspections of any sort. But that struck Kamijou as eerie. No knight inspections awaited them, nor even any that made use of the police or the military. Born Again Amakusa had prepared spells for breaking through those inspections, and now Itsuwa and the others seemed to be frowning at it.

"(Perhaps there are no knight inspections because all their forces have been assembled at Buckingham Palace,)" murmured Kanzaki apprehensively.

Unable to think of an answer, though, they saw no point in adhering to the question. They had no choice but to feel relieved that their forces hadn't been whittled away before they clashed with the main enemy camp.

Kamijou sat in an uncovered truck bed, the cold autumn wind hitting his face.

There were no other people or vehicles on the main streets in London, perhaps attributable to the level of takeover. Because of it, the truck they were riding in was ignoring the speed limit. Empty cars seemed to be sitting in the middle of the road in places, as though the people had fled quickly when the takeover happened, and the truck sometimes had to weave among them like a snake, rocking Kamijou and the others back and forth.

Kamijou cast a furtive glance at the Puritan faithful riding with him.

None of them seemed very interested in who held political power. It didn't matter who tried to get their hands on the country's reins, as long as the people of the United Kingdom could go on living like normal. However, it also didn't matter who wanted to become leader—if they tried to build a new order that bluntly permitted acts of homicide using the military, the Puritans wouldn't allow it. Their determination to fight Carissa would never waver.

To extend the hand of salvation to lost lambs.

In that sense, the Puritans' goal was pretty explicit.

"I'll do a final briefing," said Kanzaki, who was riding with them. "Our goal is to speed into Buckingham Palace as quickly as possible, then suppress the coup d'état's leader, Carissa. As for the fastest way to do that—I propose that we destroy her Curtana Original."

"…Right, so if the knights lose their leader and they even lose control over the Curtana, they won't be sure anymore whether they believe in the second princess's strength, right?"

Kamijou wasn't quite grasping it, but Vilian, sitting elegantly nearby, nodded. "…The Curtana Original is the very symbol of her coup. If we destroy it before their eyes, the knights' spirits will crumble. My sister's monstrous power is supported by the Curtana. If she loses the sword, she should go back to being a regular person."

"Let us assume there are terrorists who wish to change the country with nuclear warheads," suggested Kanzaki. It was an incredibly frightening example. "If they lost the warheads, the centerpiece of their plan, who would try to continue it?"

"Well, I guess that's true, b-but…" stammered Kamijou.

Index, sitting next to him, added, "The coup d'état will end with the Curtana by itself. But I think it's easier said than done. After all, inside the all-British Continent, the head of state using the Curtana Original acts as the angelic leader Michael and can wield powers far beyond that of normal humans."

"...Yes. Even with all our remaining forces in one place, it might be hard to break the sword through normal methods."

Kanzaki's words had a weight that went beyond their meaning. Was it because she'd personally experienced a battle with the angel Misha Kreutzev before?

"So if our enemy is out of the ordinary, we'll have to rely on someone out of the ordinary, too."

"Y-yeah, I thought so." Kamijou winced slightly under her straightforward gaze. "My right hand might be able to bust up the Curtana Original, since it's just an object made with magic. But Carissa is probably stronger than you and Acqua, right? If you guys are all whooshing around superfast, I won't be able to touch it."

"Yes, we understand that. I'm not saying that a normal high school student should come with us for a battle with someone stronger than a saint." Kanzaki nodded. "Instead, we will use you as a slow-moving, high-power mobile battery. If Carissa tries to confuse us with high-speed movement for her attack...Amakusa and I, a saint, will respond with our own speed, then try to repel her in your direction."

The Puritan remnant forces consisted not only of the Born Again Amakusa but the former Agnes unit and independent sorcerers such as Sherry. However, the Born Again Amakusa, which was centered around a saint, was still the most suited for matters of speed.

Now, the match would be decided on whether or not the speedy Born Again Amakusa could coordinate successfully with the long-range attacks and support magic used by the other members.

"You don't need to think so hard about it," said Kanzaki to Kamijou, who had fallen silent. "Survive until the end. That is the most important mission given to you."

Everyone shared that mission.

To settle things without losing anyone by the end.

Touma Kamijou, his gaze falling to his right hand, asked again, "…But will we be all right? There are, like, five hundred of us all moving in. But there haven't been any knights, and that bothers me. Carissa controls this city, so if she notices us…"

"Yes. She has probably detected us by now," Kanzaki confirmed smoothly. "At this rate, a large battle is bound to start before we arrive at Buckingham Palace."

Kamijou looked at her, startled.

"But even if she has," she went on, "if she can't pull off an actual interception, we won't have a problem."

"Ah?" Kamijou frowned.

Inexplicably, Kanzaki pointed to one of her ears. "It's starting. It would be wise to cover your ears."

2

The Atlantic Ocean.

The aerial fortress Coven Compass had moved farther northwest from Islay, and now it waited above the water just outside the UK border.

By exiting the UK, it had temporarily cut off the attacks from the knights, who received extra support from the Curtana and the all-British Continent.

Black smoke billowed from several spots on the giant disc-shaped fortress, and the whole thing was tipped diagonally, as though the balance-controlling Soul Arms had taken damage as well. Still, in defiance of the laws of physics, the fortress still floated in the air. Its major systems were still working.

On the midnight-black sea floated an island made of steel.

It was the sea fortress the knights had prepared. But unlike the Coven Compass, its cruising functions were completely destroyed, and it was almost ready to sink. The Puritan witches had certainly gotten their two cents in.

The witches protecting the smoking Coven Compass and the knights trying to capture it glared at one another.

Many of the knights who left the national borders and went back to normal had been shot down by the broom-riding witches. Several of the defeated rocked about in the waves even now, sending out strobe-like distress signals and waiting for rescue.

Outside the border were the witches—and inside it were the knights.

Two forces, struggling against each other, separated by an invisible line defined by man.

Meanwhile, Smartveri, one of the witches, cautious of the long-range spells intermittently flying at them from the other side of the border, had turned her attention to her communication Soul Arm.

The operator's voice continued.

"——*Preparations beginning for large-scale flash bombardment at Buckingham Palace. Designated witches are advised to move out of its firing trajectory and be cautious not to lose control of one's broom during the spell's preparations or the chaotic airflows caused by its firing.*"

After listening to the businesslike words, Smartveri unthinkingly whistled to herself. "Over five hundred kilometers of straight-line distance...Over one and a half times the range according to its design specs. And this will be a direct attack, so we can't use the relay points for mana guidance, either."

Smartveri's tone was relaxed.

"And with the jumble of stuff in the way that could cause interference, like the ruins on the Isle of Man, at that...I'm surprised those stubborn bastards approved of it," she muttered to herself.

Another witch, her colleague, interrupted her via a different communication line. "*What's more unbelievable to me is that we got permission to fire on Buckingham Palace.*"

"But the third princess seems to have used her royal family influence to railroad the annoying paperwork through. Well, guess I've gotta hand it to the gung-ho authorities in a situation like this."

"*...Speaking of gung-ho authorities, the coup d'état's leader, the second princess, is pretty similar.*"

"Hey, maybe they're more alike than anyone thinks, eh? They just face in different directions."

Gzgzgzgzgzgz!! Her communication Soul Arm made a strange noise, interrupting the conversation. At the same time, Smartveri's broom rocked. She hastily regained control, then heard her colleague's surprised voice from the Soul Arm:

"Zz, zz...Has it—started...?!"

A light, so impossibly white it couldn't have been part of the natural world, drove the darkness away from the Atlantic waters.

The Coven Compass's top surface. From the middle of the disc-shaped aerial fortress, at a point about twenty meters above in the sky, a pure-white orb of light appeared. The enormous sanctuary had created a massive ball of energy, which then expanded the air around it, which made changes in air pressure give way to storming winds. The Coven Compass, also the witches' carrier, had begun to start up its other trump card.

A carrier below and artillery on top.

The extensive flash bombardment, which actually possessed half the giant fortress's power and role, creaked and cracked into position, aiming at the capital of the United Kingdom.

"Zz, now that it's...aiming, do you...think the knights...zzz-zzz... will interfere?"

"A bit, probably, but I don't think any stupid heroes will jump right into the firing line. If they had that much guts, they would have brought their entire army outside the border to attack us."

Actually, had the Knight Leader still been in the fight, they might have done just that.

When Elizard was still in power, many would probably have done so gladly.

...And that's the limit of how far violence takes you, eh, new queen?

Smartveri let out a short, scornful laugh as she watched the unmoving knights.

Then, the operator's voice reached her ears.

"——*Commencing bombardment. Destroying Buckingham Palace!!*"

3

Boom!! All the windowpanes in the buildings around them shattered.

In the night skies above London, above the racing truck, a beam of light over five meters thick pierced through the air.

Even with both of his ears covered, Kamijou felt his sense of equilibrium threaten to overturn as the impact rattled the very core of his brain. Either the driver, Itsuwa, had been surprised by the thundering sound, or the truck itself had been physically shocked—its huge frame skidded unnaturally sideways.

There wasn't only one shot.

There was a second, then a third…At intervals of a few seconds, shots fired one after another in the direction of Buckingham Palace.

Kamijou shouted at the top of his lungs at Kanzaki, who was right in front of him, hoping to be heard over the din. "Hey…?! Is this what you meant when you said, *Even if she detects us, as long as she can't intercept us?!*"

"Yes. If Carissa's side is tied up defending against the bombardment, we will be able to cross the battlefield in the meantime. Artillery support from afar is a fundamental component of ground combat," said Kanzaki, her expression calm and unchanging amid the booms and bangs.

Then, from a different direction, another bombardment assailed Buckingham Palace. This time, it was like a thin, sharp darkness, piercing through the starry sky and nightscape. But there were a lot of them. Curtain fire, containing anywhere from one hundred to two hundred shots, arced through the air and plunged toward the palace area.

"You had more than one fortress?!"

"That must be the Silkie Aquarium, currently cruising on the seafloor near Dover. I heard that four silkies withstood the knights' assault and remain operational—one, two, four, and five. Three and eight are operational, too, but they seem to be concentrating on fighting back against the knights and the Royal Navy commanded by Carissa."

Apparently, it was like a submarine mothership for the sorcerers, who were active underwater like mermaids. When there had been decisive movements at the British-French border, they'd been standing by so they could act on a moment's notice. Now, they seemed to have come here to provide artillery support.

I mean, I'm glad they're helping us with these humongous attacks, but...

"...Honestly speaking, if anyone was in Buckingham Palace like that, they might seriously die, wouldn't they?"

"Actually, you'd do well to assume that even this bombardment isn't enough to take down Carissa. That's the sort of enemy we'll be crossing swords with."

"Freaking monsters," muttered Kamijou in wonder.

Concentrated fire with something like a battleship cannon wouldn't take her down. And they wanted a total amateur to run in with just his fist? He was headed to a reckless battlefield, even by his standards.

"...Anyway, there's not gonna be any collateral damage with all that shooting going on, is there?"

"The area around Buckingham Palace is basically a great big park, so I don't think we have to worry about any stray bullets," answered Index, as though matching it up to her own perfect memory.

Kanzaki agreed with the statement. "And Carissa's side is probably guiding the populace to specific places to make the residents easier to manage. They're gathering everyone in the city into hotels, theaters, and churches. Even if they accidentally blow up a house, there's little chance of anyone getting hurt right away.

"...Still, we obviously can't let ourselves be inattentive," she finished, as though she'd even given thought to unexpected tragedies.

But that meant the chances were still high that Buckingham Palace itself would be destroyed. Kamijou didn't know how much the buildings or artwork were worth, but everything in that palace, as well as the palace itself, was probably a mountain of national treasures.

As he thought about it, Kamijou glanced at the third princess's profile.

"...It doesn't matter," she offered in a steady tone. "Everyone—all over the United Kingdom, not only London—is sharing the pain. We would be pushing our luck if we wanted the British royal family alone to emerge unharmed...And if it meant calming this nationwide disturbance, we would smash that sort of palace into little pieces."

Kamijou sensed something off in Vilian's voice and expression. He'd just met her, so he didn't know the details, but he felt as though she was different from that time in Buckingham Palace when she'd been so jumpy and withdrawn.

"Yes—I have been made to realize something," said Vilian upon the boy's gaze going to her, as she checked the parts of the crossbow she held. While it was a crossbow, it wasn't made of crude metal. Instead, it could have been a custom-made item for the royal family, fashioned out of wood that gave off a caramel luster, the sort that might be used over a bar counter. The scope attached to it had an antique impression, too. If someone had told him it was something da Vinci had used regularly, he might have believed them.

"Those servants and cooks can't use any sorcery, but they put themselves in harm's way to let me, someone who fears battle, escape. And I'm sure that mercenary fought that group of knights to ensure my own safety, too."

The crossbow was large, over a meter long. It looked difficult for her slender, feminine arms to pull the string. However, perhaps in consideration of that, a slide was attached to the underside, like the kind on a pump-action shotgun. It probably used gears and pulleys to make it easy to draw it back.

"If running away from the fight would protect them, I would hide myself wherever needs must. But if doing so won't change the danger they face...then fighting is my only path."

Vilian, who had tied up her sleeves and slung a quiver over her green dress like a hunter from ancient times, returned Kamijou's gaze with a modest but firmly rooted one of her own.

"As for you…what will you do? I doubt you have the obligation to risk your life for the crisis facing our nation, and you've also rescued your acquaintance from the disturbance for the time being. There would be no issue if you were to withdraw to a safe zone, as they call it. Why do you still go to this deadly battleground?"

"…I don't have a crazy reason or anything," began Kamijou, looking up at another pure-white flash streaking through the night sky. "I mean, I don't like going to dangerous places if I can help it. If I could abandon this stuff, believe me, I would. If everyone who got caught up in this conflict was just disposable cannon fodder, I'd abandon them and find a way to get back to Academy City, too."

Unlike Vilian, he didn't have anything to prepare. All he had to do was tighten his right fist, and he was ready.

"But they're not, are they?"

She might not have been able to hear him over the continuous booming, but he pressed on anyway.

"I don't think anyone is that easy to understand or that convenient, you know? Everyone carries stuff heavy enough to break them, and they're running all over the place just to hang on to it… Can't just leave them and go home, can I? It's not an issue of some crazy reasons or obligations or anything. I think that if you want to stand up for something, you might as well do it."

Vilian watched Kamijou for a time. Eventually, she said, "…Even without a perfect set of principles or ideology, you can hear everyone around you, no matter where you are. And no matter what the situation, you'd spare no effort to find the best choice…"

"?"

"You're a mercenary…like William, but a different kind."

Kamijou opened his mouth, intending to repeat the unfamiliar name to her.

But before he did, something happened.

Fwup-fwup-fwup-fwup-fwup-fwup-fwup! A continuous chopping noise rang out overhead.

A helicopter…?! wondered Kamijou at first, but he was wrong.

White.

It was a giant object, without any color, like an unfinished plastic model. The huge fan-shaped thing gained buoyancy by spinning very quickly.

As for its size, it was fifty meters in radius, and the fan angle was about ninety degrees.

Kamijou remembered the odd color of this absurdly large structure.

"...A remnant of the omnidimensional slice from the Curtana Original...?!"

Right after he shouted, it happened.

The giant fan, which had been staying parallel to the ground and spinning at a high speed, suddenly went *clunk*...and tilted sideways. With all its buoyancy gone in a flash, the spinning object began to descend toward the ground in much the same way as a helicopter crashing.

Yes—it fell, as if aiming for the large truck Kamijou and the others were riding.

With its giant whirling blade, it could chop down trees in an instant.

"Shit. We didn't have any inspections on our way here—is this what she was after?!"

"*...Gzz-gzz...Please hang on tight...!!*"

The voice of Itsuwa, who was in the driver's seat, echoed through the radio tied onto the truck bed.

Then, a moment later—

The whirling blade was essentially one hundred meters in diameter, with its axis anchored to its bottom tip. The transport truck swerved violently to avoid it, tossing everyone around in the back. The spinning blades sank about twenty meters in one swipe, ripping out not only the asphalt but even the underground subway structures and throwing them all over the place.

They just barely managed to avoid a direct hit.

But then an impact struck the side of the truck.

The giant spinning blades had changed direction after hitting the ground. They had run into the side of a building and bounced above the ground, squirming and writhing without regularity. The top of one of the whirling blades, veering randomly, had caught the truck in the side.

It had been a sideswiping blow.

The ten-ton truck was sent flying away from the road and over the sidewalk before crashing into a building wall.

"Gwaaahhhh?!" Kamijou shouted as the heavy impact ran through him.

He wasn't thrown out of the truck bed, but the truck itself was now bent in the middle. It would be impossible to start driving again.

And then even worse news came.

Fwup-fwup-fwup-fwup-fwa-fwa-fwa-fwa-fwa-fwa! The booming noise was like helicopter rotors.

But not only one.

When Kamijou, his entire body tensed, nervously looked up, he saw four, no, *five* of the hundred-meter-plus fan-shaped spinning blades flying at them like Frisbees.

"Shit!! Run away!!"

The others didn't need Kamijou to shout it—they'd all jumped down onto the destroyed road, trying to run as far away as possible. Dragging his stinging body, Kamijou grabbed the hand of Index, who was at a loss, and jumped off the truck.

That was when it happened.

As the many whirling blades flew at them, tightly packed, they crashed into one another. The group bounced around in midair, setting them on trajectories that were random and thus even harder to avoid as they soared down at them.

…*???!!!*

He couldn't even manage to make a noise.

Countless blades tore away the asphalt and mercilessly ripped down building walls. Index's hand, which he was sure he'd grabbed, fell away…and as soon as he realized it, his own body was launched into the air. He avoided a direct hit from them, but the asphalt had burst upward, sending him flying.

He had no time to take the fall gracefully.

He slammed into the ground so hard he nearly suffocated.

Guhhfh?! Sh-shit...

"In...dex...? Kanzaki, Itsuwa!! Damn it! Where is everyone?!"

The landing impact had sent clouds of dust into the air, and he couldn't get a good view of anything. Hacking and coughing irregularly, he shouted his friends' names, trying to get his voice above the surroundings.

Only the sound of an explosion came back to him.

A whirling blade, having achieved buoyancy and dancing in the night sky at a fixed speed, had collided with a thick ray of light shooting in from afar, causing an immense flash of light in the air.

Hopelessly casting about, Kamijou heard a frail voice.

The words belonged to someone he knew.

"Over...here..."

"Itsuwa?!"

"Y-yes..."

Kamijou tried to run to her, but it was a dead end. Or rather, strictly speaking, the entrance to the back road was blocked off by a collapsed building wall. Her voice was coming from the cracks among the rubble.

"In any case, could you follow Her Highness? Right after everyone scattered, I saw her heading to Buckingham Palace by herself."

"?!" Kamijou looked around, but he couldn't spot anyone who looked like Vilian. Had she really gone ahead at a time like this?

Damn it!! He glanced toward Buckingham Palace out of reflex, but then he realized something and returned his gaze to the pile that housed Itsuwa. Then, on the other side of the wall, Itsuwa, possibly guessing something from a subtle sound or his pause, spoke to him.

"Ah-ha-ha. I'm not buried alive or anything, so no need to worry. We'll take different roads to get to Buckingham Palace. I doubt we'll be able to find you soon, so let's meet up again at the palace."

"But hey, are you okay? You're actually okay, right?!"

"Everyone else must be finding their own routes to get to

Buckingham Palace...For now, please get moving. Staying in one place will only get you sniped."

She left him with that, and he heard footsteps running away on the other side of the debris. It looked like Itsuwa really was trying to get to Buckingham Palace by taking the alleyways.

What about everyone else...?! Kamijou looked around.

He saw several figures running farther down the main road. One was jumping from rooftop to rooftop—probably Kanzaki. Index, in her arms, was shouting something in his direction, but it didn't reach his ears.

Kamijou felt relieved for now after seeing her familiar face...But a moment later, his face drew back again. There was a green scrap of fabric on the jagged edge of a piece of destroyed concrete, as though it had caught Vilian. The small, violently torn cloth seemed an awfully ominous metaphor...but Kamijou quickly shook his head to drive away the groundless premonition.

According to Itsuwa, Vilian had gone on ahead by herself. So for now, all he could do for the mission was run to Buckingham Palace.

He was pretty sure it wasn't even two kilometers away in a straight line. However, those two thousand meters had changed into a path of hellish suffering.

Bonk!! came a dull sound.

By the time Kamijou looked up, startled, a sphere over twenty meters in diameter was falling toward him—a smooth white sphere without color. Once it made landfall about a hundred meters in front of him, blocking his path, it sank unnaturally deep. It had probably even crushed a subway line underground.

But then it appeared to bounce and rise into the air again.

It crushed passenger vehicles abandoned on the road, caused them to burst apart, slammed into a building wall, then rolled off in the other direction...It was heading for Kamijou with random motions, like a living creature.

"Damn it!!"

Kamijou immediately pressed himself against the wall of a road-facing building.

That was when the giant twenty-meter sphere charged in.

In pitching terms, it was a fastball. It flew straight at the ground on a course that would roll him over, crushing him.

But Kamijou made it out without dying—all thanks to the principles of geometry.

When a sphere is put into a cubical box the same size as its diameter, there will be gaps at the edges. By backing up against the building wall, he'd slipped into that gap.

But the destruction didn't end there.

The building wall overhead, which the giant sphere had pushed into, came crumbling down. Kamijou outran the rain of debris, moving only forward. A rumbling rang through the ground all the while, pieces ever chasing him, about to crush him from behind.

He had no time to rest.

Several more spinning, fanlike blades were shooting at him.

With their centers of gravity skewed, the giant pillars writhed unnaturally, like self-righting dolls, and smashed the road.

Several buildings collapsed, blocking Kamijou's way.

None of these structures by themselves has a very complicated shape, he considered, gritting his teeth as he ran desperately forward. *But they're absolutely enormous! They're basically like battleship cannons at this point!!*

Even after pouring all his energy into dodging one or two "cannon shots," he couldn't rest easy. He had to close the distance as fast as he could and stop the "shots" themselves, or else he and all the others who had been separated from one another would remain in this crisis.

Maybe the fact that there were none of the knights in London, and the fact that the other residents had all been confined elsewhere, was in preparation to let her attack like this whenever she wanted.

Kamijou dodged among piles of debris, plunged through a curtain of dust, jumped over the fissures in the collapsed road he could see the subway line through, and continued to run on and on through the London night.

Itsuwa had said Vilian went on ahead, but no matter how far he ran, he could never see her. He even started to wonder whether she'd actually gone through this fierce battlefield to begin with.

In the meantime, the Buckingham Palace property finally came into view.

The big fence surrounding the park had caved in and been blown away, possibly thanks to the magical bombings from the Coven Compass and the Silkie Aquariums. The entire short-cut green lawn had been turned up and exploded, like a giant had missed a golf club swing—it was now a crater.

Kamijou slipped through what remained of the broken fence, charging onto the palace grounds without hesitation.

And then something chilled him to his core.

He almost stopped running for no reason.

It was past three in the morning, but the palace, bathed in illumination from the ornamental lights on the ground, stood out very clearly against the midnight dark. The bombings from afar had taken out about a third of the palace's right side, and he could see the extravagant furnishings inside from all the way back where he stood. It was such an unrealistically gorgeous building that any sense of tragedy was gone. It looked like someone had removed the roof and wall from a giant dollhouse.

Yes.

As Touma Kamijou stepped onto the palace grounds, the sight of the half-destroyed palace wasn't the main attraction.

He was looking at the garden that surrounded the place.

They were probably creations of the Curtana Original. Several giant, mysterious, white objects, created as an aftereffect of omni-dimensional slices, were buried in the ground like stakes. And since they'd fallen onto their sides, the grass and the asphalt both lay in overturned ruin.

Two women stood amid it all.

One was Third Princess Vilian.

A white-skinned, blond-haired woman wearing a green dress with a widely spread-out skirt, like a princess from a picture book. In her hands she held a fairly large crossbow, but it had a shotgun-like slide on the lower part to allow even the delicate woman to pull the firm string.

The other was Second Princess Carissa.

A woman wearing a red dress interwoven in places with leather. In her hand was a sword without blade or tip. On her cheek were bits of black soil and dirt, which must have hit her in the process of defending against the bombing by some way or another. But it didn't look the least bit disgraceful. The mud mixed with her own sweat only increased her intimidation.

"...!"

"......"

They were arguing about something—no, it was more one-sided than that. Vilian was snapping at her, and Carissa seemed to be smoothly brushing it off.

Despite the crossbow Vilian held in both hands, she hadn't pulled the string or aimed it yet. She held it like a trophy from an awards ceremony, a weapon that didn't function as an actual weapon.

In contrast, while Carissa was letting the blade-less, tip-less sword dangle at her side, her hand never quivered. Her muscles were perpetually prepared, and she looked as though she could fling out an attack this very moment.

And perhaps it symbolized their stances.

Vilian neglected her weapon in favor of pushing dialogue to the forefront, whereas Carissa was completely focused on handling her weapon and passing off dialogue out of hand.

Which meant it was clear what was about to happen.

Kamijou couldn't tell what they were talking about from where he was, and he didn't have the time to hear them both out.

That idiot...!!

He ran full speed, then jumped at Vilian from behind to push her away.

A moment later, without hesitation, Carissa's Curtana Original moved.

Ga-bam!!
With a roar, every dimension in the spot Vilian had just occupied was cleft through.

A belt-shaped, unnaturally white object appeared, a hundred meters long in total. It was the three-dimensional "cross section" cut away from every dimension in that spot that could be expressed with a whole number, and after a few moments, it slammed down onto the ground.

Getting up from on top of Vilian, who was flabbergasted at the sudden event, Touma Kamijou glared at their powerful enemy.

The second princess of the United Kingdom.

The coup d'état's leader and the one with the most military prowess of the three sisters.

And the one who'd used the Curtana Original and the all-British Continent—the one who wielded the power of an angelic leader.

"Carissa!!"

"Congratulations. Your fine actions are worthy of a medal. I'd even like to show you to my own weak-kneed knights. My sister's virtue really does show up in the strangest places. I need to stop making light of it."

Carissa answered Kamijou's shout with a steady expression.

All the lights that were normally for making the extravagant palace stand out in the dark were now bathing the elder sister in their luminescence. She reigned within that light as though the effect were natural.

Touma Kamijou kept his eyes on her body.

His gaze wasn't caused *by* her body, however. What would happen if he let his attention slip, even a tiny bit?

The young amateur could physically sense the answer.

"What of the others, by the way? Is your whole army buried under rubble?"

Kamijou's face drew back into a scowl, but he fought the terrible idea out of his mind with a growl.

They were safe. They would come for sure. His only choice now was to act on that assumption. After all, drawing Carissa's attention would stop the giant structures' cannon fire and get them out of danger.

But then, as if to stamp out his optimistic hope, Carissa put the Curtana Original on her shoulder and grinned a broad, wicked smile.

"If they are, then the Puritans certainly disappointed me, too. They're making me look like a fool for having gone through all that preparation, so."

"Preparation…?" muttered Vilian, as though a bad feeling had bubbled up from her heart and made it out her mouth.

It was a moment later.

Boom!!
Some sort of incredibly huge object passed overhead.

The object had a hang glider–like form.

But it was big. Close to eighty meters long. It rivaled the Skybus 365, a jumbo jet, in length. And after it passed over their heads once, it looped back around in a wide arc, aiming its nose at them.

"Oh, don't act so surprised. Did you think the Coven Compass and the Silkie Aquariums were the only two mobile fortresses we had? I'm sure you at least know that most of the major facilities of the UK are in my hands. The knights, especially. They have all kinds of Soul Arms, big and small, for engaging in direct combat, so. I very much doubt it will bore you."

As if to interrupt the grinning Carissa's words, several more booms and bursts streaked through the night sky. Like before, they were eighty-meter "fortresses" that looked like hang gliders—twenty of them, slowly circling over Buckingham Palace. Silver-colored metal parts were attached to reinforce certain areas, looking like armor or protective gear.

The second princess gazed up at the fortresses, painted in the same crimson red as her own dress, and said, "The mobile siege fortress Gryphon Sky."

Kamijou looked up at the mobile fortresses. He had no idea how they'd attack, and as he stood there dumbstruck, only Carissa's voice reached him.

"They can't fly at high altitudes like the Skybus 365, since they're made for attacking castles on the ground, and they don't have the flexibility or adaptability the Coven Compass has, thanks to their being unmanned Soul Arms, but their coordinated attack patterns are number one of all our nation's fortresses, so. They're stupid but obedient. Truly the best option for someone engaged in military affairs."

Is that...all of them?

Kamijou gaped at the sight, which far exceeded the scale of person-to-person combat.

They're mobile fortresses like the Coven Compass...and there're twenty of them...?!

He brought his gaze away from the night sky and back to the battle before him.

On top of the floating arsenal, the actual enemy, Carissa, had overwhelming attack power in the form of the Curtana Original. And the Knights' forces must have been standing by somewhere close, as well.

He could maybe break the sword with one hit with his right hand, but could he and Vilian fight alone in this situation?

Unconsciously, he remembered the Soul Arm called Robin Hood that had shot the New Light sorcerer Lesser. He glanced into the surrounding darkness, his caution mounting by another degree.

But Carissa had this to say about that: "No, nobody's going to ambush you. I mean, I did use that little live-relay tactic already, so."

"...?"

"Having the Curtana Original run out of control after defeating the Knight Leader and getting the knights to doubt my legitimacy as head of state...Several coincidences may have helped you, but I still have to say it was a pretty brilliant psychological tactic."

Carissa whirled the Curtana Original around and rested it on her shoulder.

"The knights were on the verge of collapse, and you forced me to reignite their passion, so. Though I did use somewhat rough methods."

A live relay. Rough methods.

Kamijou had a bad feeling about this—and then he saw it. A few drops of dark-red liquid clinging to the Curtana Original's blade-less body.

"You...You didn't..."

"Mm, it was a bit of a punishment. The security level around Buckingham Palace will drop, but it's still better than the whole Knights faction collapsing after taking control of the entire nation and losing their very support structures, so...Besides, the head of state uses the angelic leader's powers. To be honest, I don't need a royal guard anyway."

"You killed them?! You killed your own allies?!" yelled Kamijou in shock.

Vilian's shoulders shook, as though she'd remembered it happening.

But the second princess's answer went even beyond that.

"Don't worry about that. Killing someone too quickly doesn't give the imagination time to catch up, so...I made it a bit of sport—to give them the greatest performance with the least amount of mana spent."

A fate worse than death.

That was the phrase that came to mind, and Kamijou couldn't even visualize it. He gritted his teeth. "...The knights had things they believed in, too, and that's why they were following you this whole time. They're the comrades who fought at your side—and you're talking about 'spending' them?! What the hell is wrong with you?!"

There was a dull *creak...!!*

It was the sound of Touma Kamijou's right hand tightening unconsciously.

"Come off it."

In response, Carissa's face remained steady.

"Why, pray tell, do you think I gave them high positions and rewarded them with so much taxpayer money? It's so that when a national incident happens, they work themselves to the bone doing every little bit they can to steer the UK out of the crisis. That is exactly what every knight desires."

"Y-you..."

"And they truly were useful. The other cowards were ready to run away, and they prevented them from defecting."

Carissa slowly lifted the Curtana Original from her shoulder and readied it again.

Then, as though criticizing a difficult child acting too old for his years, she said, "Still, though. They were never more than a bunch of chickens who wouldn't head to a deadly battlefield on their own anyway. Now, I'll just have to pave the way myself and make them believe again that this coup d'état *will* succeed!!" the woman shouted, with many a giant fortress dancing in the sky behind her, the half-destroyed royal palace at her back, and the legendary sword in her hand.

It was the signal that the battle had begun.

4

If they beat the second princess, this coup d'état would end.

Kamijou reaffirmed the thought.

The Knight Leader was absent now, and his subordinates were wavering about whether to proceed with the coup or to stop it. Carissa had thence secured them by way of punishment. Therefore, even though their ranks were temporarily unified, were Carissa to lose her power, the whole thing would come crashing down.

Compared to going all over the UK and taking down every single group of knights, they could settle the score by defeating a single major boss. It could be no easier than that.

Forcing himself to think positively, Kamijou considered trying to loosen the tension in his body, but...

"You'll die."

A voice came from directly behind him, already with a sound of cutting wind.

She hadn't just gotten behind him in the blink of an eye.

The Curtana Original was already sweeping in a horizontal arc toward Kamijou's neck.

"...?!"

He didn't have the time to turn around. He simply dropped his body straight down, avoiding the strike by a hairbreadth. Or at least, it looked that way; in the end, a scalding pain ran through his ear. Vilian saw it and let out a short scream.

And then, another strange *gwkeee!!* resounded.

A smooth, unnaturally white object appeared along the sword's horizontal path—the debris that was created as an aftereffect of the omnidimensional slice. It weighed more than a lump of steel, and it was about to fall naturally onto Kamijou, who had dodged downward.

Sh...it...?!

Kamijou rolled out of the way of the debris's landing point.

Wh-whump!! The awful rattling shook Kamijou's gut.

And then...

"Too slow, pig. You'll be sliced in two."

Roar!! The Curtana Original swung.

A downstroke, from high to low. The strike, which cleaved through every whole-numbered dimension, created a giant slash that extended in a straight line out twenty meters from the Curtana.

On a route that would sever Kamijou's upper half from his lower.

He immediately stuck out his right hand in panic.

There was a crack like a whip, and the slashing attack vanished midway there.

It...disappeared...?

Kamijou leaped to his feet, then tried to close the distance to Carissa. If he could land even one hit with his clenched fist, the Curtana Original should break.

But before his fist could get there, the second princess swung her sword again.

She kept its tip facing up, then brought it from right to left as though opening a window. It created a wall-like white debris object that looked like a shutter, which blocked his fist.

A dull pain came back to his bones, like he'd just punched steel.

Kamijou's face twisted at the sensation. *Didn't work that time! Shit, I don't know what I need to do to erase them!!*

He was overcome by a chill. After all, his opponent's weapon was a strike that severed every dimension.

If he misread it, it wouldn't just be his right arm—it could cut his whole body in half.

But he didn't have time to be worrying about something like that.

He didn't have any room to relax and think of a strategy.

"Hu," came Carissa's breath.

At the same time, there was a massive blasting sound.

The second princess herself had kicked into the air, the white wall separating them.

The debris shield, heavier than steel, easily flew over ten meters into the air with one hit.

Carissa didn't bring her foot down.

She fired off a second kick after the first that plunged mercilessly into Kamijou's stomach. It wasn't so much a human martial art as a human machine gun.

Whump!! went the terrible sound.

Kamijou's body was easily flung several meters away, and then he began bouncing irregularly off the ground.

"Gah, brgh, aaaahhhhhh???!!!"

The urge to vomit rose within him, and he threw up red-colored chunks.

As Kamijou writhed in agony, Carissa twirled her blade-less, tip-less sword around like a baton, grinning as she threw the thin debris object to the ground. Vilian had finally tried to get her crossbow ready, but the situation had changed to something so dizzying she seemed unable to take careful aim.

Guh...Shit...Gffhh...I...knew I couldn't keep up with that speed...!!

With a very strong feeling he'd lost a huge chunk of stamina, he still got back up. His fingertips tremored unnaturally.

"Hey, what's the matter, eh? I was holding back on that one, too." Carissa's expression hadn't changed. It was like she was saying that nothing would change whether or not he got up. "Accidentally sealing massive amounts of telesma inside you does tend to give people side effects like that. Well, at least as long as you don't build a spell to remove the shackles, I think."

She was...holding back...? Kamijou's eyes took on a look of pure disbelief.

Carissa swung her sword around, using the dulled tip to point in a certain direction. "Anyway, are you all right? It's dangerous to stop thinking, you know."

Kamijou hadn't realized what was approaching him at that moment.

A Gryphon Sky flying in the air. Eighty meters long, the crimson hang glider hadn't changed significantly. However, there was a change in the giant shadow cast on it by the moon. As though spinning around, it changed shape—and in a completely impossible turn, its shape and weight transformed into those of a knight's lance, its color became pure red, and it floated right down near the ground.

And it seemed like the fortresses overhead were moving in tandem with the red jousting lance on the ground.

In that state, the Gryphon Skies made a pass over Buckingham Palace.

And, of course, the twenty-meter stake moving in tandem with them shot off, skimming across the ground at an intense speed.

What now?!

*   *   *

Ga-bam!!
Touma Kamijou took the hit directly and flew, bent over, into the air.

"Dhgh...bgh...?!"
The pain was so intense that it caused a malfunction and almost numbed him instead, tearing through his upper body. The boy flew over fifteen meters through the air without a single bounce, then, once he hit, continued to roll over the earth.

Then, like beating a dead horse, the pain came in on him afterward.

"Waaaaaaaaaaaaaaaahhhhhhhhhhhhhhhhhhhhhhhhhhhhhhh?!"
Kamijou writhed in intense agony, but then when he saw another stake flying toward him like a cannonball, he frantically rolled. He thought he'd clenched his teeth, but red liquid spilled from his mouth.

However, it was Carissa, the one who had done the damage, who gave an unhappy look.

"Great. The Soul Arm's automatic decision-making. This thing was originally for straight-up destruction of castle walls, so why can't it at least cut someone's top half from their bottom half? It's made to automatically calculate a target's strength, then cut out all excess and destroy it with minimum expenditure, but it looks like that worked against me."

After saying that much, the second princess's face took a turn as a sadistic grin appeared on it.

"Keh-heh, ha-ha-ha!! But silly mistakes in judgment won't save you any longer! ...Switch to manual decision-making. All weapons, fix your destructive force to anti–Windsor Castle levels. See? Now these attack Soul Arms can rip your flesh apart from just the slightest touch!!"

A chill ran up Kamijou's spine.

That had been her holding back.

Now that the Soul Arms' limiters had been released, taking the same hit again would make his body into mincemeat.

*Damn it! I couldn't find a clue for how to beat even just Carissa with her Curtana Original, and now...*Coughing up blood but still clenching his fist again, Kamijou glared directly ahead of him. *On top of that, twenty mobile castle-breaking fortresses flying around? How the hell am I supposed to come up with a way to turn the tables?!*

But then—

From the distant Coven Compass came a fierce pillar of flashing light shooting straight at Carissa. The attack had enough punch behind it that just by passing overhead, it completely shattered glass windows on the London streets.

Meanwhile, Carissa didn't even look that way.

She just held out her hand horizontally, then twirled the Curtana Original once like a baton.

There was a booming *ga-shhh!!*

In tandem with her sword's motion, every direction was cut. In all, it covered a disc with a radius of about twenty meters. The debris object appeared in the form of a cross section; as it scooped deep into the ground, it changed into a giant circular shield.

And then the large-scale flash spell collided with it.

There was a massive *bang*.

But the shield didn't break, and the flashing pillar of light, without anywhere to go, dispersed in every direction. The aftermath plucked out the great trees in the garden, bent streetlights over themselves, and churned up the asphalt. Several of the Gryphon Skies overhead raised their altitude for a time, almost reluctantly, trying to get away from it.

That was all.

The second princess, Carissa, was unharmed.

Are you kidding me...? For a few moments, Kamijou was stunned. *That crazy laser cannon can't even put a scratch on her. The head of state with the Curtana Original...Are you telling me this is the kind of monster that makes—?*

"Why does that surprise you?" said Carissa, as though breaking off his thoughts. With another snap of her wrist, she twirled the

Curtana Original, which had formed the shield. "Can any human kill the leader of angels?"

Zggeee!! The second princess stabbed the Curtana Original's end into the disc shield.

From above the debris object that had been created by cutting through dimensions came, perhaps, the result of cutting those dimensions again.

As though stabbing a fork into a giant potato, Carissa used just one hand to swing the Curtana Original to the side—

—while it was caught in the giant, twenty-meter-radius disc shield.

"Oh...shit...?!"

Kamijou reflexively used his hands to protect his face, but there was no point.

Ka-thoom!! Then came the crash of thunder.

Carissa had forcefully swung the Curtana Original around while about half the disc shield was buried. The ground immediately collapsed as though a giant construction machine had shoveled it up. The black earth, the concrete, the asphalt, the roadside trees, the water and gas pipes running underground—all of it lumped together. As a river of dirt and debris, it plunged toward Kamijou like a tsunami.

There was no way to avoid it.

The overwhelmingly enormous chunk of mass simply sent Touma Kamijou flying.

The earthy wave's front end pushed away his body, knocking him easily ten meters back. As it did, the earth bit into Kamijou's lower half like a living creature's jaws. As he screamed at the immense pressure, he saw out of the corner of his eye the disc shield slipping out of the Curtana Original. The giant structure flew through the air, collided with Buckingham Palace, and did even more damage to the almost collapsed building.

"Guh, ah, ahhhhhhhhhhhhhhhhhhhhhh!!"

Kamijou yanked his legs, buried up to his thighs, out of the gravel. He felt something awfully hot on his right thigh. He looked and saw a broken tree branch, about as thick as a ballpoint pen, stuck in it.

Vilian, who had run toward him, shouted something to him, but the pain was so intense it was giving him vertigo, and he couldn't tell what she was even saying. She seemed to be frantically wondering how to aid him.

Kamijou bit his own sleeve as hard as he could so he wouldn't bite his tongue.

And then, he put his hand to the branch stuck in his leg. With trembling fingers, he gripped it—and then tore it out all at once.

His scream wasn't audible.

While no shortage of blood flowed out, Kamijou gritted his teeth so hard he thought he'd break them.

"Don't you think your ideas were a bit naïve?" said Carissa calmly, watching Kamijou as he endured the incredible pain. "You might have a bit of strange power in that hand of yours, but a mere unarmed human trying to touch an angelic leader? Could you be more presumptuous? The first condition, the 'thing you need to do to win'—you were mistaken from step one, so."

Such a difference in power that he couldn't touch her even once.

Though it was restricted to the UK, the one wielding the power of Michael, the angels' leader.

Right now, the second princess probably had at least as much power as Acqua of the Back. The actual logic and tech might have been completely different, but the strange objects created when she sliced dimensions somehow reminded him of Misha Kreutzev's watery wings.

"I don't mean thinking you could fight and win was a mistake."

Carissa lowered the Curtana Original's tip once.

He heard the sound of hissing gas from within the black soil destroyed by her last attack.

"You may be acting in defiance, but if you seriously wanted to run away, you'd survive—*that* is the level of thinking you're making a mistake with. That's what it means to be the angelic leader, the head of state."

No mercy for those who rebel.

Judgment from heaven would unilaterally rain down annihilation. The only path available to those who faced it was to fervently prostrate themselves and wait for the wrath to pass as soon as possible.

The scale of this battle was already in mythological territory.

This woman would create a legend just by standing where she was.

And that was—

"...The second princess...Carissa..."

"That's *Her Majesty* to you, fool."

Carissa made a displeased face just for a moment, then tapped the tip of the Curtana Original, which she'd lowered to the ground, on the ruined and broken asphalt.

The hissing noise of leaking gas stopped.

Attached to the entire city's supply—

Ba-boom!!

A moment later, the night behind the princess erupted into a crimson explosion from horizon to horizon.

The flames themselves didn't reach Kamijou. But the shock wave blasted past Carissa and slammed relentlessly into his body.

"Guh...bfrt?!"

It was like he'd been smacked by a wall. His breath caught, and his feet hovered off the ground. Vilian, who was next to him, had been pushed into the air in the same way.

They remained there for over a second.

Meanwhile, Carissa, despite being closer to the blast wind engulfing her than Kamijou was, didn't seem in pain at all. She smirked at her floating targets, then kicked lightly off the ground and came near, as though it was actually a comfortable tailwind pushing her.

Yes—even the flames and blasts spreading around them weren't her "attack."

Even this was no more than a simple way to bolster how she wanted to move.

With her one light step, an explosive sound rang out, one even more awful than the gas.

Bwa-gaahhhhh! Carissa jumped, smashing the ground. The way she moved was more like stabbing through space than advancing normally. Kamijou, who had finally stumbled in trying to regain his balance, was almost entirely defenseless.

Immediately, he swung around his right hand, but it wasn't going to do him any good.

Rather than using brute force, Carissa sharply followed Kamijou's movements, twisted the Curtana Original's trajectory diagonally, and went for the neck—the blind spot in his defense.

Along the blade-less, tip-less sword's path, every dimension was sliced through.

A belt-shaped debris object followed after the sword.

The strike could unquestionably cleave through the nuclear shelters of science and the grand cathedrals of sorcery. Kamijou kept his eyes on it and wondered:

The threat was never just the Curtana Original.

This was a person powerful enough to pull off a coup d'état in the United Kingdom, a country that had maintained a very solid system, almost perfectly.

The second princess was incredibly well versed in military affairs. Why *wouldn't* she be acquainted with martial arts?

"Die."

The one single word reached his brain.

A moment later, there was a dull *whump* as that brain was rocked.

Touma Kamijou's vision teetered and blurred.

His feet left the ground, and he couldn't perceive gravity anymore.

His breathing stopped.

And...

I'm...alive?

Kamijou finally snapped out of it when he felt someone grabbing the back of his clothes.

The place he'd just been standing in seemed a little distant. Carissa's swing of the Curtana Original had connected with empty air, and the second princess was growling at the result.

This was undoubtedly something impossible for Touma Kamijou's physical skills.

And as proof...

"...I was finally able to return a debt normally."

...he heard a woman's cool voice.

Simultaneously, the sensation of someone grabbing him in the back vanished as Kamijou was gently let onto the ground. He looked and saw that Vilian had been picked up along with him. The third princess was looking in blank amazement at the person who had protected her.

Kamijou turned around.

Standing there was...

"Kan...zaki...?"

"Not only me. Everyone else will be here soon," she said smoothly, glancing away from Kamijou for just a moment. "Index. I request a magical analysis. It is possible that pressure from the Royal Family faction has created a bias in your 103,000 grimoires, so you may not have any record of Curtana-related spells. Would you be able to do a reanalysis based only on your existing magical knowledge?"

"To either take away control, or to seal it. I'll do it."

Index, who had been moving with Kanzaki after their transport truck got wrecked, had arrived as well. When Kamijou stared at her dumbly, she gave a snort of pride.

One of only twenty saints in the world, and a magical library with the knowledge of grimoires from across the world stored within...

They were both highly valuable for the sorcery side, but their reinforcement didn't cause Carissa to lose her composure.

"Foot soldiers who couldn't even reach the main battlefield properly. And now you think to play a major role?"

"A certain ignorant princess doing quite a number on the city delayed us somewhat. We found it necessary to intercept several structures threatening to crush a theater full of civilians."

She had stopped structures reaching a hundred meters wide while unarmed.

After saying something so tremendous with utter calm, Kanzaki reached a hand for her katana's grip.

"...And I don't plan to solve everything myself. I now have comrades with whom I can trust my back."

5

The saint Kaori Kanzaki and the second princess, Carissa.

A searing tension spread between the two women.

No concrete physical occurrence would be the trigger.

It simply began when Kanzaki was the first to move.

"‼"

"‼"

She pulled out her two-meter-long katana—or, rather, pretended to—while she manipulated seven wires with that hand.

Seven Glints.

"Holding back against me, are you?" Carissa gripped the Curtana Original as the metal wires shot at her from all directions. "...I'll end you."

There was an ear-shattering *gkk-keeee!!*

The next thing Kamijou knew, Kanzaki and Carissa were at super-close range, their blades pushing on each other. They'd only run straight ahead and swung their swords, and yet that simple motion was impossible for Kamijou to see.

"Competing with my omnidimensional slice? Two blades that can sever all things—it looks like the two laws may have created dissension or contradiction."

"...You're moving differently than before. I will return your advice—if you continue to hold back, it will trip you up."

Her words seemed to be supporting Kamijou's side, but the boy himself refuted them in his mind.

He could tell by instinct: This princess, skilled as she was in military affairs, would control herself—but she wouldn't go easy.

"It is an unmanageable shrew, after all," Carissa explained. "Obviously I'd try to produce the necessary results by paying a cost appropriate to the situation—that way, I'll create no needless side effects or openings. Decreasing consumption and preventing exhaustion is yet another required skill for tactics."

Boom!! Their two weapons bounced away, and then they swung again.

Bodies blurred.

What happened next was an offense and defense that made it hard to even grasp where they were located. *Tak-tak-tak-tak-zzz-zzz-tak-tak-tiktiktik!!* The blasts fired off like a machine gun, with glints of light dancing between them at the same time. Around Kanzaki were torn-up wires, and around Carissa were debris object fangs that were sliced one after another out of her mobius strips from the garrotes.

This wasn't the sort of situation Kamijou could add himself to in any direct fashion. But the Imagine Breaker still doubtlessly presented an irregular threat to the Curtana Original.

Then there's something I can do!!

After making up his mind, Kamijou ran in a large circle around their battle—moving outside Carissa's field of vision—so that, even if it was impossible to directly interfere, Carissa would still have to spare a little mental energy for him.

"Heh. Very admirable for you to go that far, so," said Carissa without turning around, realizing his intent as she traded blows with Kanzaki with lightning speed. "But—go to hell."

Ga-boom!! came the sound of an explosion.

The debris objects were naturally created during their skirmish thus far. She used her heel to kick one of them, a thing with an incredibly sharp tip, backward—straight toward the spot where Kamijou stood.

It was like a javelin thrown by a brawny soldier.

"?!"

Kamijou hastily twisted, but still ended up with a wound streaked across his cheek. It wasn't a cut from a sharp blade—it was a dull wound, as though he'd tripped in a rocky area by the seashore.

When Kanzaki saw it, she ignored her own crisis and shouted, "Touma Kamijou!!"

"Don't mind me! Push her back!!" yelled Kamijou angrily, stopping Kanzaki as she was about to change her tactics out of concern.

Meanwhile, reinforcements had arrived.

——The Born Again Amakusa-Style Crossist Church, centered around Saiji Tatemiya armed with his flamberge and Itsuwa with her Friulian spear, with ancillary members equipped with various swords, spears, axes, hammers, bows, and staves.

——The former Agnes unit, composed of Agnes with the Lotus Wand, Lucia with her giant wheel, Angeline with several coin pouches, and other nuns armed to the teeth with a myriad of Soul Arms.

In addition, Sherry Cromwell had come with her golem in tow, while Orsola Aquinas and others had gathered as well. It looked like just about everybody had showed up when they charged in.

The latecomers seemed faintly surprised at first when they saw how Kanzaki and Carissa were fighting, but they stood their ground and joined the fray. Some targeted Carissa from a distance, weaving attacks into the intervals of the ongoing fight, and others challenged her as a group in close combat, intending to lighten the saint's burden.

Carissa gave a soft slick of her tongue. "Seriously. Now you're making me pay more than I need. Maybe I should have left some knights to have them ward off the small fries."

And yet the second princess still didn't fall.

There was a great *boom!!*

While ceaselessly skirmishing with Kanzaki, Carissa began to work even the trajectory of debris objects into her tactics. Sharp, pointed structures that looked like giant fangs or ribs flew out in all directions. They blocked the attacks shooting at her from many directions at terrifying speeds, becoming a wall to hold back their assault, then turning into projectile weapons to counter their strikes.

It's like a game of beanbags, thought Kamijou while he, too, avoided attacks on his life.

Carissa had only two hands and only one weapon. And yet she dealt with dozens, even hundreds of enemy strikes and movements at the same time. The common sense instilled in him from back-alley brawls said that if you used a big enough group of people as a wave, it would wash away a single person. And yet, that didn't apply here.

And to top it all off, the Gryphon Skies overhead interrupted as well.

A giant, twenty-meter jousting lance skimmed just over the ground, moving in tandem with the crimson fortresses above them, and shot toward Ellis—the golem that Sherry controlled—then rammed into it head-on. After taking the maximized attack, the hunk of boulders broke apart in midair and rained its pieces down on the heads of the former Agnes unit.

Seeing Agnes, Lucia, and the others frantically avoiding them, Kanzaki clicked her tongue. Then she said to her comrades in Born Again Amakusa, "Let's split into a Carissa team and a Gryphon team! The mobile fortresses are up about twenty to fifty meters... Peter-type aerial attack spells will work at that altitude. Ushibuka, Kouyagi, Nomozaki! Can you construct spells to bring them down by yourselves?!"

"We'll try, but they're probably guarded by huge shields of their own. No guarantees we can whittle them away!!"

Despite Ushibuka's and the others' replies, they moved swiftly.

The Gryphon Sky that had destroyed Ellis swung around again and began to plunge toward Born Again Amakusa—only to abruptly lose its balance and skew. The giant jousting lance skimming over the ground rammed into the black earth, scattering a tsunami of dirt. Since it was a Soul Arm, it displayed more massive destructive power than even its apparent mass and speed would imply.

But they didn't completely bring the thing down.

The Gryphon Sky that they'd shaken around got back up and tried to launch another attack on the Amakusa group.

"Shit—!!"

"No, that was all I needed!!"

Kanzaki interrupted Ushibuka's shout, charging ahead with a saint's leg strength. The giant jousting lance had slowed after aiming into the ground. She grabbed the side of it with both hands, then turned from the waist and swung it around as hard as she could.

The Gryphon Skies were currently set up to move in tandem with the giant stake's "shadow." Since Kanzaki had grabbed and swung around the jousting lance, the Gryphon Sky overhead also started revolving like a tornado. Perhaps the jousting lances really held a way to sever and split the magical tandem movement, for fear of one hitting a durable fortress and getting stuck in it. But it wouldn't have mattered. Kanzaki was using more than just arm strength to swing the Gryphon Sky around. She was both using advanced sorcery to interfere with its emergency release and putting her arm strength as a saint to use at the same time.

Swinging the Gryphon Sky around in a wide circle, she strung along about four of the ones in the air, and after making them into a clump, she changed the axis of her swing, dropping them all down in a straight line.

It was a supergiant morning star.

And, of course, she'd aimed them at the Curtana Original–wielding second princess, Carissa.

There was an enormous *ga-baaam!*

But it didn't happen because of several massive aerial objects falling to the ground.

It was the blast noise of the second princess, having thrust the Curtana Original from low to high, severing the morning star with a single attack.

"Shit!! That hammer was made of five mobile fortresses!!" shouted Isahaya in place of Kanzaki as she ground her teeth.

However, Itsuwa, readying her Friulian spear, raised her voice to energize everyone. "B-but she's proven we can bring them down! Split into more teams and launch attacks on the Gryphon Skies as well. If we reduce the number of mobile fortresses and get more people able to concentrate on Carissa, that alone should raise our chances of victory!!"

They nodded, and without anyone speaking, they split into two groups and headed for their own enemies.

Then Kanzaki temporarily withdrew from the front line, leaving the fight to her comrades. Even as she caught her breath to restore her stamina, she jumped smoothly toward Kamijou.

"It pains me to say this, but it looks like we will indeed need to rely on your right hand. Carissa's slashes—can you cancel out the omnidimensional slice attacks themselves?" she asked him in a low voice, repelling white structures flying at them sporadically. "They are both powerful slashes and a way to create projectile weapons. If you can erase even one, it will throw off the second princess's tactics, and it may provide us with an opening."

"I mean, I can try, but I can't make any promises!" Kamijou clenched his right hand again. "I can't seem to figure out the rules. A bunch of them hit me before you got here, too, but there were times I could erase them and times I couldn't."

Just then, a curtain of jet-black fire from the Silkie Aquarium mobile fortresses, fired from afar, shot one of the crimson Gryphon Skies out of the air. With the hulk approaching them like a crashing passenger plane, Kanzaki grabbed Kamijou by the back of the neck and jumped over two hundred meters.

"There is a legend about three swords in China. The strongest of them would cut without feeling like it cut, and the person cut wouldn't realize it, either, and go on living as though nothing had happened…Well, it is a fable that appears in educational ideas, but it seems like the Curtana has taken that fable and made it reality."

"?"

"To the point—if a slash is truly too sharp, there will be a time lag between when it slices the object and when the result appears. In concrete terms, debris objects appear in three-dimensional space as cross sections one-point-two seconds after the omnidimensional slice."

"…You had the time to *analyze* that?" Kamijou was baffled.

"It was necessary," answered Kanzaki perfunctorily. "The dimension-slicing ability is the only magical phenomenon. The debris objects are no more than physical phenomena born from it. It is, for example, like the relationship between a magical fire and its ashes after it's burned out. Your right hand can erase the slashes themselves, but it probably can't deal with the debris objects created as a result."

"Which means…"

"If you attack the point through which it passes within one-point-two seconds of the Curtana's attack, you'll be able to erase the slashing attack and prevent any debris objects from appearing."

One-point-two seconds.

Precise decimal times like that were beyond what a simple high school student could perceive.

"…And if I mess up, it immediately puts me in danger of a fatal cross counter."

"I'm not saying you need to beat her. Think of it like this—if the Curtana Original tries to slice through dimensions on a wide scale and at a long distance and create a giant structure, if your hand will reach it, then reach out."

"Got it. Stay calm and wait for my chance, right?"

Kanzaki patted Kamijou on the shoulder once, as though signaling that she was trusting her back to him. Then she put strength into her legs once more and jumped back to the main battlefield where Carissa and her Curtana were dancing.

But the situation didn't wait for her.

Ka-bam!! With a rumble, a giant flower blossomed with the second princess in the middle of it. Its petals were those of death, woven with sharp, white structures. Projectile weapons, fired in every direction, blasted the close-combat unit at the heart of Born Again Amakusa far away.

"Itsuwa!! Tatemiya?!" shouted Kamijou.

But before they could answer, Carissa spoke. "Come on, now. Leaving your precious lambs behind for a strategy session? It's like you want me to shoot them or something, so."

As her words ended, the second princess jumped.

Perhaps borrowing telesma from the Curtana, her straight jump was over ten meters high. In the air, she readied her blade-less, tip-less sword, and as she fell, she aimed for her "target." Kanzaki moved immediately.

Touma Kamijou's right hand had an important role in the quest to destroy the Curtana Original.

That was why Kanzaki figured Carissa would go after the boy first and foremost.

"No! It's not me!!"

And when Kamijou tried to bump Kanzaki out of the way, Carissa swung the Curtana in midair. It created a smooth, white plank in the air, to which the second princess delivered a mighty kick.

The trajectory changed to an acute angle—

One veering away from Touma Kamijou and toward the third princess, Vilian, who had been watching in a daze.

"?!"

Vilian immediately tried to bring up her crossbow, but it was too late.

With a *boom*, Carissa landed right next to the third princess, then used one hand to drag her younger sister down to the ground. By the time Vilian looked up, the Curtana Original's end was already at her throat—the sword that had no blade or point but could still cut through dimensions.

"And why is someone like you, who can barely use magic, even here in the first place? Have you been spurred on by an odd sense of justice? Or were you just too scared to wait on your own, left behind by the main force?"

The arrows for Vilian's crossbow, possibly on advice from the Puritans, had been modified somewhat. But from Carissa's point of view, holding the Curtana Original, one of the United Kingdom's greatest Soul Arms, it was the same as trash. Red, blue, yellow, green…It seemed to be glowing with four-colored magic lines, trying to form various sorcery based on their distribution, but it wasn't even as effective as a little kid's love fortune.

"Rather than operating spells others started, you triggered a spell to harm someone with your own strength for the first time in your life, using the subway to make my Curtana Original go out of control. Bet you're on cloud nine now, aren't you? ...You're so innocent, so happy over a single coincidence. But that's really as far as you could go, isn't it, my incompetent little princess?"

Essentially straddling her, Carissa laughed derisively.

But then her face froze abruptly.

"...Perhaps it is. So this was what those sinless servants and cooks, and William, faced in order to let me escape. To think it was this terrible."

The third princess returned her sister's stare dead in the eye.

To directly convey her will to win.

"Then I will stop hiding and stand up as well. As princess of a nation, I will be a roof to protect everyone from this kind of torment and fear!!" she shouted, readying her crossbow.

Ignoring the sword at her throat, she took aim at Carissa overhead. Then, as though saying she was prepared for them both to kill each other, she unwaveringly pulled the trigger.

She'd fired a special arrow, one with an arrowhead whose tip functioned as a Soul Arm.

"?!"

For the first time, Carissa's face changed.

All she'd done was swing her neck aside.

But the second princess, Carissa, had used all her strength to avoid her sister's arrow.

Even though the crossbow was modified to be easy to use, even for feminine, slender arms, it was still over a meter long, and loading the next arrow would require about five seconds at the least.

Meanwhile, if Carissa gave the Curtana Original the order, she'd slice every dimension apart, along with her sister's neck.

"Rest in peace, dreamer," declared Carissa, her face different from before, now terrifyingly impassive.

Then...

*   *   *

Pa-ga!!
The night-streaking arrow Carissa had dodged landed a direct hit on the Coven Compass's large-scale flash spell.

Originally, Vilian's arrowhead had been modified to grant a magical effect. Carissa was sure it was the sort that caused wounds to expand, but...
When the arrow hit the large-scale flash spell, it morphed.
The pure-white light turned into a mass of water that weighed dozens of tons. It rolled and undulated eerily in the night sky. Far too enormous to be a whip, its supermassive tip curved like a radio tower and shot toward Carissa, engulfing some of the crimson Gryphon Skies in the air as well.
A combination attack?!
Vilian, on her own, didn't have the strength or the knowledge to substantially control sorcery. However, that changed if she used the mana the Coven Compass was launching over a long distance. She didn't have to prepare some incredible spell to cause a huge explosion—all she had to do was use her own strength to trigger the detonation.
Plus, the Puritans had the Index of Forbidden Books on their side. With advice from several sorcerers, just imitating them and weaving a magical signal into the arrowhead had made it possible to cause such phenomena.
"Damn your cheap tricks!!"
Carissa rolled with all her might to escape the giant mass of water. In the meantime, Vilian forced her slightly shaking hands to calm, pulled the shotgun-like slide, and nocked her next arrow.
"Were you not aware? Just as you excel in military affairs, they say I excel in virtue."
"Justifying your reliance on others? It sickens me to think we're sisters, so!!"
Zwoh!! Something invisible spurted out into Carissa's surroundings.

Without backing down, Vilian pointed the crossbow up to the night sky above her sister's head. The arrow she fired once again struck a large-scale flash spell from the Coven Compass, but Carissa didn't even watch it. Instead, she ran straight for Vilian.

The giant pillar of light burst, then became a collection of golf ball–size spheres, raining down upon Carissa like a deluge. But having borrowed the Curtana's power, Carissa executed movements that were beyond human territory. With short zigzagging motions, she dodged through the rain, always closing the distance to Vilian.

"This is the limit of relying on others!!"

Now that Vilian didn't have any other way, Carissa swung the Curtana Original.

With this timing, it would be impossible to dodge or defend.

All that was left was for the third princess's head to fly, but…

"Yes, this is the pinnacle of reliance upon others, my sister."

There was a thundering *drr-bam!!*

It was the sound of many footsteps. Vilian's body disappeared from before her eyes, and in exchange, the close-combat team at Born Again Amakusa's core, including Tatemiya and Itsuwa, jumped at her.

This was clearly different from their earlier speed.

The foot soldiers were flitting about three or four times faster now. As Carissa swung the Curtana Original with reckless abandon, creating debris objects to intercept their attacks, she gritted her teeth.

To think that deluge was really—not an attack but a physical ability–enhancing spell!!

Even as the high-speed battle continued, she unconsciously set her glare on Vilian, who was now farther away.

The third princess, after getting out of the saint's arms, said, with confidence she hadn't possessed until now:

"I told you so. I'm the one on the side of virtue."

"Silence! You think you've won with this pathetic cleverness?!"

Carissa made a long jump backward, then swung the Curtana Original around in a wide arc again. The spell borrowing the Coven Compass's power reinforcing the foot soldiers' physical abilities had buried itself in the ground in the shape of bullets. In that case, if she created a giant hundred-meter-long debris object and turned the entire earth over with it, she'd break the hundreds of cores supporting their spells.

It's over, Vilian. Once I stop them from moving, I'll have you drawn and quartered in front of the people!! thought Carissa, swinging the Curtana Original around with all her strength, her entire body in it.

But all the other dimensions didn't get cut.

She felt the attack slip away, like it went through air, and frowned.

The cause was a single boy, Touma Kamijou.

Yes.

Just as he'd planned with Kanzaki, there was the crack of a whip, and the halfway-sliced dimensions reverted.

Then, in time with that misfire—

—the third princess, Vilian, pointed her crossbow at the night sky again and fired an arrow.

This way...?! Carissa automatically readied the Curtana Original overhead to prepare for the Coven Compass's powerful combo attack.

But the third princess's "virtue" didn't stop there.

After that, these words rang out.

"BTD, CD!! (Bend the trajectory, change downward!!)"

Those were the words of the girl who had precisely memorized 103,000 grimoires. It was a method called "spell interception," used to interfere with others' magic.

However, it hadn't been for the Curtana Original Carissa held.

Index hadn't yet completely analyzed the Curtana's magic. What she *did* have, though, was a communication Soul Arm linked to the Coven Compass.

In other words—

The large-scale flash spell, which should have been traveling in a straight line, was what had bent.

"Wha—?"

For the first time, the second princess looked surprised instead of angry.

As if to dodge Vilian's arrow, the giant pillar of light the Coven Compass fired swerved at a right angle. When it changed trajectory in the air directly downward, it pierced mercilessly through the Gryphon Sky along the way, then plunged straight toward Carissa, weaving through the Curtana Original's blind spots.

An explosion went off.

An intense explosion that knocked over even the sorcerers spread out around her.

It nearly blew out Touma Kamijou's hearing.

A massive amount of dust danced up into the night sky. With the spot the large-scale flash spell struck at the center, it had left a crater of over forty meters in diameter. The close-combat team members, centered around Born Again Amakusa, coughed and wheezed, but Kamijou could still tell they got up.

It was so extreme that Kamijou wondered if they'd gone too far.

It was enough to make him accidentally worry about the enemy, but something made him revise that idea right away.

"...All right, that one worked, so."

An awful chill ran up Kamijou's spine.

In an instant, the air of relief spreading through everyone vanished. Because:

With the whooshing of a whirlwind, the clouds of dust blew out from within. Standing there, with the Curtana Original in hand, was the second princess, Carissa. Her leather-decorated red dress was pocked with mud, and some parts were torn. Something red and oozing was visible on her skin. But Carissa was healthy. The Curtana hadn't broken, either.

Are you serious...? Kamijou felt a shiver run through his legs.

He imagined being made to fight a monster with extremely high health in an RPG forever.

She took something of that level to the face? I don't know the details, but that was a cannon blast from a fortress. Might not be that practical or that good in regular combat, but the pure power could've been more than Kanzaki's attacks. And even when it hit her directly, it only gave her a few scratches?!

"…As I thought," said Kanzaki to herself, her face bitter. "As long as we don't destroy the Curtana Original, we can't do anything."

Of course, a bigger problem then arose—how was Kamijou's right hand supposed to get close against someone whom they couldn't defeat even with *that*?

In response, Carissa put her beloved sword on her shoulder once and looked around easily at the night sky.

There had been almost twenty Gryphon Skies at the start, but thanks to long-range artillery fire from the Coven Compass and the Silkie Aquariums, plus attacks from the Puritans on the ground, they were nearly wiped out. Even the final one, which was barely flying despite its damage, lost its balance while Carissa watched it, and it began to plummet.

"I suppose that's as far as unmanned ones can go, so. Actually, they were designed for attack, and I used them for the opposite, for interception. Their specs might not have been the only issue here."

"Either way, you're the last one," said Kamijou. "If we can keep pushing you back…"

"Oh, well. Beat up the grunts and leveled up, have you? That's quite a low estimation of the head of state armed with the Curtana."

Carissa returned her gaze from the night sky to set her eyes on Kamijou, the sword still on her shoulder. She reached a hand into her dress's breast pocket and pulled out a small radio.

"And I don't recall saying those were the only grunts I had."

"?!"

For a moment, he thought she was going to call in more mobile fortresses, and he focused his mind on Carissa's radio.

But his prediction was wrong.

If he'd thought calmly, he would have known why she took out a radio and not a magical Soul Arm. Either way, this was what she said:

*   *   *

"Orders for the destroyer *Wimbledon* currently patrolling in the Strait of Dover. Prepare the cruise missiles loaded with bunker cluster warheads. Set the warheads' detonation depth to negative five meters, aim them at Buckingham Palace…and fire at once."

The first one who grimaced and stiffened up was Touma Kamijou—from the science side. "B-bunker clusters?!"

"You know them? Special warheads, designed to destroy entire military shelters. They do scatter about two hundred smaller bombs in the air, after all. If I fired them while the Gryphon Skies were up, they'd hit them; they would have toned down their destructive force."

With her right hand holding the Curtana Original and her left hand holding the radio linked to the destroyer, Carissa smiled a more wicked smile than ever before.

"I was originally planning to put you in more of a crisis to lure my mother, Elizard, here and then fire them at her, but you destroyed the Gryphon Skies ahead of schedule. I had to move it up."

"Shit!! Those warheads'll blow away everything in a three-kilometer radius!! It won't just be Buckingham Palace. If even one of those things hits, it'll wreak havoc on London, too!!"

"You may wail if you wish, but cruise missiles are quite fast. Concords, Eurofighters—France and the other EU nations pester us quite a lot for development costs, but thanks to that, our nation's supersonic-related technology got stronger. We kept up with the foldable wing concept, and I think they were saying the cruise missiles with them can reach up to Mach 5 even at low altitudes. A hundred-kilometer distance wouldn't even take a minute."

"Damn it…!!"

Three kilometers in sixty seconds. Normal human legs wouldn't carry a person outside its range in that time. Maybe it was a different story for a saint like Kanzaki, but most of the Puritans here wouldn't make it.

"I will not let you."

The one who interrupted was Kaori Kanzaki.

"I'll create a defensive barrier in the air to intercept it," she went on, checking the wires in her hands. "A three-kilometer effective radius and two hundred smaller bombs…If that's all, the scale certainly shouldn't be impossible!!"

"Yes—if you use magic power, you might be able to do something about the bunker cluster," noted Carissa with a smirk.

She herself stood before them only because she'd borrowed the Curtana Original's power, and she was probably confident she'd emerge unscathed even from those blast winds.

Then, with her left hand holding the radio, she gestured to the night sky.

There was a point of light up there, man-made, clearly different from the twinkling stars.

"…But you don't have much time to spend preparing."

"!!"

Springing into action at those words, Kanzaki strung out her seven wires in the night sky. They depicted a three-dimensional magic circle, through which a pale-blue light ran as it tried to cover the entire city block with a giant, thick wall.

It was the kind of insane sorcery only saints could use.

But…

"You're defenseless. Just as planned, so."

"…?! Kanzaki!!" shouted Kamijou instantly, but Carissa, licking her lips, brought her Curtana Original to bear faster.

Ga-bam!! With the sound of every dimension being sliced, everything began to collapse. Kanzaki barely managed to avoid the hundred-meter cross section, but her spell preparations were stopped as a result, and the thick wall that was supposed to cover the night sky was pierced through by a ray of light.

It was the approaching cruise missile.

Kanzaki tried to reconstruct her defensive spell, but she didn't make it.

At around four thousand meters up in the air, the cylindrical missile split into four. Then the compartments shed their shells, and out of them appeared two hundred bombs that had been packed within. They scattered into the air, then plunged down like lances.

Carissa had set their detonation depth to negative-five meters. Even though they were meant to displace massive amounts of earth deep underground, she'd purposely made it so they'd explode over the surface, in order to blow away Kamijou and everyone else who was at ground level.

He thought he heard someone scream for everyone to run.

Kamijou, unable to move his body, simply stared dumbly at Carissa.

His enemy.

The United Kingdom's second princess had her arms stretched wide, as if to accept divine light. As she watched the two hundred specks of light in the night sky with satisfaction, she seemed to notice Kamijou staring. She brought her gaze in front of her again, then gave him a smile, a real one—completely different from any he'd seen her give—and said something.

Kamijou couldn't tell what it was.

A moment later, the bunker cluster assaulted Buckingham Palace.

There was no noise.

Only pure white, blanketing his vision.

But he felt, somehow, that his body had been thrown. Most of the bombs didn't explode in midair or on the surface; they buried into the ground like they were originally designed, plunging beneath the surface before detonating.

His consciousness blacked out, then flickered back on.

For a while he moaned; his fingers twitched…and then, somehow, Kamijou came to the realization that he was still alive.

"Guh…urgh…"

He heaved like he was coughing, but his own voice didn't get to his ears. He tried to turn his neck, but his body wouldn't move the way he wanted. And yet, with awkward, jerky motions, he moved his dirt-caked hands and feet, wobbling unsteadily up. This was the first time he'd ever really considered it miraculous that his limbs were all still attached.

He looked around.

Surprisingly, the catastrophic devastation hadn't spread to the London streets. Maybe it was thanks to the defensive barrier Kanzaki built halfway, but in reality, most of the two hundred smaller bombs had misfired in midair, and what had come down on top of Kamijou and the others were the leftovers that slipped through the cracks in the barrier sliced open by the Curtana Original. And even for those that got through, the other sorcerers would have immediately tried to use their own defensive spells to lessen the force of the blast wind.

But...

"In...dex...?" he muttered, not caring about the mud all over his face.

There was no response.

"Kanzaki? Itsuwa?"

Only the boy's voice rang out in the cold.

He was buried in the dirt, buildings were collapsed, and his own limbs faltered. In the middle of the burned, thoroughly destroyed area, Kamijou somehow managed to move his shaking lips.

"Sherry, Agnes! Oriana!! Shit...Orsola, Lucia, Angeline! Tatemiya, Vilian!! Damn it. Someone...someone answer me!!"

He heard several groans in response, but there were no clear words.

Almost everyone was down. Some might have been buried in the dirt. That scene did much more damage to Kamijou's heart than the shock wave had done to his body. It was too hard now to imagine how many tricks their enemy had at her disposal. Kamijou's mind was starting to lose track of the situation.

In the midst of all that, just one transcendent figure stood there.

The second princess, Carissa.

The woman in the red dress, Curtana Original on her shoulder, spoke.

"All right. Do you still hold out hope?"

She smirked, then brought the radio in her other hand to her mouth.

As if to show off, she spoke mercilessly into it.

"Orders for the destroyer *Wimbledon*. Prepare to fire another bunker cluster."

6

The first princess, Limeia, had taken off her trademark monocle. In its place, she was peering through an antique telescope, the kind a ship captain might have used during the Age of Exploration.

...Well, well. This nation's sorcerers should at least know, as a matter of course, how terrifying the head of state is with the Curtana Original. Well, I suppose they've been shown in full color now, and the Puritans' remaining forces seem to be on the verge of annihilation.

As she lay in hiding on a London rooftop, even while she looked at the distant battlefield, a smile came to her lips.

Then, a voice reached her ears from her communication Soul Arm.

She'd refrained from using it before, but with Carissa's attention now focused on the Buckingham area, she'd decided the mana source wouldn't be detected.

"Hey, young lady. I'm havin' the young ones scour the Edinburgh region, and it looks like things're exactly as you suspected."

The words were like those of a good-natured father, lacking in due consideration for someone with royal blood. But Limeia's face broke into a smile anyway. Indeed, for she was the type of person who became very honest toward people who didn't know she was the first princess and who didn't try to take advantage of her position because of that.

"It's as I thought, then...Things are headed toward 'the cemetery,' I suppose?"

"It's keepin' itself small, but the sheer precision is nothin' to shake a stick at. Don't think there's much doubt about it—it's on par with a monarch-class 'cemetery.' Bet it's like what you'd get if you squeezed King Khufu's pyramid into a one-room apartment."

After he said he'd send her the data, black ink-like dots began to appear on the parchment paper Limeia had out next to her. Like an invisible feather pen was writing, diagrams and smooth cursive handwriting continued to be written on it in a tightly packed manner.

Limeia put her monocle back on. As she looked over the concrete values, she nodded, satisfied.

"I see…Then we've essentially found the ringleader's goal," she said to herself, moving her gaze away from the parchment for a time as though thinking back. "I suppose it makes a certain amount of sense that that woman hasn't killed them."

"…*Question for you, young lady. From where in the world are you gettin' all this dangerous info? If I remember right, you claimed you were from an ancient sorcerer clan tasked with the preservation of Stonehenge, but are you really—?*"

"Oh-ho-ho. If you want to learn a beautiful woman's secrets, you should do it after you're a little more well acquainted with her," she scoffed offhandedly, and then ended the call.

Immediately after, Limeia changed its aim and booted up the communication Soul Arm again.

Thanks to her dependable friends she'd gained without revealing her identity, she had the necessary pieces.

Now, all she had to do was take action befitting the brilliant first princess.

Meanwhile.

All the knights who had been serving as the second princess's guards at Buckingham Palace had fallen. The Knights faction had been prepared to flee after the Curtana Original went out of control, and so in order to bring them all back together, some received "punishment" as examples.

It was true, to be honest, that they'd nearly lost hope in Carissa after she failed to completely handle the Curtana.

But that had been naïve.

202 A CERTAIN MAGICAL INDEX
The Curtana Original may have gone berserk for a time, but Carissa, the one who wielded it, was so overwhelmingly powerful that the young knights were left without any options.

Among them, something stirred restlessly.

One person, in all the suits of armor covering the floor like refuse, had slowly stood up.

He wondered where he was.

He was no longer inside Buckingham Palace, its walls splattered with blood. It seemed to be a large building, though, with light flashing sporadically in the distance. From where he stood, he could hear the sounds of explosions and feel rumbling...Those phenomena arrived at different times, though, like distant thunder and lightning.

The young knight dragged his aching body, moving his head as though searching for something. Something had stimulated his mind from its previous unconscious state—a woman's voice, which he could hear through his communication Soul Arm.

"Listen to me. I am the first princess of the British royal family, Limeia."

Normally, someone breaking into their transmissions warranted a degree of businesslike caution. However, the young knight was in a daze from all the intense pain. He couldn't even build that routine, businesslike process in his mind. He just waited idly, letting the words flow into his ears.

"Thanks to reports from spies in Edinburgh, we've grasped the true aim of this coup d'état's leader, Carissa. My sister has most likely kept her real goal to herself and not told any of you knights of it."

The young knight took a slow look around.

Heaps of corpses surrounded him in a tragic scene. He seemed to be the only one who had survived.

Why he'd survived the damage he had endured to his muscles, his bones, his organs, and his mind at the hands of the tyrannical Carissa—and also who had brought him, while unconscious in Buckingham Palace, to this place.

However, he didn't try to think too hard.

Whatever the reason, they'd put their lives on the line and done everything they could for the second princess's "revolution," but in the end, they'd been no more than disposable pawns in her game. They'd been betrayed, but he couldn't even muster the energy to be mad like he should have. All he felt was an overwhelming sense of exhaustion that threatened to make the young knight collapse again.

"As a representative of this nation and steward over its military affairs, she felt more responsibility than any other to do something about the threat the people of the United Kingdom were facing from the forces of Rome and Russia. Others used the EU as a tool, stealing our nation's military might with a disguised ban on cluster bombs and other weapons. They used the Eurotunnel explosion to provoke this very nation, driving her into a corner. And Carissa reached the following conclusion."

The young knight, ready to drop, then heard something small.

…He wasn't the only one here.

At the sound of scraping metal, the young knight turned around. There he saw his colleagues, trying to somehow get up, even in their dazes, just like him.

"That at this rate, the United Kingdom would have its value and dignity stolen. An age where simply being a citizen of this nation would be a source of ridicule and oppression by other nations. And so, Carissa thought this: The times would change drastically because of war, and in order to prevent the destruction of the British people, the only way to retain our value and dignity as a nation is through military force."

At first, they hadn't been listening too carefully to Limeia's words.

The incredible pain shooting through their bodies didn't allow it, and more importantly, they had just been tyrannized. Anything that defended Carissa seemed fraudulent.

"And at the same time, Carissa worried. Because she has such excellent capacity in military affairs, she understood more than anyone how strong and how terrifying the Curtana is… Without the Curtana in the head of state's hands, without the absolute rule needed for

it, then perhaps she would have bent her ear to the people and corrected this country's course before the war with the Roman Orthodox Church grew any more severe."

However.

The young knights were slowly realizing something.

Their joints, organs, and bones should have been damaged. That should have been Carissa's goal when she'd enacted her "punishment." She'd granted them a terrible pain worse than mere death, then held together by fear those watching…Supposedly, that was the only reason she'd crushed them inside and out.

But then why could they all stand up like normal?

They hadn't been disabled via broken bones, nor had they sustained any lasting effects that would drag on for the rest of their lives…It was as though she'd been aiming away from any of a person's vital spots.

And…

With that level of violence and cruelty, why, exactly, hadn't a single one of them died?

"When Carissa resolved herself to wield the Curtana Original as her trump card against France and the Roman Orthodox Church, she did so meaning to completely seal away the ultimate weapon after the fighting had ended—in order to create a system where someone could stop our nation's mistaken course. To do that, she couldn't only completely destroy the Curtana."

Only Limeia's voice continued.

"Even if she murdered the entire royal family now, even if she destroyed both the Curtana Original and the Second, a new royal bloodline could emerge a century, a millennium from now. Someone might analyze the destroyed wreckage to develop a Curtana Third or another Soul Arm we can't even imagine in this day and age—and in reality, after a very long time, the Curtana Original, which had supposedly disappeared from history, passed into Carissa's hands. It not only gave her an advantage, it was the source of her suffering."

Unable to answer his own questions, the young knight simply listened to the speech.

"Leeway was built into our monarch-knight system of government, constituting the Curtana and the all-British Continent, from the start. Extra space was intentionally left over for people to create a Second, so even if the Original was lost, the government would live on. Think of it as a safety, so that if someone had been able to analyze the Original to create a Second, then activated the Second while the Original was lost, the all-British Continent's framework wouldn't be thrown into chaos and conflict...Not only was Carissa trying to completely seal the current Original and Second, she was even trying to prevent the possibility that another Curtana would be created after a long time had passed."

The young knight saw.

Out the window.

Carissa's back as she fought in the ruined palace grounds.

They were kilometers away, but they were armed with a long-range sniper search spell, so the distance meant nothing to them. They could see the fierce battle unfolding at Buckingham Palace as though they were standing there.

Wielding the Curtana Original's power without reserve, using even cruise missiles loaded with bunker clusters, it was like Carissa reigned over the center of a storm. And for some reason, she looked, to the young knight, to be strangely alone.

"Carissa's goal is to murder the royal family for their ability to use the Curtana, then interfere with both the currently existing Original and Second to eliminate the possibility of someone analyzing them to make a Third. By doing so, she would perfectly avoid the worst scenario—that a new monarch and Curtana appear only to lead the United Kingdom astray. Destroying Buckingham Palace wasn't merely an attack on the Puritan faction. It was to thoroughly destroy all the coded documents and artwork as yet undecodable by sorcerers, thought to be how the Curtana Second was produced, thus annihilating any possibility of a Curtana Third appearing later in history...After the war with France and the Roman Orthodox Church was over, Carissa was prepared to personally seal and destroy the Curtana Original and Second, then spend the rest of her remaining life deep in a cemetery."

Someone slowly stood up.

It was mysterious that he was able to.

It wasn't because of the knights' power by itself. Carissa had made arrangements for it from the very start: to let the Knights faction survive after cooperating with the coup d'état, the second princess became a solitary tyrant, shouldering on her own the blame that should have rested on the knights.

The young knight had an honest thought. He wanted to fight for a person like that. But he also thought that didn't mean obeying Carissa's orders and making her coup succeed.

"*This is the conclusion: Carissa has two goals. The first is to make herself an overwhelming tyrant to eliminate France and the Roman Orthodox Church, protecting the United Kingdom even if later generations would call Carissa a dark stain on the nation's history. The second is to seal away the ultimate, most terrible weapon, the Curtana Original, and, by removing an incompetent monarchy, make it so the will of the people could halt the nation's rampage…Even if, after it all, the stars aligned to create a new system of monarchy different from ours—if that monarch tried to make the wrong decision—she wanted to leave them a 'weakness' that would make the monarch bend their ear to the people. It is for those goals that Carissa, now a tyrant, tries to shoulder alone the sin of wielding the wicked weapon Curtana and massacring foreign enemies wholesale.*"

If Carissa was still the kind of person who wouldn't even kill the subordinates who looked at her with disappointment…

…then they couldn't let her stray any farther from the path.

There had to be a way to overcome the crisis with the Roman Orthodox Church even without the Curtana Original's power.

Yes.

If the queen of the British royal family and the three sisters, including Carissa, were able to all work together.

And.

The Knight Leader, standing on the building rooftop, had been listening to the words of the first princess, Limeia.

"I will not force you to act in a certain way," she said. "I know you all have family, friends, and spouses you have to protect apart from the nation. I will not deny your right to flee to prevent their sadness."

He was quiet, his eyes shut.

Ignoring him, Limeia wrapped things up. "However, if any of you have pity for my sister Carissa…If any knights wish to help one woman, regardless of her position as second princess…Will you not take up your swords once more? I am sure there is a woman for whom that thought alone will be her salvation. It matters not how much strength you wield. Someone would be fighting for her sake in the truest sense. There is a woman who only needs to know."

For a while, there was silence.

The same silence had surely visited the rest of the United Kingdom.

They would think in silence, then come to a final decision.

As a knight, as a man, as a human…A decision made freely.

We no longer even need to give orders to the United Kingdom.

The Knight Leader nodded without a sound, then drew a sword from out of nowhere.

It was a silver longsword, which no longer drew power from the Curtana and the all-British Continent and now couldn't even shift colors to red. But the naked steel looked more reassuring than it ever had.

Even without orders, we know what we must do.

It was a knight's sword, its original purpose regained.

With it in his hand, the head of the knights began to swiftly jump from building to building.

Limeia smiled thinly.

The Knight Leader had been standing behind her for a while, but she never once turned around.

She trusted nobody who knew her status as the first princess.

But that wasn't exactly the reason she hadn't turned around. In fact, Limeia wasn't the type to show her back to those she didn't trust.

...Carissa has changed enough to execute a coup d'état for her love of the people, and Vilian has seen the people suffering for it and grown, she thought, checking on the battle situation through her telescope again. *Perhaps I, too, have grown a little stronger after everything that has happened.*

7

Without even wiping away the mud tangled in her hair, Vilian, currently fallen on the ground, directed her hazy gaze to a certain boy's back.

To the one boy in the Puritans' near-annihilated remnant forces who had continued to desperately oppose Carissa.

Vilian, who was unable to move and on the verge of death like many of the other Puritans, heard the transmission from her older sister, the first princess, Limeia.

Had the boy heard the same broadcast? He might have, from a Soul Arm fallen on the ruined battlefield. He also might not have.

And yet, he hadn't wavered.

Only he had not hesitated, among all the Puritan remnants when they had learned of Carissa's intentions.

"Well, now what?" Carissa goaded. "The second bunker cluster was already fired! Unlike before, the sorcerers don't have the reserves to create a defensive barrier!!"

"!! Damn it! I'm not giving up!!"

"Ha-ha-ha!! Do you think if you break the Curtana Original, it'll send the missile a self-destruct signal for lack of orders from me? It's not a nuclear weapon! Unfortunately, that warhead doesn't have that feature!!"

"It's not over!! Not if we use the barrage from the Silkie Aquariums!!"

"I guess that's somewhat more realistic. But if they could do that, they would have intercepted the last shot, too. French trash would be one thing—they were so stubborn about domestic development and production that they lost their versatility. But the cruise missiles I deal in won't be brought down so easily!!"

The boy was a mercenary who, unlike William Orwell, had no doctrine or ideology. He wouldn't be able to make the right decision every time. After all, he'd been tricked by Carissa and the knights and hadn't been able to stop the coup d'état from happening.

But the boy didn't dwell on it.

Even if he was wrong, he'd never give up. No matter how bad the situation got, he would always look at it and try to find the best plan he could to turn the tables.

Therefore.

This situation wouldn't cause the boy to waver.

He might smile and accept things, but he'd never let surprise make him hesitate.

Someone who always tried to be completely correct from the start and someone who tried to make it so everyone could smile in the end. Which one was more precious?

"See? The bunker cluster is here."

Even with her intentions exposed by Limeia, Carissa tried to continue her reign as tyrant, spreading her arms and looking up into the night sky.

A speck of light in the dark sky had appeared—not of another star but of a missile.

"I'll blow you ignorant plebs away!! This is what my military expertise can do!!"

"!!"

As though betting on a slim possibility, the boy was looking around for a communication Soul Arm that connected to the Coven Compass or a Silkie Aquarium. But finding one on palace grounds—now a missile-racked mountain of debris—would prove difficult. And he barely knew anything about magic to begin with, so he might not have spotted one even if it was right nearby.

In the meantime, the cruise missile approached a spot directly over Buckingham Palace.

At this rate, its two hundred smaller bombs would scatter, and this time, the entire city in a three-kilometer radius from the palace would be blown to smithereens.

And then…

"Zero!!"

A new voice reached them from afar.

A moment later, before breaking into four and blasting apart into so many bombs, the cruise missile malfunctioned. Even after reaching the predetermined location, it didn't open. Instead, the flames spurting out the rear suddenly vanished, and it fell like a wild pitch toward a road outside Buckingham Palace property. It was supposedly quite heavy, but rather than stab into the road, it bounced several times across it.

It was an unnatural phenomenon, like someone had stolen every bit of the weapon's attack power.

As the third princess watched, dumbfounded, she heard the sharp sound of something slicing through the air.

A debris object created by the Curtana Original.

A sharp stake, about three meters long, one of the ones Carissa had kicked away during the battle. *Boom!!* It headed straight for Vilian's face—but never penetrated it.

From just beside her:

The Knight Leader, who had suddenly jumped in, had punched away the three-meter stake with his right hand.

With an awful *gwkk-keeee*, dark-red blood spurted out from the gaps between his fist's fingers.

But there was no change in the Knight Leader's face. He simply glanced at his fist, then watched the result.

"…As I thought, it won't work against the Curtana Original or any of the phenomena that derive from it."

"Knight Leader…?" called the mud-covered princess in a shaking voice.

But he didn't turn around. The head of the knights, who had

appeared with a large number of men from the Knights faction, said to Vilian, his back to her:

"I will accept any punishment. When this coup d'état is ended, you may sever my head from my body if you wish."

His words had no hesitation.

The Knight Leader, for the first time, had called what he'd been doing all along not a "revolution" but a "coup d'état."

"However, allow us to at least make the preparations for my punishment. And if I may be so bold…I pray that the whole British royal family once again comes together to face France and the Roman Orthodox Church the correct way."

As the Knight Leader spoke, his bloody hand reaffirmed its grip on his sword.

Cut off from the power of the Curtana Original, it was merely a knight's longsword, no longer able to wield its original abilities.

"…Princess Carissa is the type of person who is able to do everything by herself. If she can use that power justly and cooperate with the others in the Royal Family faction, she will no doubt drive away the Roman Orthodox Church."

When Vilian saw the Knight Leader about to head off for a deadly battlefield at a clear disadvantage, her lips moved in spite of herself. As she dragged her aching body up, she called out.

"You will wait."

The words had spirit in them, so much that they barely seemed to belong to the third princess, and the Knight Leader unconsciously stopped. Vilian already held within her the strength to force the head of the Knight faction to stop and turn around.

"A selfish demand for death is nothing but a nuisance. If you truly wish to atone, then I will have you do something worth being happy about. I want each of you to think for himself about what he should do. Do not do it reluctantly, because you were forced—because there is meaning in acting for yourself first."

The Knight Leader mulled over those words for a few minutes.

Then, without hesitation, he stepped in between Kamijou and Carissa, who were still fighting.

"Split into two teams. One to recover and restore the wounded Puritans in the area and the other to attack Princess Carissa to stop her directly."

At the Knight Leader's short orders, the wound-covered, armor-clad men moved swiftly. They weren't obeying a set of orders numbered one to ten. All of them, from their leader down to their lowest rung, were acting on their own volition.

"...We promise victory. *We cannot leave Princess Carissa alone any longer.*"

As Kamijou dodged the giant white structures, trying to nullify Carissa's omnidimensional slashes when given the chance, the Knight Leader stepped up next to him.

"My apologies. I've left the fate of my nation and the princess in your hands."

Kamijou's answer was simple.

He didn't look at the Knight Leader—he just commanded:

"Right, then. You're gonna help me stop her."

They moved at the same time.

Kamijou would nullify the omnidimensional slice. The Knight Leader would plunge directly in and bar the Curtana Original itself from moving.

The Knight Leader was gripping a longsword with an eighty-centimeter-or-so blade meant for fighting on horseback. He glanced at the weapon he wielded and muttered bitterly, "...As I thought, its expansion has been sealed. I can't use the pattern-type sorcery that combines chivalrous spells from around the world. Only natural, with its power supply from the Curtana cut off...So what I've got left are Thororm's Spell, since I created it myself, and the fast-movement support spell. But Thororm's Spell won't work on the Curtana or any phenomena derived from it. Even my swordsmanship is looking at large decreases in power without the Curtana's power supply..."

His clearly disadvantageous situation came to mind, but the Knight Leader smiled a little.

A slightly offended smile, as though he'd regained his usual manner.

"...At most I'll have half the speed. But I want to stop her without killing her—so I'm thankful!!"

"I see. I hadn't expected the charismatic, virtuous Vilian to be followed by my sister the intellectual!!" shouted Carissa, as sword clashed against sword.

Yes—the Knight Leader's longsword had repelled the Curtana Original. He'd accurately struck the flat of the blade, which wasn't generating the omnidimensional slicing field.

"She waited for the perfect time to make that speech! The knights and the Puritans were both just about to give in to the Curtana Original's power! That's why it worked so freaking well! Just like having a sweet drink after eating something bitter!!"

Nevertheless, Carissa's fierce attack didn't stop.

Against the monsters, the Knight Leader, and the Knights faction, she continued her skirmish, freely controlling it.

"Plus, that wasn't even aimed at the entire Knights faction! She just made it look that way—she delivered that message with you individually in mind! I mean, obviously. You're their leader, their pillar of support!! Your individual decisions can greatly influence the Knights faction's outlook. Instead of telling each of them to choose freely, she knew swaying *your* opinion would make the entire organization's movements easy to predict. Her speech was as shrewd as she is!!"

"I do not care."

In response, the Knight Leader, while avoiding Carissa's attacks, kept his face steady.

His determination was already unbreakable.

"It does not matter how calculated it was, as long as it gave me the motivation to save you, Princess. Being made to dance by the intellectual princess, Limeia, is entertaining in itself!!"

"Is it your pride as the Knight Leader? But with your power supply from the Curtana Original cut off, you can't bring your true abilities fully into play. Or did you think you could keep up with me with only the weak trickle from the Second?!"

"My personal power is a triviality! It will not cause me to waver!!"

"Ugh. You disgust me!!"

Even as she shouted, Carissa could feel the knights' will to fight had recovered—no, even expanded beyond what it was originally, as they attacked more fiercely than they had before. Even the fallen Puritans, their physical states aside, had probably undergone a complete mental recovery. They were a more close-knit group, and on top of that, with additional knights from all over the United Kingdom gathering, fooling around any further seemed like it would cause even her trouble.

I hate to say it, but I can't spare any cruise missiles!!

After swinging the Curtana Original around in a wide arc to ward off attacks, Carissa took a giant leap backward to gain distance.

When she created that slight temporal "space," Kamijou and the knights moved to gauge the distance again. Carissa watched them, resting the Curtana Original on her shoulder.

"I wanted to save some to attack France with, but it looks like I'll have to use up all my bunker clusters here and now, so."

Carissa's hand held the small radio.

Kamijou was shocked, but the Knight Leader took a challenging step forward.

"The Thororm's Spell I use isn't advanced enough to seal your Curtana Original or the phenomena caused by it, but it can zero the attack power of something like bunker clusters. Will you still insist on wasting them?"

"Yes, I believe you told me that the defensive spell you use can nullify the attack power of any one chosen weapon target that the caster perceives." Carissa sneered, almost like she was asking an employee to tell her what their job was.

As she did, she brought the radio to her mouth.

"Then I'll send this order—prepare the cruise missiles loaded with bunker cluster warheads. Of the destroyers on standby in the Dover Strait, the *Wimbledon* will fire twenty-four, the *King Henry VII* will fire twenty-six, the *Sherwood* will fire twenty, the *Hastings* will fire fifteen, and the *Shakespeare* will fire fifteen. To all whom it may concern, aim at Buckingham Palace and fire a total of eighty bunker clusters on my command. Now then—out of those, which do you think I will hide with an illusion spell?"

"...!!" The Knight Leader froze.

Carissa responded with a wicked smile. "It might just be a bluff, but if it slips past, that's it. And I can guarantee it by pressing the issue and attacking with the Curtana Original at the same time. With everyone dead if you let even one through, I will test the essence of the United Kingdom's knights and judge whether they can repel my blade."

"Gah! We have to stop her!!" insisted Kamijou to the head of the knights, trying to charge in at Carissa with his own fist clenched, too.

But the second princess's fingertip moved, pressing the Call button faster.

Before Kamijou's fist could reach her, Carissa gave the order for destruction through the small radio.

"All five named destroyers, I order you to fire the cruise missi—"

Kamijou clenched his teeth, but in response, Carissa suddenly frowned for some reason.

Then her head came up in surprise and she jumped straight backward a moment later.

And then...

Dpshhhh!!

The giant antenna tower used for military communications plunged right into the spot where Carissa had been standing a moment ago.

Kamijou had been about to head for Carissa, but the blast wind forced him backward, knocking him to the ground. As the dust billowed around the giant antenna tower stuck in the center of the

debris, he saw someone standing on its wreckage. The large figure looked down at the second princess, Carissa, and spoke.

"Now, now, you cannot give reckless orders to the British Armed Forces. They, too, are people of the United Kingdom. Without explicit instructions from a dictator, they would never fire cruise missiles at the capital of the nation they should be protecting with their lives."

"I see how it is. You're all starting to piss me off...!!" growled Carissa, her voice more bitter than it had been before now—and possibly the most spiteful it had been for the entire coup d'état.

In response, the tall man jumped down from the antenna tower, landed between Kamijou and the Knight Leader, and said this:

"I see I am late. I had to learn a bit about science. It seems to have taken me some time to find all the nearby military antennae and destroy them," he said.

And then a certain mercenary brought his giant sword, over three meters long, back to the ready again.

The mercenary who was experienced not only with individual combat but with larger-scale conflicts finally joined their ranks.

With, as always, such detestably amazing timing.

INTERLUDE FIVE

In the end, it was just one stupid thing after another.

It hadn't been one specific, unique moment. The rails heading toward the worst possible conclusion were something she'd been getting glimpses of for a long time now.

"By majority vote, we hereby forbid the usage of the aforementioned weapons."

It wasn't just the bunker clusters.

The Roman Orthodox Church now had the EU assembly under its thumb. They had been approving one prohibition treaty after another, pinpointing only the weapons that the United Kingdom was currently developing. It was a clear message the UK was being dismissed as an outdated fossil of a nation and there was no fear of retaliation no matter what they did.

However.

The beginning of this decision had come before Carissa had taken over as the head of military affairs, during the time of her mother, Elizard. In those days, only the UK's nuclear weapons had been prohibited—France's had not. What separated the two was supposedly the difference in their explosives' destructive power, but after that, the UK was prevented from even developing specifically less-powerful nuclear weapons. Ultimately, they'd decided that all UK-made nuclear weapons should be handed over to France. The apparent excuse was that France, now the only nuclear power in the EU, had the technology to safely dismantle them, but the real reason was obvious:

The attack had started.

Carissa was now witnessing the tragic result of the escalation of those attacks.

In the shadows, the EU member nations were probably whispering things like *We have no problems as long as we have the Roman Orthodox Church's support,* and *The United Kingdom can criticize all it wants—but it would never challenge an organization two billion people strong in a straight fight.*

A once great but obsolete nation.

Your prosperity ended at the beginning of the twentieth century.

In other words: *Our value as a nation has fallen,* Carissa thought.

Her mother, leader of the nation, had said they didn't need to respond to these clear provocations. But as a result, the neighboring nations had begun treating the UK with contempt, steadily building an environment where they could do anything to the UK without any repercussions. If this state of affairs continued, eventually the United Kingdom would lose even its status as a sovereign state, and the citizenry would be mocked and ridiculed simply for being British, ushering in an age where their people had to conceal who they were just to make a living.

She needed to stop that from happening.

She could not lose this age, in which her nation's people could live with smiling faces.

Carissa had been preparing for it for many years now. There were probably several different methods, but she'd naturally gravitated toward one of them from the beginning. After all, she'd never excelled at anything but military matters—she knew nothing but how to stand on a battlefield, covered in mud, sword in hand. The only option that seemed realistic for her to succeed was to stage a coup d'état.

But these had been preparations, and that was all.

Without several conditions having been met, she would never have had to execute them.

Perhaps if their leader, her mother, could have restored their national pride by wielding her diplomatic skills, it wouldn't have been a problem. If their neighbor countries had withdrawn from Roman Orthodox support—if they'd led their nations each on their own intentions—then this crisis in which she had no choice but to act might have vanished naturally.

However.

The Eurotunnel connecting the UK and France had been bombed.

Then, as if timed, a hijacking incident had occurred, closing routes into the UK.

The checkpoints and border lines she'd set as strategic points beforehand had all been crossed in the worst way possible.

Carissa had decided that there wasn't any more time to spare.

The princess had decided that if she didn't act now, the value of the UK citizenry would fall to a level worse than slaves.

As a result, Carissa had taken up the Curtana Original.

It was a kingmaker that she detested.

But the princess had quietly resolved to become a tyrant.

For a woman who was only ever talented when it came to military affairs, one who knew nothing but how to fight with a sword in her hand, there was but one way to change the nation and the world.

Carissa decided this for herself, without telling a soul.

She had resolved: When the war was over, she and the two Curtanas would disappear into the annals of history. She would hide deep in a crypt she'd created herself and sleep there until the end, unbeknownst to anyone.

CHAPTER 8

Queen and State: The People's General Election

Union_Jack.

1

Acqua of the Back and the Knight Leader stood side by side.

Acqua gripping the Soul Arm Ascalon and the Knight Leader his lone longsword, the leftover core of his larger Soul Arm.

The Knight Leader spoke under his breath, low enough to be talking to himself but high enough to be addressing his old friend.

"...To think the time would ever come again when I entrust my back to you."

"I see you cannot shift it into Hrunting. Try not to slow me down too much."

"Bah."

With only that, the Knight Leader waved his longsword and looked ahead.

There was no longer a need to admit superiority, nor to closely examine the other's gaze. Like the times they had crushed many a strong enemy together, he offered some words hesitantly, as a bridge of trust.

"To battle. Let us each inspect what the other has gained in his decade of study."

*   *   *

Bam!! The earth split.

When the two of them began to run at the same time, the ground could no longer hold itself up.

Acqua from the right and the Knight Leader from the left:

Closing in from either direction, at a blur, they darted toward Carissa, swords brandished.

"Ugh."

In response, the princess reacted to Acqua first. As she twisted to avoid his three-and-a-half-meter longsword, she took advantage of the movement to wheel the Curtana Original around. The debris object it created shielded her from the Knight Leader's longsword.

"Your head—it will fly," she whispered into Acqua's face.

Bam!!

Their slashes collided.

Carissa struck diagonally from the shoulder, while Acqua responded with Ascalon. Considering the Curtana Original's power, he didn't let the blades touch. Instead, he parried using his sword's hilt against hers.

Ow...?!

Until now, Carissa had had a decisive upper hand, but the unexpected recoil shocked her.

The pure impact it created pushed their bodies backward. They hadn't retreated, but rather their feet had scraped across the earth.

But they were both still within range. Another pair of killing techniques flashed.

"!!"

"?!"

Disregarding the size of his sword, they both unleashed an attack to deal a fatal blow. It was like a Wild West standoff—victory would surely be decided by the slimmest of margins.

However...

"...Don't think...you two...are fighting alone!!"

"Wha—?"

From the side, the wound-covered Kaori Kanzaki had charged in—working her body to the bone after it had been slammed with the blast winds from the bunker clusters despite her having blocked some of them with a barrier. With the other Puritans still unable to move, she alone could stand up—probably due to her characteristics as a saint. What she'd unleashed was her Single Glint, which could slice through even angels. Carissa, driven to a corner and absolutely unable to ignore such an attack, twisted her sword's trajectory to defend against it.

Which, of course, left her open to Acqua's attack.

And to add insult to injury, the Knight Leader had moved in as well.

"Whooooooooooooooooooooaaaaaaaaaaaaaaaaaaaaaaaaaaaaa!!"

Their shouts overlapped, creating a unique gale.

As its impact electrified the battlefield, several shadows passed the speed of sound.

Carissa kicked at Acqua's leg to throw him off balance, slightly bending his sword's course. Without waiting for Ascalon to just barely pass her by, she used the Curtana Original to deflect Kanzaki's Seven Heavens Sword, after which she leaped back to avoid the knight's follow-up attack.

Unlike before, she was dodging with everything she had.

But the three superhumans wouldn't sit quietly and let her.

Gk-gk-gk-gk-zk-zk-zk-zk-zk-kik-kik-kik-kik-kik! A storm of sparks followed Carissa as she retreated in a straight line. As the attacks approached from various angles, Carissa kicked up rubble and debris objects on the ground, swung the Curtana Original, stopped one attack after another, twisted, parried. In response, Acqua and Kanzaki cut through the rubble and fired the debris objects back, trying to create an advantage.

There was a moment's span before the Curtana Original could create a debris object from its slash. With speed that made the debris late to appear, the four combatants continued to slash.

A sharp intake of breath reached Kanzaki's ears.

In this fight that wouldn't allow discrete syllables, much less a conversation, it displayed Carissa's intent.

The second princess kicked up two debris objects at her feet, then slammed them together like symbols, destroying them herself.

Ga-boooom!! The fragments scattered like fireworks.

"?!"

Everyone paused for an instant, pushed by the shock wave. Only Carissa moved, taking advantage of the momentum to gain fifteen meters' worth of distance.

For monsters like them, the distance was one they could close in the blink of an eye.

"...I see..."

A bead of red blood traveled down Carissa's forehead.

It hadn't been Kanzaki, or Acqua, or the Knight Leader who had hurt her. A fragment of the debris she herself had created—that was what had drawn blood from her royal personage.

"This is getting to be more than a trifle to deal with. No matter how much special power I've gotten, it's still a pain in the ass fighting three saint-level monsters together."

"You shouldn't think that being a 'special human' allows you to do everything," rebuked Kanzaki, recovering her stamina with a special breathing technique. "We can only use our full power because there are those who support us. With many sorcerers constantly targeting you from every direction, you will naturally always need to be conscious of attacks in blind spots, which will narrow down your vast array of options."

"Maybe," said Carissa, her eyes turning to glare at the other woman. "From a military perspective, some battles are fought and won by the number of allies you have."

She set her stare on the sorcerers trying to fire long-range magic in between the saints' and the Knight Leader's attacks when they saw an opportunity.

"But didn't you think that would give me an opportunity to beat you?"

*　　*　　*

Chill.

Something, something like a wave of sadism unlike anything before, began to emanate from the second princess.

A moment later:

With incredible leg strength, she kicked a block of rubble up in the air. Equipped with a limited portion of the angelic leader's power, the object, heavier than metal, shot up five meters.

But she hadn't aimed it at Kanzaki, Acqua, or the Knight Leader.

She had purposely sent it reeling toward the group of knights on the back lines giving aid to the fallen Puritans.

"Wha—?"

With a huge *boom*, several figures went flying.

In the instant Kanzaki's gaze went to them, Carissa gave the Curtana Original another large swing. What appeared was a hundred-meter-class debris object. It was a rectangular plank, twisted in the center part, reminiscent of the blades of a wooden helicopter toy.

Carissa caused the edge of that blade to explode, then used the momentum to spin it like a giant propeller. At a forty-five-degree angle, the whirling blade ripped up everything in its path, approaching the crowd.

"Damn!!"

In response, the Knight Leader jumped out in front of the propeller at a supersonic speed and tried to knock away the whirling blade.

And then, with a *thud*, came an impact from directly behind him.

It wasn't an attack from Carissa. He'd been paying the utmost attention to her killing intent.

The strike that hit him was from one of the Puritan sorcerers, supposedly an ally, having forced his wound-covered body to move and firing desperately.

"...Ah..."

He turned around and saw that he was making a flabbergasted face of his own.

He hadn't done it out of malice. It had been a stray bullet.

However.

The Knight Leader had lost his balance, and the giant whirling blade was shooting right for him without mercy.

"?!"

He frantically tried to intercept it with his longsword, but with his balance gone, he didn't have his normal strength. The heavy impact slammed him into the ground. The whirling blade, its trajectory altered, squirmed around like a living creature. And that caused the damage elsewhere to expand.

"No matter how many people you have in your group, it doesn't change the fact that a group has connections among each and every person."

Carissa waved the Curtana Original in a wide arc above her head. The giant debris object it produced changed into a huge suspended ceiling tilted diagonally, which tried to crush all the sorcerers from the skies.

"Which means that whatever the organization, there's always a chance to split the individuals apart. That property never goes away—even if magical thoughts or scientific brain waves link them together."

Kanzaki immediately attempted to slice it apart with her wires, but the second princess leaped on the action. Her leg whipped out and caught Kanzaki in the stomach, sending Kanzaki flying.

"Groups perfectly unified as a single unit, a single being, are naught but the product of fantasy."

Dozens of ranged attacks stabbed into the hanging ceiling, just barely finishing it off before it crushed the sorcerers. In the meantime, Acqua jumped about, swiftly slipping between the land and the ceiling as it crashed, upheaving the earth. He charged toward Carissa, greatsword in hand.

"In fact, the more you have, the more strands of the web there are to cut."

An ear-shattering *boom!!*

It was the sound of Ascalon and the Curtana Original clashing against each other at a spot close to each hilt.

However.

With this much of their cooperation ruined, the battle had devolved from a group fight to an individual one. And in terms of individual strength, Acqua had severe wounds from the battle in Academy City, so Carissa, who could use the angelic leader's power fully within the United Kingdom, was his better.

Gk-gk gree-gree-gree!! After several slashing attacks crossed, Acqua's body skidded backward. He didn't fall, but dark red began to ooze from a spot on his side.

"Bring a thousand, bring ten thousand. I still won't waver," declared Carissa, resting her sword on her shoulder.

This was no quarrel between children.

One wasn't always at an advantage. But if there was a chance she'd lose hers, Carissa would immediately prevent it. By stopping everything before the tide changed, her advantage would never be overturned.

"And I'm quite used to fighting groups, so. Did you forget how talented I am, even among the royal family, when it comes to military affairs?"

Those words signaled the restarting of the nightmare.

2

People were watching their fight.

Those people were not so-called sorcerers. But neither could one declare them completely unrelated civilians. They were the retainers, the servants, the cooks, the gardeners who had been working in Buckingham Palace for the royal family.

The only ones who could really get the closest to the members of the royal family were mainly expert interceptors polished in a magical sense as well, like the Guards Maids and armed attendants, but those here were different. Most of them were truly of common birth, people whom the third princess, Vilian, had invited in.

They'd been able to step all the way into London, but they couldn't charge into the central battlefield, Buckingham Palace. Their hesitation now exposed them as amateurs; after all, this place where they thought they were safe was just one more position that Carissa could blow away on a whim.

Without realizing that, they gazed at the battle.

Their days up until now had been filled with more happiness as a United Kingdom citizen than they deserved. They wanted to protect Vilian for giving that to them, and they purely wished to fight if it was for the British royal family.

However.

With this overwhelming sight before their eyes, what were they to do?

Whether they looked at the coup itself or the large-scale magical battles, the servants' hearts and minds were already long past maximum capacity. They'd wanted to fight in the subway tunnel, too, but in the end, their legs trembled and they couldn't act at the most important time. It was the same now. Shame, reputation—none of it mattered. They were, to be honest, tiny normal people, and they were *scared* of the battle unfolding before them. This feeling wasn't something to be spoken of in the same dimension as courage or a sense of justice. This was, perhaps, the proper way of thinking as the humans they were.

Carissa's tyranny was a true symbol of hopelessness.

Even now that the true reasons for her actions were out in the open, the regular servants felt so hopeless they could only tremble.

On the destroyed Buckingham Palace grounds, monsters like Acqua of the Back and Kaori Kanzaki were fighting at the same time. And despite the greater part of the Knights faction having left her, the second princess's sadism showed no signs of abating. In fact, most of the sorcerers they called "professionals" had already fallen to the ground.

This battle would not be easy to jump into.

Most likely, if they joined in, what they would find is instant death. Because they'd dragged their feet, the professional sorcerers had been the ones to fall, and that could lead to a major change in the fight's outcome.

When they started to think about it like that, standing and watching was all they could do, unable to break out of the civilian realm.

"What else can we even do?" someone mourned.

They were all simple people. Once nonsensical magic started appearing, there was no room for them. And even among the civilians, there was a boy, squeezing his right hand into a fist and fighting. But that was because he had a special power, wasn't it? He had the strength from the beginning to oppose sorcery. If they were the kinds of people who could fight terrorists hijacking the Skybus 365, they'd run in here without hesitation, too. But they didn't have any special powers to call their own.

So what else could they even do?

"Do you truly believe that?"

That was when they heard a voice. Hastily, the servants turned around and saw a familiar face there.

"Do you seriously think that boy's right hand is the only difference separating you from him?"

"…"

With someone else asking the question again, the servants fell silent.

In truth, they knew: That boy wasn't fighting on this crazy front line because he had special powers. In fact, it seemed more logical to them that he only happened to have anything at all. That, in other words, was their answer: The ability to take part in this civil war was decided by courage and nerve.

"Do you have that?" the woman asked again. "It doesn't matter what your personal feelings are. It doesn't matter what objective reasons you have. Do you have that measly bit of courage to stand up to overwhelming terror and save our nation from this crisis?"

At the question, someone looked up.

They decided they didn't need to hang their head, so they looked up.

They knew their answer.

At the very least, the servants didn't want to lose to that boy in strength of will. They understood they were scared enough to quake in their shoes, but that wish to be in there, fighting, had managed to keep them in place, keep them from running away. That had been linked to why they were watching the battle.

So in the end, they decided:

They wanted to fight alongside the rest, too.

"Very good," acknowledged the woman.

Elizard, queen of England, gave a reassuring, captain-like grin that reached across her whole face.

"Then come with me. I will make up for everything you lack."

Everything she needed was now in place.

This was where their comeback story would begin.

3

A tremendous *kaboom!!* rattled through the Buckingham Palace grounds.

"...!!"

Quickly, she readied her Curtana Original to respond, but she still felt her hands tingling. Carissa looked at her assailant, who had charged in from a distance, faster than the speed of sound, and gave her loudest shout of the night.

"So you finally showed up—the cause of everything, my mother!!"

What had slammed into her was the Curtana Second, with the exact same shape as her sword.

As Acqua and the Knight Leader were on the back foot, the true head of state had stepped in, wielding the other kingmaker of a sword.

The two Curtanas clashed against each other, each royal owner glaring into the other's eyes.

"I don't mind you doing what you want," Elizard began, "but if you're going to do it, do it one hundred percent—and make a better plan than mine. It seemed like this was turning out worse than mine, so I came here to stop you."

"Stop your prattling!" Carissa barked. "Does the root cause of all this want her throne that badly?!"

Then came an unpleasant *zzzk* sound.

Between the Curtana Original and the Second, the Original of course had more power in it. They wouldn't even have a good clash of blades—the Original's blade was sinking slowly into its little sister's.

When it had gotten about a centimeter in, both swordswomen moved.

Ka-shing, ka-shing, ka-shing!! They traded just three quick, short blows.

Each time, sparks flew from the Curtana Original's blade. It seemed as though they weren't even the same material hitting against each other; it was like Carissa was whittling away at soft gold, like she was carving it.

"...Despite all the setup, despite all the groups fighting each other, in the end it comes down to a clash between Curtanas. I feel like an idiot for thinking so hard about everything, so," said Carissa with a self-deprecating grin, the unscathed Curtana Original in her hand.

Both women's strength was manifest.

"But a fight between Curtanas is a fight I cannot possibly lose. My Original has over eighty percent of the power, and your Curtana has less than twenty. If we're using the same type of power, the pure quantity will decide the outcome. Don't you understand that?"

In response, Elizard gave a little smile. Not a purposeful act—but one that honestly seemed to have slipped out by accident.

"...You are a more small-minded woman than I thought, my daughter."

"What?"

"All to take responsibility for a foolish monarchical system and protect the British people...You'd become a tyrant, crush all hostile nations in Europe, and then hand over the government's reins to the people. Your plan seems to be quite large-scale, but have you caught, around its edges, the glimpses of your small-mindedness?"

Carissa didn't answer with words.

Instead, she swung the Curtana Original with a massive *boom*.

Elizard parried with her own sword, but this time it left the Second with a bigger gash in the blade than before.

Elizard's expression was unmoving. "Do you really want to change this country? Do you want to protect the people, even if it means breaking the great pillars forming our government? Then don't rely on systems that are already in place. If you're going to do something—then at least do this much," she said.

The queen gave a great swing of her Curtana Second, then let it go, flinging it hard and straight at Carissa. Carissa hastily knocked it out of the way—only to realize a moment later what it all meant.

The Curtana Second, its trajectory altered, bounced off in a different direction and vanished into the dark.

Queen Elizard had purposely let go of the magical sword that supported her power.

"What...are you thinking?"

The sheer recklessness, the defenselessness, actually made Carissa tense and ready herself.

With the Curtana factored into her tactics, that option would, thinking normally, be absolutely impossible.

Yet the queen had willingly chosen it. And then, with absolute confidence, she answered:

"A revolution."

At that moment, Elizard stood more grandly in that spot than her daughter.

"A revolution is what you need before you realize something that has yet to be realized. Abandon all delicacy. People who try to overturn stagnant theory don't cling to that same theory. If you see something happen for the first time in history and you're surprised, then you're still tied to the thick pillar of this nation's idea of exceptionalism."

Is she trying to say she has more nerve than I do?

Carissa decided that instead, it was part of a plan to rile up the hesitating masses. And she had to give it to her—it was effective. It wouldn't be strange if stupid people mistook Elizard for being braver.

But…

Then I'll respond with a tyrant's methods. If I kill her in front of everyone, it's over!! With her mangled corpse on full display, they'll crumple into despair for real, so!!

Her conclusion reached, Carissa raised the Curtana Original to slice her in half vertically, to create the kind of corpse that would be most effective at inducing terror.

But then she noticed it.

And she was so late she had to wonder how it had slipped by her.

"Wait…This…No…"

The Curtana Original was acting strangely.

When she turned her glare on the one who knew the cause, Queen Elizard answered:

"Didn't I say it already? *This* is a revolution."

Flap went the sound of cloth hitting the air. Elizard held a large cloth in her hands—a flag. On the front of it was the national flag of the UK, and on the back was a flag in white and green—once used as the national flag of Wales.

"The United Kingdom's flag adopts designs from those of England, Ireland, and Scotland. As for Wales, at the time this flag became established, it had been absorbed by England. This flag respects their culture by placing it on the reverse side…Of course, the trick was getting to the British Museum to pick it up."

England, Scotland, Wales, and Northern Ireland.

Symbols of the four cultures comprising the United Kingdom.

And the basis of the Curtana Original's power.

"Of course, not everyone could actually pull it off…but you made a mistake not prioritizing my assassination. *This thing* is one of the national-level sorceries designated for exclusive use by the British royal family."

Elizard flapped the flag out and spread it wide across the night sky.

Union Jack.

After speaking the spell's name, the queen took just one deep breath.

"By my name."

And then she raised her voice high, loud enough so that it would resound everywhere.

"I hereby command the power gathered within the Curtana, that used for the all-British Continent, constructed from four cultures: Release your power and redistribute it evenly among all the British people!!"

4

With Elizard's words, the Curtana Original lost its power.

Well, not exactly.

The power accumulated inside it began to flow out from the tip to other places.

"Together with this power, I, Queen Regnant Elizard, proclaim this to every citizen."

The Curtana's power gave strength to a pyramid of power centered on the ruler and the knights. But what, exactly, gave a monarch the right to the throne?

If you investigated that question's deepest implications, you would come to see the true form of *the spell* Elizard demonstrated.

"Because of this coup d'état, much has happened this day. The army mobilized, cities were taken over, destroyers were let loose in the Dover Strait, knights engaged in combat, and then bunker clusters bombed our capital. Many of you have no idea what is truly happening, but you probably have incurred strange damages."

Yes: At the beginning, any British citizen would have had the right.

"But now you all have the power to resist."

The British royal family was formed long ago after many battles. If the events of history had played out even slightly differently, someone else who also lived in Britain might have started the royal bloodline. And considering emigration and political marriages, the potential for a completely different outcome simply become greater.

Which meant only one thing was important: whether or not you were a person of the United Kingdom. It wasn't an issue of bloodline or citizenship. It was whether you loved Britain, and whether you wished to make it your homeland.

"I cannot explain the details as to why, but for tonight and tonight alone, you all have an equal chance to become heroes. You are now able to fight against the strange events you've seen but don't understand the reasons for why it is happening! You are now able to do anything!! And I want you all to choose. Think for yourself and decide who you want to fight for, and who you want to fight alongside!!"

On top of that, the queen gave that right to them—

To those people who might have become kings and queens.

To the ones who might have been sitting on the throne, if only history had been slightly different.

"I will gratefully accept all who wish to help me! You are even free to side with the usurpers! If you can show us a completely different alternative path, feel free to do so!! And you don't need to force yourself to fight simply because you have the power!! If you don't want it, you can will it to *return*. If you decide you trust someone else more than yourself, you can will it to *transfer* and it will!! In every sense, in this moment alone, this great power is *yours*. If you want to fight, or even if you want to flee, you can decide for yourselves!!"

She told them that the fragments of power they could have had were there for them.

That the power needed to change a nation was there for them.

"Don't let yourselves cater to the whims of others telling you what to do or that something is right! Reject even your own words!! Think about everything with all the information at your disposal, without any objective priorities, and after you've finished considering it all, stay true to the justice and courage and nerve you have left at the end!!"

Perhaps what Queen Elizard had surrendered was something very

simple. One could interpret it as the most important thing, the most crucial element for a democracy.

"…I know you're all tired of the bigwigs doing whatever they want and having to pay the price for their actions, aren't you?"

It was a single, tiny vote.

But the people now held the power to influence an entire nation, and the queen of England, Elizard, shouted to them.

"It's time for a national general election from right out of the age of warlords!!"

At that time.

…In one place, a boy looked up. He didn't know whether this emergency was from some sudden terrorism or a war. He'd been dragged outside by the arm by someone from the military, then brought on a vehicle into this movie theater. Warned that they'd be shot if they left the building, all the boy could do was tremble alone in the darkness. But when he heard the voice ringing inside his head, he slowly stood.

…I can run away, or I can give it to someone else.

He confirmed to himself what he had learned. Fighting was only one of many choices. The voice in his head had told him several times to think for himself and make his own decision, but…

I will fight.

That was the conclusion he came to.

As he headed up the stairway passage in the dark movie theater and to the exit, the boy encountered his parents. When they looked at his face, they weren't surprised. They just gave him a single small nod.

I want to fight!!

The boys, all thinking the same thing, opened the exit door and burst outside.

Past the final line, beyond which lay the threat of death.

Whether or not they had strength wasn't an issue.

The courage they had, to take that one step, was something that only existed in their hearts.

...In one place, a soldier who had confined many people inside a large hotel clenched his fist, trembling. He'd thought, acted, and cooperated with the coup d'état for Britain's sake in his own way. And now they seemed to want him to stop the coup in order to save its leader. What had he been fighting for this entire time?

The soldier rested his back against a wall and slid down to the ground. No longer willing to fight, he watched as the entrance door of the hotel opened before his eyes and the residents of London poured out of it. They'd probably go on to become heroes like the queen said. But for a puppet who'd been cooperating with the usurpers until now, he hadn't the right.

But then it happened.

Someone walked over in front of the crouching soldier. The person squatted down. Facing him as though leveling their stare with a small child's, they talked to him.

He was probably one of the people confined to the hotel. The person, a man in his middle years, seemed to have tried to resist their tyranny to protect his family. The proper hero said this to the villain who had confined him until now:

"We need your strength. Let's fight together. You were driving an armored car, right? Please, use that to take us to the battlefield."

For some moments, the soldier ruminated on his words in silence. Eventually, he took the key to the armored car out of his pants pocket and stood up, once again, on his own two feet.

...In a certain place, the boss of a certain UK sorcerer's society heaved a sigh. Nearby, a young girl of about twelve was almost appalled at what had become an incredibly absurd situation, from the magic trade's point of view.

"What should we do, boss?"

"Moron. What, you were hoping you could leave everything to your youth and jump into the fray? She said that if we don't need it, we can give it back. So just do that."

"Couldn't we also use this change to analyze the Curtana?"

"If we do anything underhanded, that crowned hag is gonna blow her top. Let's stay out of things this time and observe the places that aren't being watched anymore, from the outside."

"All right. But, boss, your little sister, Patricia, just ran off somewhere with her chest all puffed up."

"Get her back here, you idiot!!" called out an unusually flustered voice, ringing through the midnight London streets.

...In a particular place, a girl named Bayloupe, who belonged to an organization called New Light, sat up, her body covered in wounds. After losing the battle with the Puritans, they'd brought her to a cathedral to be healed and corralled, but when the coup d'état had begun, they'd thrown her into some strange hidden room.

She took a marker out of a tidy desk nearby, then drew an impromptu magic circle to activate a communication spell.

It wasn't worth it to think about where she might be calling.

"Do you hear me, Lesser?"

"You betcha, Bayloupe. Florice and Lancis are connected, too."

The answer came back immediately.

"So for real, what do we do?"

"I'm not entirely sure..." Bayloupe stood slowly, scratching her head a little with a sigh. "Well, the whole coup-accomplice thing is way past its expiration date now...But it's our creed to do things that will benefit the UK first and foremost, right? In that case, we can't be ashamed or worried about our reputation. We have to act."

...In another place, the servants and gardeners who had worked at Buckingham Palace poured onto the battlefield. Professionals, civilians, beings out of place—the gap between them and the pros had been bridged completely. Now, as long as they had the courage to take that first step, they could fight equally.

"Princess Vilian!!"

"Are you safe, Your Highness?! Are you hurt?!"

Suddenly surrounded, the third princess was completely perplexed. Secretly, she'd been thinking to herself how different the queen, her mother, was acting, and how much sense it made that she could gather so many people together. But she'd never stopped to think about the people who would rally around her.

"...But...why...?"

Therefore, her question was an honest one.

The servants had saved her in Folkestone. They'd helped her in the subway tunnel. But now it was different. Their hearts should have all been focusing on the queen now.

Then why would they take a detour all the way over here?

"Royal family, servants—it doesn't matter anymore," she said. "Everyone needs to decide for themselves how they'll use this power. You all placed your hope in me, and I ran away on my own. I couldn't help you at all in the end. You needn't feel obligated to flatter me like this..."

"Her Majesty the queen told us to think freely and choose for ourselves," one of the servants said, looking squarely at Vilian. "Will you let us use it? The courage we couldn't show you during the coup d'état or in the subway tunnel!! Not one of us wants you to be hurt, and yet we couldn't take up our weapons and fight for you in the end. We're a band of fools!! So please, just this once! This one time, please, let us fight alongside you!!"

Upon hearing those words, Vilian felt ashamed of herself.

This was the virtue of the third princess?

She hadn't even tried to learn of these earnest feelings that had been living right next to her. The title was greater than she deserved.

"...Then I will use this power for my own sake as well," said Vilian, reaffirming her two-handed grip on her crossbow.

...And added, to herself, that it was for the sake of the future that she would walk alongside these people.

"Y-you..."

The second princess, Carissa, Curtana Original in hand, growled.

In response, the queen regnant, Elizard, assumed a barehanded stance, then grinned like a president proud of the corporation she'd built in a single generation.

"Quite a revolution, right? If we're going to change history, we have to get everyone pumped up for it. Nobody will follow you if your methods only make the privileged class happy."

The old and new heads of state glared at each other from point-blank range.

But while Carissa was furious, Elizard's expression looked relaxed. "Your childish games are over. It's time to show you what *statecraft* truly means."

"Cut the crap!! What you're doing is giving weapons to powerless citizens and sending them to the battlefield, while you watch alone from the safety of your throne, indulging in pleasure!! Are you so attached to your own privileges that you would force the citizens you're supposed to protect to take more power than they know what to do with and use them as shields?!"

"...Why won't you realize *that's* the way an arrogant monarch thinks?"

As Carissa raged, her mother's smile faded.

But it wasn't because Carissa had overpowered her.

It was the opposite. The queen had stopped smiling because she was about to overpower *her*.

"Who decided normal people couldn't hold the Curtana's power? Who decided the nation would collapse if the new queen didn't have the Curtana Original and retain total control over the country?! Winning the war with the Curtana, then setting yourself up to be stopped by the ideas of the masses—it sure sounds convenient. But in the end, your privilege as head of state, the only thing that could use the Curtana Original's incredible power, had you caught in its spell the whole time!! A small change like that will only cause distortions. If you really want a revolution to bend this nation out of its current shape, then you cannot fear how that will change your own position!!"

"What...did you say...?!"

"I'm saying this as a concerned mother—a lecture for some brat's stupid suicidal wish. And...one more thing. You gave up on this great nation far too easily. Now you'll learn that its ninety million people think so much of you that they'd choose to become heroes to save you!!"

It happened at the same time as the queen spoke.

A huge *whump* rang out. No sooner had Carissa realized it than the servants and gardeners, the people who knew next to nothing about sorcery, created an incredible march. Their footsteps had come together to form a grand threat.

Yes:

The people of Britain, assembled under their flag, the Union Jack, in order to protect their nation.

5

Index, covered in mud from the aftermath of the bunker cluster and swaying on her feet, referred to the knowledge of the 103,000 grimoires in her head. But even as she analyzed the spells pertaining to the Curtana Original, she was purely captivated by the spectacle.

Fighting in the middle of her view were Carissa, with the Curtana Original, and the barehanded Elizard, who had discarded her weapon.

And, as if to protect the empty-handed queen, or perhaps to be her weapons, a crowd of figures had fluttered into the sky. They weren't only mere sorcerers: A maid who clearly knew nothing about sorcery aimed for Carissa from a spot over ten meters in the air, and an office worker in a suit knocked away a giant stake created from debris. Scenes from the normal world and the magical one were intersecting, mixing, creating a stage unlike anything Index had ever seen.

As she watched, she saw the Puritan sorcerers, previously fallen but having received aid from the knights, stand up on their own two feet again. Either they, too, did so thanks to the queen's Union Jack spell, or they did so out of their pride as professional sorcerers, unable to stay down while amateurs were out there fighting with everything they had.

The queen watched the large force, centered around Kaori Kanzaki, Acqua, and the Knight Leader, head for Carissa as well. She smiled tauntingly. "Come on, now, Carissa! You don't look well! I'll admit, you had the upper hand in a fight between the Original and the Second...but how long can you hold on in a ninety-million-to-one game of tug-of-war?!"

"Enough prattling!! This...isn't...enough to shake the Curtana Original! Even now, my Curtana...may have lost some strength from going out of control thanks to your subway ploy, but I'm still holding on to all eighty percent of the power it has left!!"

"Indeed. But if your focus slips, even for an instant, ninety million people will snatch away all its power. Try not to get worked up, and don't neglect any of the attacks coming at you!!"

"!! Was that what you were after, you damn schemer?!"

With London teetering on the edge of darkness, completely normal people like students and sales clerks ran toward them, a continuous stream of reinforcements. Some had decided it would be difficult to cross the distance fast enough, so instead dozens of bullets of light streaked in sharp arcs from the distant skies toward the second princess.

"It's like a massive volunteer army interrupted you during a massive, precise magic ritual being performed at a giant shrine. The more control you lose over your power, the more it'll strengthen our forces. Don't forget that."

"It's all a sham!! No matter how many people arrive, they're less than twenty percent of my total power! I hold eighty percent of it, which means they can't defeat me, so!!"

Despite redistributing the Curtana's power and bestowing telesma unto them, that wasn't enough for people to skillfully handle their newfound supernatural powers. A sorcerer's knowledge was still required to understand how to alter that power and what needed to be controlled.

Of course, a mere civilian wouldn't have anything like that.

So who on earth was providing the support for them?

"I see. Then I can't leave it up to the people alone. What? I was always meant to stand in the field, not sit on a throne—and to be honest, I'm actually having fun just playing this game with you."

"?! You…That power…!! You already threw away the Curtana Second!!"

"You dolt. The queen is a member of the British citizenry, too. She has the right to cast an honest vote, same as anyone else. I may only have my fists to fight with now, but if you don't mind, I will take my spot on the front lines of the greatest stage!!"

Index's gaze was fixed on a single point:

The queen regnant, Elizard.

If anyone could pull off this feat, it was her. When she equally distributed power from the Curtana to the whole nation, she'd applied the communication spell she used for her speech to add all the telesma itself to it. By changing its traits to respond to the users' thoughts and by accepting the telesma adjusted to be conveniently safe for them and stable enough that they wouldn't go out of control, only then did the civilians gain the ability to use the power they'd obtained to perform the actions they imagined.

Putting it into words was simple. Even Index once had apparently guided Komoe Tsukuyomi to indirectly use healing magic (though she was in John's Pen mode, so the memory was unusually hazy considering she had perfect recall). But that sort of thing worked only because it was a one-to-one relationship.

Guiding the entire populace of the United Kingdom, all ninety million people, at the same time, and continuing to maintain enough stability so that not a single one would be caught in his or her own power running rampant—it would have been impossible for Index even if she had the 103,000 grimoires at her disposal to their fullest.

And that wasn't even the most amazing thing.

The students and office workers who had gathered at Buckingham Palace were now witnessing strange, fantastic things, all while fighting with the power they'd gotten from Elizard. They'd probably each try to interpret the supernatural phenomena they were seeing in their own way.

——Maybe some people thought they'd awakened to hidden powers within them.

——It was also possible some believed this had happened because their horoscope was past awesome.

——Some probably believed Elizard was an alien queen who came to Earth on a spaceship.

——Some might even decide they were borrowing power from the strange dinosaur under Loch Ness.

But there was one thing Index could say about all those theories:

Not a single one of the ninety million citizens would come to the correct answer that it was magic.

Unlike Index, who had guided Komoe Tsukuyomi by pushing her grimoires' knowledge to the forefront, Queen Elizard was thoroughly concealing any such traces of magic. She had it creep within their minds and let them use it freely, but she wouldn't let them come near its true nature. In doing so, she'd even removed the greatest risk, that of a grimoire's knowledge corrupting a civilian's mind.

Index looked around at the maids and chefs flitting about in the sky.

They wouldn't realize what it was they were truly using.

And they'd probably be satisfied with that. They were far beyond thinking about how it made sense or how it worked. It was a matter of fundamental emotion—and they'd all approach this one-night-only Halloween party with everything they had.

That was Elizard.

The true queen, flowing with many sorceries, in charge of this nation, the headquarters of English Puritanism.

What if...?

As the girl with perfect memory watched this fight, she suddenly thought of something else that she'd never bothered to think about before:

Is this one of the other reasons I was created? To support all this...?

Touma Kamijou had been watching the battle, too.

A maid, carrying a giant sword from a wounded knight, swung it around mightily. Dozens of police officers flung out, sending kicks flying at a huge, spinning, bladelike debris object, knocking it away instead.

Carissa, getting worked up as she tried to contain the Curtana's power, lost the sharp wit granted by her military talent, and as she swung her sword around with reckless abandon, she was slowly being cornered.

The actual sorcerers weren't taking it lying down, either.

The former Roman Orthodox sisters, numbering over two hundred, brandished their weapons as a single group. A giant golem, comprised of objects from all around, stopped an attack from a debris object. And just as he noticed a military transport plane had flown by in the midnight sky, a rain of rune cards poured down, creating a flaming titan as they scattered.

This is incredible..., thought Kamijou honestly.

It wasn't just the turnabout Queen Elizard had brought. His eyes were pure and sparkling as he watched all the heroes running to the scene, practically burying the Buckingham Palace grounds under them.

There're just so many actors that they're upstaging me, Index,

Kanzaki, and even Acqua and everyone else! What's with this country? How can everyone be a main character?

The real core of what he was seeing probably wasn't something trivial like Queen Elizard or the Union Jack.

Power was just another method to win.

The people of this nation, who had grabbed hold of that power and decided of their own volition to stand up and fight, were another, and, in fact, the core of everything.

Kamijou considered Carissa: the second princess, wielding the Curtana Original, brandishing one massive attack after another. At the eye of the great typhoon called a battlefield, she was never swallowed by the waves of the masses. But somehow, it gave Kamijou a lonely impression. For some reason, the term *monarch* didn't fit her right now.

In truth, Carissa probably knew as well.

Knew how much radiance slept within the people of Britain.

That was why she'd grown so desperate to protect them.

Maybe that's all this battle was, when you got right down to it, he thought.

But in the process, she'd relied too much on her military affairs. It wasn't only the people attacking the nation from outside with the intent to destroy—she'd tried to hurt even the people the nation carried within it. In other words, like an extremely powerful magnum hurting the shooter's hand.

I'll protect her.

Touma Kamijou gripped his fist once again on this battlefield.

I swear I'll drag her out of this stupid negative cycle.

And then, once again, he stepped forward on his own two feet, onto the hellish battlefield of the Curtana Original's overwhelming slashes and the whirlwinds of diversionary attacks from the giant debris objects.

Then it happened.

"STCTU! (Shift the Curtana's trajectory upward!) SAAARTET!! (Stop all attacks and redistribute the excess telesma!!)"

As soon as Index's cry rang out, Carissa's arms, holding the

Curtana Original, bounced unnaturally. Spell Interception—Index, who had analyzed the inner workings of her magic, had interrupted in an attempt to block it.

"Ugh…?!" Carissa gritted her teeth and hastily tried to bring the sword back under control.

She was probably frozen for only a few seconds at most.

Kamijou clenched his right hand again, but he wouldn't make it from here.

So he took the straightforward approach and asked allies for help—in order to pour all his strength into this greatest night.

"Acqua!!" he shouted.

The powerful mercenary responded. Kamijou kicked off the ground and jumped a few dozen centimeters into the air, and Acqua thrust out with his sword into the space between him and the ground. Kamijou planted his feet onto the giant sword's flat side, landing on it like a surfboard.

Kamijou and Acqua didn't need to exchange words, much less have a strategy session. They didn't have the time—and they both knew what they had to do without saying it.

Keeping up appearances with words wasn't needed anymore. Kamijou's resolution spoke entirely to that idea, and because Acqua had accepted the weight of that resolve, he gave his aid to someone who had once been his enemy.

"…!!"

Acqua gave a short exhalation, then whipped Ascalon around in a horizontal arc as hard as he could.

He may have been wounded, but it was still the full power of one of less than twenty saints in the world. Considering that, it would be obvious what would happen to Kamijou, who was standing on the side of the sword.

Then there was a huge *boom!!*

Touma Kamijou's body, borrowing Acqua's Herculean force, shot away like a cannonball.

Wha…?

In that moment, Carissa was, without exaggeration, dumbstruck.

The Curtana Original was about to go berserk, and its control still hadn't returned to her. And the boy, with a right hand that could cancel out all magic, had plunged among his many allies, shooting straight for her.

There was maybe 0.1 seconds before he arrived.

But in that single instant, the second princess, Carissa, saw it:

Touma Kamijou's face as he squeezed that fist ever so tightly—and the reassuring grin plastered on it.

Wha-pooooom!!

After flying a distance of over thirty meters, Kamijou's fist connected directly with the Curtana Original.

The kingmaking sword, the Curtana Original, shattered from that one attack.

Carissa didn't have the time to check and see.

The fist that had broken the sword plunged without mercy right into her face.

Like metal balls hanging from strings, this time, the momentum all transferred to Carissa, shooting her off into the night sky like a cannonball. She collided once with Buckingham Palace's nearly collapsed ceiling, then bounced upward on a different trajectory, flying farther and farther away.

Kamijou heard an awful noise from his wrist, his elbow, and his shoulder, as though the bones had all dislocated in a chain.

But before he could feel the pain and his face could twist in anguish, he proceeded over ten meters farther before finally landing. Still, he obviously couldn't stand on his own feet now, and as he fell down, he kept going, bouncing a few times.

Is it…over…?

Kamijou tried to speak, his body covered in wounds, but it came out only as a groan.

But he didn't need to ask the question—the answer had been shown before his eyes.

There was a shrill *keeeen*.

He looked and saw that the end of the sword, broken in the middle, had thrust into the black soil plowed by many an attack. As he watched it, it began to crumble, as though a mountain of time was weathering it, and eventually it flowed into the night breeze and disappeared.

The Curtana Original had been lost.

That meant the second princess, Carissa, had been defeated—and this long coup d'état had ended.

EPILOGUE
State and Mastermind: Another Strong Enemy
Next_Step.

The coup d'état was over.

With it, the power granted to the people by the queen's spell, Union Jack, was lost as well, and everyone returned to being normal citizens. Calm now that they'd lost their strength (or perhaps relaxed now that they had the freedom to think about other things, since the fight was over), the students and office workers eventually looked at the dreadful scene before their eyes, beginning to cast dubious gazes around.

"…I don't mean to brag, but I really went big with this one, eh?" Queen Elizard grinned in self-deprecation, once again picking up the Curtana Second she'd discarded earlier. The legendary sword was now missing its entire blade after the fight with the Original. Just as she was considering having that boy thoroughly break it, she noticed a figure suddenly approach.

The Knight Leader.

"It pains me to say this, having been a factor in the coup's inception… but what shall we do now?"

"You going to worry about stuff in the past forever, you bloody idiot? I thought British chivalry dictates you boast as much as you can whenever you stand before noblewomen." The queen snorted. "Besides, nothing's wrong with what happened today. All the civilians who took part will try to interpret these strange events in their own ways, but the spell's construction will never be exposed. It'll just be a good memory they can recount to their grandkids in the future."

"But we cannot reject the possibility that someone may arrive at the conclusion that it was magic."

"We'll cross that bridge when we come to it," answered Elizard immediately. It wasn't that she hadn't thought about it; it was the opposite. "If that happens, we'll simply have to admit it. Admit that magic exists in this world, and that it works in the shadows to protect them every day. We can call it a rebirth of the magical nation of Britain."

"But that would be—"

"History is ever-changing. There's no rule anywhere saying sorcery has to be hidden from people forever. Come now—it's not like we're the first anyway. There are even some African tribes where certain sorcerers make decisions for their tribes—in other words, they let them take the reins of government. That means such a form of government is far from impossible. It's one historical what-if and a revolution away from becoming reality."

Coming from Elizard—who had just faced off with a "revolution" of Carissa's making after the princess had almost completely taken over the country—those words held an incredible sense of realism to them.

Meanwhile, she, the one involved in all this, continued with a jovial tone.

"...Anyway. Let's go grab Carissa from wherever she got blown away to. Hm? Wait, now where did that medal-deserving boy go?"

The third princess, Vilian, having gone a short distance away from the Puritans and knights who had stopped the coup, looked to and fro. She was searching for someone, but she couldn't find him at all. Eventually, she ceased her efforts and said to herself, her face clouded with resignation:

"...Once again, William has already left, without saying a word..."

"..." The Knight Leader, who had walked up to her side, hesitated on how he should best respond. Eventually, he nodded. "There seems to be major activity in the Russian Catholic sphere. Important activity that relates to this huge overt battle between sorcery and science. It seems he's gained intelligence from a comrade who also left God's Right Seat and will act to stop this war from a different direction than the English Puritan Church intends."

"A comrade?" asked Vilian quietly. "You have as well, but everyone has gained many things in these ten years. I feel as though I am the only one who has failed to do a single thing."

It seemed to have hurt Vilian more than the others that William had left without saying good-bye. As the Knight Leader looked at her, a hint of bitterness crept into his face.

"...That bastard," he muttered under his breath. "He used his carefree position as mercenary to drop this troublesome role on me..."

"?" Vilian tilted her head in confusion—had his mumblings been out loud?

The Knight Leader hastily readopted a formal expression, then spoke again. "A certain mercenary has left me with a message. He prefaced it by explaining that I should tell you when nobody else was around to hear."

"What...did he say?"

"...'One day, once this war is over and the world is at peace, I wish to return to Britain. If it may be granted, at that time, I would like my escutcheon to decorate the hallway in Buckingham Palace like it should have always done. Until then, my sword and I will protect the emblem, so my wish is for you to repair Buckingham Palace and gain the strength to overcome the many ordeals that will likely bar your path...' Well, would that not be his way of proposing that you grow enough to be worthy of that mercenary's fealty?"

"...!" The eyes of the third princess, Vilian, went wide with surprise, but the Knight Leader had actually mixed into his message one or two things that William Orwell hadn't actually said.

...Well, he never does use enough words. Giving the original message would have come off as inconsiderate.

Only the man who'd directly received the message knew how much of it he'd given straight and how much he'd embellished. But the Knight Leader, while Vilian wasn't looking, secretly stuck out his tongue and thought, *You are very aware of my personality, and you still entrusted me with that artificial message. I'm sure you knew how I'd convey it, didn't you, William?*

Kanzaki and the members of the Born Again Amakusa-Style Crossist Church, who had finished giving aid to and evacuating the wounded, came to gather together after a short breather.

Saiji Tatemiya was the one to break the silence.

"...So Touma Kamijou ended up snatching away the best part again, eh? Your debts to him are ballooning like a loan shark, don't you think, Priestess?"

"Wha—?! You're talking like Tsuchimikado!! Th-this makes us even, doesn't it? I mean, we all worked together, so the achievements should be distributed equally. There are no debts or loans involved. Right?"

"Anyway, we decided to mobilize the erotic fallen-angel maid. Hm? Wait, you haven't done that yet...Which would be better to attack him with in this case?"

"Don't decide things for me! I never want to wear something like that ever again!! N-Nomozami, Isahaya, you too!! You're too old to be shouting, 'It's a double; it's a double'!!"

Kanzaki went on and on with her complaints, but the men in Born Again Amakusa were united in their feelings: *We've never seen the real-life legend, so please make her appear, right here, right now.*

Meanwhile, a short distance away from that commotion...

"...I-if he fought for everyone this time, then I can interpret that as me having a debt to him, too, right?" Itsuwa hissed under her breath. "In that case, I have, umm, a reason to...Hee...☆"

"Wait a minute. You may look pure, but your womanly desires are coming out now, aren't they?"

Even as Tsushima, another woman, pointed that out, Itsuwa wasn't one to give it much thought.

Then...

"*Heave, heave,* phewww...I have finally made the scene at Buckingham Palace..."

As Kanzaki turned around, thinking she'd just heard some strange-sounding Japanese, she saw Archbishop Laura Stuart, slumped exhaustedly over the horse she was on, coming her way.

"B-blast you, Elizard...As soon as you received the flag at the British Museum, you entrusted me with your warhorse and left immediately...I—I couldn't figure out the horse's movements and rhythm, and now my back, ohhh, my back..."

In contrast to the tired and battered Laura, the horse seemed displeased in his own right. He was giving a spirited, angry neigh as if to say he hated her, since they weren't compatible.

"Urgh...Thanks to that, I became completely useless. For what reason hath I come all this way, I wonder?"

"...That's what you say, but...You had a hand in this behind the scenes, didn't you? The Union Jack is a large-scale, national-level spell that has never been used before in history. Considering that, the Royal Family faction probably wouldn't have been able to activate it at their own discretion. Either you gave some sort of permission or you forced the lock open. It was one of those, wasn't it?"

Lying limply on her horse, Laura didn't confirm or deny her subordinate's assertion—she merely wore a meaningful smile on her lips.

Kanzaki suspected several things, but then Laura Stuart began searching for unexpected help.

"I can't go on...I cannot use any strength, nor can I stoppeth the horse. K-Kanzakiii...Stop the horse; help me down..."

"Huh? I—I can't. I'm not actually very good with horses."

"And you wear that?! You looketh like you come from a Wild West movie!"

"Well, no, these are just the items I need for constructing spells. I didn't do it out of any love for horseback riding— *Gwaaaahhhh?!* It's eating me—the horse is eating my ponytail!"

When she saw her black hair covered in horse drool, she screamed, but the warhorse seemed to have taken a liking to her. As he naturally stopped by Kanzaki and tried to play with her, Laura, with unsteady motions, finally got off the steed and settled her feet on the ground.

"R-right, then. In passing, where might be the boy for whom Kanzaki will wear that utterly erotic clothing? I had heard he hath come to Britain, and I wanted to see him at some point."

"Argh—for someone who waltzed in when it was all over, you're really trying to push my buttons! That boy got involved in a magical incident, so shouldn't it actually be *you* wearing the erotic fallen-angel maid outfit?!"

The second princess, Carissa, had fallen flat on a London street.

There was still a little time until daybreak. Her coup had ended, but its effects still remained, for there were no cars on this major road.

She wondered where she was.

How far away from Buckingham Palace property was she—two kilometers, three? In any case, she'd been knocked sky-high, so brilliantly far that she couldn't figure out where she was anymore.

"…" Carissa gazed at her right hand.

Her own hand, which still held on to the Curtana Original's hilt in desperate attachment even after everything that had occurred. But the sword had a cleft down the middle, and its magical power had been lost. The massive power of the angelic leader had probably already moved to the Curtana Second by now. Of course, she couldn't see that mother of hers being so attached to the power.

For a while, Carissa didn't say a word.

She'd been thinking, just a little, about ninety million people having the will to fight. Protect the people? They were so strong—outside countries poking them a few times would never cause their pride as people to plummet. This all meant, in the end, that the one most scared of the path before them was Carissa.

Then it happened.

"Ha-ha. Now, this *is* something. Never thought I'd see you of all people lying on the ground covered in blood and mud like that... But now that I'm actually looking at it, well, it's an even more enjoyable sight than I expected."

She heard a man's voice.

Carissa dragged her aching body to sit up. Somebody was there. A man in mainly red clothing. He didn't seem to have much of a trained physique, but something beyond that impression caused a strange, almost unnatural presence.

"Who...?" spat Carissa, putting strength into her right arm before remembering the Curtana Original was broken. She threw the sword hilt aside. "Who are you...?"

"If I said Fiamma of the Right, would you understand? If you still don't get it even with all these hints, it would be wise to dismantle your intelligence division and put together a new one."

"...!"

Fiamma of the Right.

The final member of God's Right Seat, which controlled the Roman Orthodox Church from the shadows and he was its most powerful member. According to reports, he'd partially destroyed St. Peter's Basilica with one attack in a dispute with the pope of Rome, who was apparently in an unpredictable state even now.

After gathering those data points in her mind, Carissa looked up, having suddenly thought of something. "The angel with whom you correspond is Michael, the LIKENESS OF GOD...The same quality the Curtana operates on— Were you after this sword?!"

"Hmm? Oh, I see, I see. Yes, that might have been another way to do it."

Carissa watched Fiamma closely as he continued, his tone of voice amused. She provoked him to see if she could get a reaction. "Unfortunately, the Curtana Original here has already lost its function, so.

If you wanted to use the chaos of the coup to sneak in and snatch it, you must be disappointed."

"Well, yes. It is indeed a terrible loss. In fact, what you suggested might have actually been easier," noted Fiamma offhandedly. He looked honestly impressed. "Eh, it wouldn't have worked anyway, right? I don't think so, at least. The quality of the power meets the requirements, but its capacity probably wouldn't hold out. As soon as I moved my mighty power into the sword, the sword would explode and that would be that."

"What…are you talking about?"

"Just some meaningless gossip. And if I may add—your guess is half-correct. I did take advantage of the chaos to come here and steal that which is preserved in the deepest annals of the English Puritan Church. But that item was not something paltry like the Curtana."

Fiamma gave her a sarcastic round of applause. "Well, maybe one-fourth correct. After all, going through the Roman Orthodox Church to make the French government beg and have them incite disorder within the United Kingdom was for this purpose."

"Wh-what?"

"Well, manipulating France and Britain into a real war, then recovering it from a burned-down London would have been fine, too. But you handled that quite excellently, you know. Thanks to your absurd game of playing house, I was able to achieve my goal without turning the capital into a storm of killing, pillaging, and rape."

Blood rushed to Carissa's head.

Without the Curtana, the second princess didn't have much in the way of direct attack magic. She could muster average power, but that wouldn't be nearly enough to challenge this man.

And even when Carissa tried to jump on him, Fiamma didn't move a finger.

There was just a massive *ga-pow!!* and a shock wave that carried her body over ten meters away.

"Hey, would you quit that? I've already achieved my lofty goals. I've no need to fight a daydreaming princess. That hag of a queen is one thing, but small fries like you I can let go."

Something giant had sprouted from near Fiamma's right shoulder. It was like a wing or an arm…It was a strange, incomprehensible object that seemed otherworldly.

"Damn. Failed partway through again. I have to say, I've acquired quite a troublesome companion." Fiamma walked over, his heels clicking on purpose.

"What was it…An item that would upstage even the Curtana? You caused this war, exploited it, and secretly tried to steal something—what was it for?!"

Carissa coughed up blood as she raged, but Fiamma didn't change his tune at all.

"You don't know?" Fiamma smiled like he was splitting his own mouth in two. Then, he spread his arms theatrically. "Just a little treasure. One that you royals *secretly* created, for that matter."

Carissa's body drew back in shock. She knew what Fiamma was referring to.

"Impossible…It actually…existed…?!"

"As I thought, they didn't tell you about it. It was sitting right there in Buckingham Palace the whole time. I was surprised myself. It was a secret item in the truest sense of the term. They may have told the sorcerers to bring everything crucial with them when your coup began, but if they didn't know about it in the first place, they couldn't have brought it," said Fiamma in a singsong voice, slowly moving the third arm that had sprouted from his right shoulder.

If he used *that thing*'s abilities to its fullest, Carissa as she was now would easily be blasted to smithereens.

"So what will you do, then? Give up and keep living or try a little harder and die?"

"Rubb…ish…"

Blood leaking from her mouth, Carissa slowly stood up.

Her body was already on an angle, and she had trouble keeping her balance, but the light in her eyes never withered.

"…I think I know now…why the pope resisted you until the end…"

"Do you? Then you can bite the bullet like he did."

Shhhwhh!! A massive burst of wind pressure assailed Carissa.

Dragging her battered body, she still tried to face forward, eyes wide open.

And then…

Gwrkkeeee!!

With a tremendous sound, a boy's right hand suddenly appeared out of nowhere and blocked Fiamma's attack.

The colossal power tried to blast the boy backward, but Carissa supported him from behind. Two sets of soles scraped across the floor, but they just managed to hold their ground.

"What the hell…are you doing…?" growled Kamijou, giving his right arm a swing to make sure it was still working. The simple act caused awful creaking noises that reached Carissa's ears; it really had affected his bones and joints.

As Kamijou ignored it and glared, Fiamma laughed.

He laughed hard, much harder than before, so hard he nearly had to hold his stomach.

"Kha-ha-ha!! What's going on? You were today's lucky constellation— and I seem to have hit the bull's-eye!! Here I thought you'd be the finishing touch. To think I'd get a double in a place like this!!"

"…Who the hell are you?" demanded Kamijou.

Fiamma didn't answer. He just laughed.

Instead, Carissa, who unsteadily pulled away from him and nearly fell face-first on the ground for it, told him: "It's Fiamma…Fiamma of the Right. God's Right Seat's leader, essentially, so."

The unexpected voice startled Kamijou.

Eventually, Fiamma looked at him again, still chuckling.

"Hey, at least let me introduce myself, will you?"

"Fiamma…"

The last of God's Right Seat, which bossed around the Roman Orthodox Church. The ringleader of this whole war. He was so important that the big war might end if they could just defeat him.

As Fiamma watched Kamijou unconsciously grip his fist more

tightly than before, he responded by moving the third arm stretching from his right shoulder. Then, almost licking his lips, he spoke up.

"Are we doing this? All right. I apologize for the unsightliness, but I'm warmed up now."

"Shut up!!"

With a shout of indignation, Kamijou began to run—and at that moment, Fiamma's third arm let out an explosive light.

Sound disappeared.

Only the right hand he'd stuck out took the fierce impact with a terrible *ga-bam!!*

When the light vanished, Kamijou and Fiamma were still glaring at each other.

That one attack alone had had enough destructive potential to wipe an everyday cathedral off the map.

"I see. I should have expected as much from that rare right hand I rightly desire. Now that I see it up close, I'm even more surprised at its singularity."

Fiamma's attack had been erased, but he seemed satisfied.

His third arm wriggled like an independent creature, writhing like an agonized snake, about to melt away into the air.

"Time is up, I see," said Fiamma as he watched Kamijou, who had his attention on the third arm. "Don't be so surprised. That right hand you use is similar to it. Actually, both are incomplete, so they're the spitting image of each other."

Then, Fiamma's third arm made a much more violent movement than before. For the first time, he gave a slight frown. "Well, I suppose greed is never a good thing. Let's stop here for today. Killing you now would be a simple matter, but I'm not so attached to the idea that I'd risk the slim chance of you destroying the Soul Arm I stole…I will obtain it one day in the near future anyway."

"A Soul Arm…you stole…?"

"It's pretty great. You want to see?"

The next thing he knew, Fiamma was gripping something in his hand. It was a lock made of metal.

It looked like a dial combination lock, but it had too many numbers. Actually, there were English letters carved into it *instead* of numbers. There shouldn't have been enough room to engrave all twenty-six on such a small ring, but they were all there, like some kind of unnatural optical illusion. Maybe it wasn't that each letter was engraved on it—maybe it was like a ring-shaped liquid crystal that displayed only necessary letters.

What is that...? Kamijou frowned in suspicion.

"No!! Don't let him use that!!" shouted Carissa tensely.

But the likeness of Michael didn't listen. He rolled the Soul Arm into the palm of his right hand, then used his thumb by itself to spin the dial attached to the cylindrical lock.

A moment later...

...there was a thundering *boom!!*

Something white burst out from below, tearing through the asphalt.

Had it passed through the subway or water pipes, too? A circle of asphalt about twenty meters across, centered on the blast location, pushed out of the ground and blew away. Kamijou had been standing right on the edge, and his body fell backward as Carissa came dangerously close to falling into the underground space.

Its destructive force was immeasurable.

But that wasn't what had surprised Kamijou.

Wha...?!

The thing that had suddenly attacked them—

Was a person.

A girl with silver hair and green eyes.

A sister wearing a teacup-like white habit embroidered with gold thread.

Yes.

"...In...dex...?!" shouted Kamijou in spite of himself.

Why had she appeared at Fiamma's signal? And how had she created an impossible amount of destruction given her clearly normal arm strength? —How did a girl who shouldn't have been able to use magic receive magic-like assistance?

There were two things to answer this myriad of queries.

The first was Fiamma's words.

"The safety attached to the Index, John's Pen…You could call this Soul Arm an external controller for it. Only the leaders of the Royal Family and Puritan factions possess such a treasure. Still, using it risks corruption from the original copies, so it seems they were really keeping it as an absolute last resort…But didn't you think it was strange? That despite how much she wished for it, why they placed an Index of Forbidden Books firmly into a city of science with no insurance? How is that possible? And not to mention that archbishop who created this cruel system."

The second thing was Index's own words.

"Yes. I am a libr—ary of grimoires be—longing to the English Pur—itan Church's—0th parish—Necessarius, the Church of Nece—ssary Evils. My official na—me is Index Librorum Prohibitorum, bu—t my abbreviated nick—name—*zizizizazazagagagagagaga*."

As Index muttered along impassively, she suddenly began to shake massively and unnaturally, and then she collapsed softly to the ground.

"Index!!"

"Oh? Was there damage to John's Pen as well? Well, it is a shame I won't be able to fully control her physical body, but this much should suffice…If I do some precise adjustments on the Soul Arm to raise its 'output,' I should gain free access to the 103,000 grimoires' knowledge."

Fiamma's face looked like he'd gotten a toy that turned out more boring than he'd expected.

"What did you do…? What did you do to Index?!" shouted Kamijou, voice swelling louder than it ever had before.

Fiamma spread his arms and shrugged. "I don't know. Any inadequate maintenance is your fault."

"You bastard!!"

Kamijou clenched his fist and began to run toward Fiamma, meaning to punch him away for real this time.

But before he could, Fiamma of the Right moved.

He gave an order to his third arm and fired a huge flash of light at Kamijou.

"Right, well. I need to pay a quick visit to Russia and pick up the 'materials' left by the angel, too. Until then, I leave your right arm and its management to you."

"...?!"

Kamijou automatically held back the flash attack with his right hand, but by the time his vision cleared, Fiamma was already nowhere to be found. All that was left were the blood-covered Carissa, the unconscious Index, and debris from the asphalt she'd broken through.

Patter-patter-patter-patter!! The sound of several sets of footsteps rang through the building.

Sasha Kreutzev, member of the Russian Catholic Church's Annihilatus, brought her head up in surprise. After placing on the table the thick book she'd been reading and taking a sip of the black tea that had been spiked with an ungodly amount of brandy, she slowly stood from her chair.

She looked toward the window. Vasilisa was there, peering outside.

"This isn't good. I *told* them a Roman-Russian alliance would be foolhardy. It looks like God's Right Seat's influence has gotten to the Russian Catholic Church, too. They have orders to capture you, Sasha, and now our own fellow Russian Catholic devotees have mobilized."

"Question one. Could it be Bishop Nikolai Tolstoj, wrapped up in that long thing, trying to profit from the chaos again?"

"Would *you* happen to have any ideas why that piece of shit would be tailing you?"

"..." Sasha fell silent for a moment at the question.

Thinking from a magical perspective, from a Crossist one...It must have been that time with the massive quantity of telesma that had apparently gotten into her body at some point. Sasha had no recollection of it whatsoever, but as far as she could learn from the traces…enough had been temporarily stored inside her to hold an entire angel.

Vasilisa's expression turned rather serious, too. "Hmm. You're just too gosh-darn adorable, Sasha. Maybe that's why he's trying to pull you away from me…If that's the case, beheading that old fart would be too good for him."

"Ignoring that absurd opinion to answer you—this is probably the result of the Roman Orthodox Church wanting to capture me for some reason and bargaining for me with the Russian Catholic Church now that it's a puppet. Question two—what do you intend to do now?" asked Sasha in a brusque tone. "To explain further—though Bishop Nikolai Tolstoj may have ambitions elsewhere, should the Russian Catholic Church officially order it, you may be obligated to obey him. If you cooperate with me any further, you will be punished alongside me."

"*Mweeen!*" Vasilisa made an incomprehensible noise.

She took an old sheaf of papers out of her personal bag. They looked like some kind of work-related contracts. She may have been rotten, but she *was* her superior, so there were a lot of painful-looking documents in there.

"Hi-yah!"

Rp-rp-rp-rp-rp-rp-rp-rp-rp!! Vasilisa suddenly started tearing up all the contracts into little pieces.

"Wha—? You— Question three, what on earth do you think you're doing?!"

"Well, um, betraying the Russian Catholic Church, rebelling against the state, and breaking my contract to various state-related people, I guess?"

As Sasha's mouth gaped like a goldfish in shock, Vasilisa responded with a creepy wink.

"Yay! We made an enemy of a pretty big part of the world, yeah?! Now I don't need to listen to the Church's orders, so I can be on your side forever and ever!"

"A-are you drunk? Question four, are you in your right mind right now?"

"Oh, poo. Don't mind me—get out of here already. Go! Look, I packed everything you'd need for your escape, like clothes and money, into this bag here, so take it and escape out the window!"

As Vasilisa continued the conversation on her own, she opened the window, took out a different bag than the first, then hurled it at Sasha, who was hesitating by the window. *Splop!!* came the incredible sound as Sasha vanished out the window, thrown clear outside the building.

Underneath was a deep layer of fresh snow...so she wouldn't get hurt too much when she fell.

Vasilisa sighed slightly—and at that very moment, the door and its lock were destroyed and the remnants were thrown into the room.

She looked over to see a bewitching woman come forward—another member of Annihilatus.

"Oh my. I had heard Sasha Kreutzev had come here."

Skogssnua.

The name came from a Russian fairy. They lived in the forest, weren't particularly aggressive, and sometimes fell in love with humans...but their sexual activities were so forceful that they'd cause their partners to die.

The woman wore a straitjacket—and not the functional kind, either, but one made of lace and leather with maximum emphasis on sex appeal, stretched tightly over her upper body. She was an expert in every possible form of sex magic.

"Oh! That is an attractive outfit, very much my type...but for you to be dispatched to the one staying faithful to Sasha, this must be one of that piece of shit Nikolai's pranks, hmm?"

"Well, I wanted to 'play' with this Sasha Kreutzev myself, too. I'm not currently in the mood for the whole old-lady thing, but I have to do what I need to or else I'll be in trouble. The higher-ups seem to want to cozy up to the Roman Orthodox Church, after all. Sorry about this, but would you mind giving up?"

"You've got me," said Vasilisa, her tone leisurely. Then, she put an index finger to her lips and asked, "Oh yes—why, do you think, did they make me the coordinator for Annihilatus?"

"Eh?"

"...It's because I'm the strongest one in the organization."

Roar!! Something invisible started to storm and swirl.

As the something spurted out from Vasilisa, Skogssnua frowned.

"Man-eating woman in a one-legged house, please grant me strength for the sake of your unfortunate, faithful daughter," sang Vasilisa in an unnaturally youthful voice.

Vasilisa's name originated from a heroine in one of Russia's most famous folktales. The unfortunate heroine is abused by her stepmother and older sister, and a man-eating witch living in the forest takes a liking to the girl's faithfulness, which continues to remind her of her own late mother. Instead of taking the girl's life, the witch gives her several magical items, allowing her to achieve happiness.

"Man-eating woman in a one-legged house."

Softly:

Vasilisa removed her index finger from her lips. Then, as though grabbing a huge glass of brandy, she curled her fingers in the air, palm up.

In order to execute, by the hands of the witch, *the way by which to achieve happiness.*

"Please give me the death's-head lamp, the death's-head lamp to spit flames and burn my faithless stepmother and sister to death."

Ba-boom!!

With an explosion, the two sorcerers began their battle.

After falling into the snow from the window, Sasha Kreutzev decided to run along the freezing land, even as it pulled hair out of the back of her head, in order to not waste Vasilisa's determination.

The temperature was negative-five Celsius.

And this was still on the warmer side. Though it was moderate for Russia, the temperatures around here boasted minimums as low as negative-twenty Fahrenheit, which could stop some tanks dead on their treads.

While using magic to maintain the bare minimum thermal insulation and heat retention, Sasha advanced across the land as the snow burst up off the ground and danced in the air. When a gale blew across and whipped up the lighter snow, it could completely blanket your vision in white.

And yet her pursuers had a clear read on Sasha's position.

A light flickered in the distance. No sooner had she seen it than a crater-size clump of snow right by her blew into the air. Sasha quickly dropped into hiding. A second, then a third explosion hit, caused by long-distance projectile weapons.

She knew that as they prevented her from moving, another team was approaching her in the meantime. Sleipnirs—eight-legged metal horses designed to be used in these frozen lands. Riding on these Soul Arms was probably a pursuit team comprised of Annihilatus members.

At this rate...!!

As Sasha gritted her teeth, someone plucked her up by her slender arm. The person yanked her into a standing position before addressing her.

"Over here. Seriously, this is getting annoying."

It was an odd woman with all-yellow clothing covering her whole body. She wore thick makeup on her face and even had piercings on it.

Her outfit, of course, was unnatural, but...

"Q-question one: Where did you—?"

"Over there. The cave entrance is hidden under the snow," said the woman in yellow as she tugged on Sasha's arm. "I knew it was a good route choice to go to Russia instead of Britain. Considering the situation, I knew that bastard Fiamma would come looking for this girl."

"U-um...Question two: Who are—?"

"Where did I come from, who am I—what are you, some sort of novice sightseer who has to be right up the ass of your tour guide at all times? Where were you going to escape to if I hadn't shown up, anyway?"

The words caught in Sasha's throat as she fell silent, her expression one that would make Vasilisa writhe in pure glee.

The thought *Run away, run away, just run away now* had been at the front of her mind. She hadn't been thinking about an actual plan at all. Of course, being suddenly marked in Russia meant you couldn't blame her.

But the woman in yellow looked clearly fed up. "Whatever. Russia is feeling the effects of God's Right Seat thanks to the Roman-Russian alliance. Anyway, you won't be able to rest until you leave this country."

"..."

"The closest border to us is the Elizarina Alliance of Independent Nations. It's not like I have an obligation to help you this much, but I can't stand the people who want to get their hands on you. If it'll make them foam at the mouth, then sure, I'll do something I'm not used to."

"Question three: What is the Elizarina Alliance of Independ—?"

"I told you: I'm not your tour guide. Anyway, it's a group of small countries that declared independence from Russia recently because they didn't like its methods. In there, it won't matter if you're with the Russian Catholic Church or the Roman Orthodox Church."

"No, not that...To repeat question three—we must be of the utmost importance for the Roman-Russian faction to retrieve. If we head for another nation, would it not cause a pretext for war—no, for a military act of invasion?"

"Too late...An attack has already begun on the Independent Nations with Russian forces at the forefront."

Sasha gasped in spite of herself.

"Align with the Roman Church and you'll win wars—that's how the overeager Russians seem to be taking it," the woman in yellow continued. "They've already started invading the Independent Nations, declaring themselves rulers of a new world. Even if we stayed here, they'll be fodder for indiscriminate bombings soon enough."

"But that's...However...Answer one—that shouldn't be a good enough reason to bring in the tinder that will have a one-hundred-percent chance of burning into tragedy."

"It's the opposite, you blockhead," said the yellow-clothed woman, cutting down Sasha's viewpoint without mercy. "If most-wanted people like us are in their territory, the Russians won't be able to indiscriminately bomb, shell, and massacre. They can't kill us when they need to capture us, after all. At the same time, the English Puritan Church and Academy City want to stop the ambitions of God's Right Seat—or rather, Fiamma of the Right—and this will make their eyes naturally shift toward the Elizarina Alliance of Independent Nations. It's a great chance. We can make them intervene in the international society and pretend we don't know anything. As a result, there's a fair possibility we'll shackle the Russians and prevent their violence."

"Question four: In that case—?"

"Well, we will be living where we're going away to hide. Paying the rent is only polite."

Sasha didn't know who the woman was, but she'd made an unforeseen ally. She nodded honestly.

Then the saffron woman noticed Sasha's clothing and her face crinkled, appalled. "Anyway, what is with that straitjacket? We're going into hiding, so couldn't you put on something a little less conspicuous?"

"Answer two—in terms of clothes, I don't believe someone wearing all yellow has a right to say that. Anyway, my boss gave me a set of things I'll need," she said, opening the bag Vasilisa had given her and pulling out the change of clothes.

It was the dress suit worn by Magical Powered Kanamin.

"Wait a minute, why are you trying to go back? …What? You're going to give your asshole boss a piece of your mind? Hey, wait, stop, stop stop stop stop stop stop!!"

Touma Kamijou stood there in a stupor.

As Index lay on the road, many people had come around them. Even the English Puritan Church's professional sorcerers had bewilderment on their faces.

The unconscious Index wasn't waking back up, no matter how long they waited.

Kaori Kanzaki, who had knelt beside her, looked up at him and said, "Her breathing and pulse are normal. There shouldn't be any threat to her life."

Hearing that didn't put Kamijou's mind at ease. What on earth had happened? His understanding hadn't caught up yet.

"…What is this?" came a voice.

It wasn't Kamijou. The words belonged to Stiyl Magnus, who was edging closer to Laura Stuart a short distance away. The first thing he'd seen after finally joining up with everyone else was Index lying there.

"What is this?! Just how…how much more are you going to deceive people? How much more are you going to hurt that girl before you're satisfied?!"

All notions of superior and subordinate gone, Stiyl grabbed Laura by her collar and seethed. But there was no major change in Laura's expression.

"Give it a rest. We needed to place several safeties on the Index to secure her basic human rights," interrupted Elizard from beside them.

Stiyl remained silent, so the queen continued. "If we hadn't created a way to control her remotely from London, we would have always needed to consider the threat that someone might make off with the Index. For example, we would have had to confine her in a Tower of London room forever or cut off her limbs to prevent her from escaping."

"Are you…being serious?"

"The 103,000 grimoires cannot be managed through our personal feelings alone. If we hadn't made her fully controllable and the mechanism safe, should she be caught in a crisis, we wouldn't be able to argue against the opinions that it would be safer just to kill her because the Index is a threat…An extreme argument, but to stop it, we had to prepare several safety mechanisms."

"Shit!!" swore Stiyl, shoving Laura violently away.

What's going on? wondered Kamijou.

Hadn't everyone been brought together as one just a few moments ago? Wasn't this supposed to have a happy ending? Just because that Fiamma of the Right guy showed up, everything turned into this. Everything scattered apart in an instant, and now they were glaring at one another.

The final member of God's Right Seat.

Fiamma of the Right...

"We could never have predicted that the Imagine Breaker would so easily destroy the Collar, an important factor comprising John's Pen, from the planning phase," explained Elizard to the still-frozen Kamijou. "We'd never tested using the remote-control Soul Arm while the Collar was broken like that, and this was how it malfunctioned. If Fiamma accesses the knowledge in the Index of Prohibited Books now, it will likely place great stress on her body."

As she spoke, she squatted next to Index as she lay on the road. She picked up the girl's body in both hands.

"You know what you need to do, right?" said Elizard pointedly. "We'll take care of the Index for the time being. We were the ones who built the Index of Prohibited Books and her system, so we'll have experts apply healing to her and work to block as much of Fiamma's influence as we can. But that won't be enough. Unless we defeat him and completely destroy the remote-control Soul Arm, we can never guarantee her safety."

"..."

The queen couldn't leave this place. She had to protect the United Kingdom.

That was a very correct choice, and Kamijou had no way to argue it.

But he didn't intend on insisting that she help him.

"Stiyl," said Kamijou to the red-haired sorcerer, "I'm gonna go give Fiamma a beating. Can I leave Index to you in the meantime?"

"...Are you bloody serious? Are you telling *me* to sit by and do nothing to the person who did this to her?!" shouted Stiyl, looking like he was about to have a row with Kamijou himself.

But instead, Kamijou grabbed Stiyl by the collar and pulled him in close.

Bringing his mouth to Stiyl's ear, he whispered so only he could hear:

"…Excuse me, but do you have any proof the people plotting all this bullshit aren't going to do anything to Index in the future?!"

"…?!"

"…I don't know anything about how it works from a magic perspective, but even if I was with Index around the clock, I could miss cheap tricks. If they tell me not to enter a magical facility because of my right hand, that's it. That's why I'm asking you to do this! A sorcerer I know will protect Index until the very end, no matter what the situation, without letting the bigger organization's plots throw you around!!"

After saying his piece, Kamijou pushed Stiyl away.

He didn't like thinking that way, but he had to. The kind of malice emanating from Fiamma made Kamijou remember the faults among individuals in a group that he knew had just been connected.

Feeling bitter, Kamijou turned to Queen Elizard and spoke. "…He could have been trying to mess us up on purpose, but if what Fiamma said is true, he'll be going after Sasha Kreutzev next. God's Right Seat uses angel magic, right? Sasha would be too tempting for him to pass up…After all, she had an actual archangel in her body once before."

"I'd like to keep as tight a lid on losing control over the Index as I can. Which means you won't have a just cause to save her. In other words…"

"…If it's cooperation you mean, then I don't need it," said Touma Kamijou.

It wasn't that he felt nothing. The anger boiling out from his heart was finally being expelled into the outside world.

"I'll get there myself. I'll go to Russia, then beat that shithead Fiamma to a pulp for you."

There were two things Touma Kamijou hadn't said.

The first was that he'd lost his memories regarding the Index incident.

The second had to do with the third arm, another right arm, that had come out of Fiamma.

It was like an actual right arm had broken through the skin—an incomprehensible object of power. Fiamma himself had said that the two men's right hands were similar to each other.

He had a lot of questions he needed to ask.

So, quietly, he vowed to himself: he'd ask them all, then punch him without hesitation.

AFTERWORD

For those of you who have been keeping up since the first book, it's good to see you again.

For those of you who read all twenty books at once, it's a pleasure to meet you.

I'm Kazuma Kamachi.

The twentieth book at last! And it's the conclusion of the British royal family arc!! Which means this afterword will be about what happened in Volumes 17 and 18! How did you like the story revolving around the legendary British sword, the Curtana? With a certain mercenary's appearance in Volume 17, I made the term *knight* stand out, but in Volume 18, I used the Curtana to bring the *queen* to the forefront. By the way, this Curtana is a sword that actually exists, so it's worth checking out. It's actually still used today for crowning the head of state and stuff.

Elizard, the queen of this story, is my personal ideal ruler. Basically, she's a perfect queen equipped with all the strong points of the first princess, Limeia; the second princess, Carissa; and the third princess, Vilian. The queen herself complains in the book that her daughters are all so extreme, but that's something she can say because she has a good balance of all three. There might have been a very strong image of storybooks and fairy tales for the princess team under her. Especially the healthy third princess, Vilian, bullied by her big sisters—she's an archetypical storybook heroine.

Aside from the royal family, some of Sylvia's settings peek through—she appeared in the second short-story volume—and a certain sorcerer's society boss who has been active in a magazine called *Dengeki Bunko Magazine* also slipped in there. If you have the time, please check those out as well.

I'd like to thank my illustrator, Mr. Haimura, and my editor, Mr. Miki. I'm sure it was difficult reading through nothing but troublesome battle scenes, but really, thank you so much.

And I'd like to thank all my readers. The protagonist Touma Kamijou was able to walk this massive path laid before him only because of your encouragement. I look forward to your support in the future.

Well then, as you close the page here for the moment,
And as I pray that you open a new page next time,
For now, I lay down my pen.

How many kinds of strange maid outfits exist in this world anyway?

Kazuma Kamachi

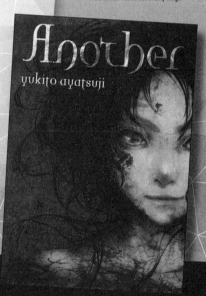